WINGS of LIGHT

LAURA BINGHAM

Sweetwater Books
Springville, Utah

ISBN 13: 978-1-59955-492-1

Published by Sweetwater Books, an imprint of Cedar Fort, Inc., 2373 W. 700 S., Springville, UT 84663
Distributed by Cedar Fort, Inc., www.cedarfort.com

LIBRARY OF CONGRESS CATALOGING-IN-PUBLICATION DATA
Bingham, Laura.
 Wings of light / Laura Bingham.
   p. cm.
  Summary: Sixteen-year-old Erin and her twin brother, Bain, have recently become immortal elves but when old enemies threaten their quest to find their mother, Erin must turn to new friends for help and learns that some magic is better left unexplored.
  ISBN 978-1-59955-492-1
  1. Brothers and sisters--Juvenile fiction. 2. Twins--Juvenile fiction. 3. Magic--Juvenile fiction. 4. Elves--Juvenile fiction. 5. Fairies--Juvenile fiction. 6. Fantasy fiction, American. [1. Brothers and sisters--Fiction. 2. Twins--Fiction. 3. Magic--Fiction. 4. Elves--Fiction. 5. Fairies--Fiction. 6. Fantasy.] I. Title.

  PZ7.B5118169Win 2010
  [Fic]--dc22
                                                    2010040627

Cover design by Megan Whittier
Cover design © 2011 by Lyle Mortimer
Edited and typeset by Melissa J. Caldwell

Printed in the United States of America

10 9 8 7 6 5 4 3 2 1

Printed on acid-free paper

For my kids, who keep magic alive.
For Parley, who is always there for me.
And to everyone who took the journey with me by reading
Älvor. *May this new adventure be even more fantastic.*

Praise for *Wings of Light*

"Warning: If elves, spells, dragon-riding, intrigue, mystery, danger, romance, and intercontinental pizza hopping are too much for your heart, you should NOT read this book. Otherwise, pick it up, take it to the cash register, pay for it through whatever means possible, take it home, lock the door (you won't want any interruptions), and read it—NOW! Laura Bingham has penned another novel that fantasy readers of all ages will devour."

—J. Scott Savage, author of the Far World series

"One of the hardest things for an author to do after writing a great story is to expand on it. Quite often an author will turn a great book into a mediocre series. Not this time. Bingham's *Wings of Light* delivers a sequel that may be even better than its predecessor, *Älvor*."

—Dave Lateiner, thelateinergangbookreviewspot.blogspot.com

Praise for *Älvor*

"*Älvor* will leave you with a sense of wonder and make you think a long time after you've finished it. An excellent book."

—James Dashner, author of *The Maze Runner*

"I would definitely recommend *Älvor*. . . . This has been one of my favorite books to read, and I can't wait for a sequel!"

—Flamingnet Young Adult Book Review, Top Choice Award

"I closed the book last night knowing that while the book gave me a feel for some favorites I have known, *Älvor* is in a class all its own. Unique in its own right. This book was everything I had hoped it would be."

—Sheila A. Dechantal, bookjourney.wordpress.com

"It is one of those books that I could not put down. I did not stop reading it until I passed out with the book on my lap. An amazing, colorful story of a set of twins who enter a magical world that is so well described and detailed, I wish I was there. A must buy."

—Dave Lateiner, thelateinergangbookreviewspot.blogspot.com

Contents

Contents

1
Nothing's Changed

ERIN WONDERED WHICH WAS WORSE: HAVING MAGIC, OR NOT being able to tell anyone about it. Christmas music drifted from the black CD player tucked away on the old entertainment cabinet. Erin tried to ignore the cheerful lyrics as she stared out the window at the steel gray sky. Snow hadn't reached the Pennsylvania hills, but soon ice would frost the world for what would seem like forever. Thanksgiving leftovers sat in the fridge, Christmas decorations already littered the walls, and Grandpa Jessie insisted on dragging the fake Christmas tree out and decorating it while the two of them were in town, even though it was only November. Another year, another holiday, but this time, it didn't feel real.

Erin looked over at her twin brother. At least he hadn't blown their cover. Bain seemed content as he sat on the floor shelling pistachios and flipping through pages of a magazine. Untouched issues from the last three months were stacked on the floor next to him. He turned a page, and she almost smiled that he used his hands to do it instead of magic. In the last few days he had only used his magic a couple of times.

Normal. It was something neither she nor Bain would ever be again, but how were they supposed to keep their secret forever? Grandpa Jessie would never believe in the älvor butterfly fairies, magic, or immortal elves. Every minute she spent with Grandpa Jessie now felt like a lie. When she was home, her life *was* a lie.

The fire crackled as a log tumbled softly off the burning pile and settled on the bed of ashes on the woodstove floor. Grandpa

Jessie's face hid behind the local section of the newspaper. It was hard to believe that today was her last day home.

She swallowed against the hard lump in her throat, wishing she could make the uneasy feeling go away. If she didn't ask him now, she wouldn't get the chance again for at least another month. The song changed to one without words, and she tried to let the melody infuse her with its relaxing tones.

"Grandpa?" She hoped her voice sounded comfortable, but with the way her stomach twisted, she doubted it was possible.

He collapsed the newspaper and peered at her.

"Tell us about Mom." She tried to pull a small smile, but her heart thudded in her chest as if it were trying to escape. Four days ago Grandpa Jessie had told her she looked like her mom. It should have sounded like a compliment, but instead her world tilted on its side. How could she look like her mom? She didn't even look like herself anymore. Becoming immortal could do that.

She waited, watching the flames lick the dark wood through the glass walls of the circular furnace. Bain glanced up at her quickly but then turned his eyes back down to the magazine.

Grandpa Jessie set the newspaper down and leaned back into the leather recliner. "Well, Erin, I suppose the best way to explain your mother is to look in the mirror and then put a bit of Bain's personality into the equation. She looked just like you, love. Maybe more of a free spirit, though. She had seen most of the world before she met your father—could tell a story about any continent."

"But she was more like me then?" Bain asked. He closed the pages and reached for another handful of pistachios.

Grandpa Jessie smiled. "Well, she was more likely to get her hands dirty. And she wasn't afraid of anything."

"Did you ever see her ears, Grandpa?" Erin asked. The answer to this question could change everything. She folded her arms tightly against her chest as if to keep her churning stomach hidden.

He scratched his chin as he contemplated the question. "Sorry, love. I think I lost track of her ears. I don't know that anyone ever thought about her ears with all those auburn locks getting in the way."

Bain reached up to his ears, but Erin shook her head slightly, hoping he would get the message. Grandpa Jessie probably hadn't noticed their ears either. Bain hadn't cut his hair since June, and now his thick blond hair fell in waves to his jawline.

"Why did they leave?" Erin asked, staring intently at the fire.

Grandpa Jessie looked over to her. "You mean, the last time?"

"Yes." Erin did not lift her gaze from the flames. She'd heard the story before, but it had been a long time. Maybe there was something she missed.

"She was taking your dad to see her family. Not her parents, mind you, but her extended family. The flight was to Ireland. It was only going to be for a few days. It was as much a getaway for the two of them as anything. You two were doing so well, they decided they could afford a week away."

"But they never made it to Ireland," Erin finished.

"No, love, they didn't." Christmas carols filled the air as Grandpa Jessie drifted into silence. "But it was said that their deaths were instantaneous. It happened so fast that no one had time to feel anything." He watched her face before continuing. "They never meant to leave the two of you. They loved you more than anything in the world. If they had it to do over, I know they never would have gone."

"I know, Grandpa. I just think about them and wonder so many things." Erin fiddled with the pages of the book on her lap.

"I do too, love. I do too." Grandpa Jessie pushed the foot of the recliner down and pulled himself out of the chair. He crossed the room to the CD player but paused before his fingers touched the buttons. The music paraded on as he turned to face them. "Your mom and dad loved you. Always know that. Always remember that. You two were their crown jewels." A tear escaped and he quickly brushed it away. "I'm going upstairs."

She could have rushed to him at lightning speed and hugged him, but she sat as if gravity held her to her seat. "Love you, Grandpa." It seemed so simple compared to the tornado of emotions that whirled inside of her. Someday she and Bain would have to tell him the truth, but she didn't know when or how.

2
Time to Go

ERIN SAT ON HER BED, WADDING UP A CREAM-COLORED SCARF. Practically everything she owned was packed in the purple suitcase on the floor. She doubted she really needed to wear her coat and gloves, but the neighbors would notice if she went out in the cold without all the accessories; another masquerade to keep the questions away and make everyone believe that she was the same Erin as always.

"What do you think about Mom?" She stared at the suitcase, hoping Bain would talk about it. They never discussed their parents. What was there to say? Neither one of them could remember their mom and dad. But things were different now, and it was time to break the unspoken rule.

"I don't know what you're talking about." Bain sat on the floor of her room, absently rolling a baseball back and forth. He used his magic to propel it around, never letting it touch his fingers.

Erin wondered if he even realized he was using magic. He hadn't practiced much in their short time back home. Not that she had expected him to, but it was encouraging to see him doing something with his magic without being compelled. "Bain, don't you wonder why Grandpa didn't freak out when he saw us at the door a few days ago? And don't you think it's odd that he says I look just like Mom?"

She wished she knew what her mom looked like. In all of the pictures they had of their mom, not one showed her face. There were plenty of partial profiles and even more where her back was turned. It was completely unfair.

"I don't know. I didn't really think much of it. You've always looked kind of like her. You know, her hair, her color. At least I didn't inherit the albino skin."

Erin directed the baseball into the air and suspended it in the space between Bain and her. "Bain, we look like elves. Don't you think we look a lot different than we did last August? Like, so different that he shouldn't have even recognized us?"

"What are you trying to say, exactly?"

She let the ball drop to the floor. He wasn't going to put the pieces together on his own. "I think Mom was an älva."

His eyebrows pulled down, making him look older than a barely sixteen-year-old boy.

"Bain, I think Mom was an elf. That would explain how she traveled the world. And why Grandpa Jessie thinks we look just fine. Just like our *mom*."

"But it's impossible," Bain answered.

"How do we know she's not an älva? What do we know about what's possible and what's not? Haven't you ever wondered why we don't have even one decent picture of her? Why we've never even seen her relatives? Why all of our lives, no one from her side of the family even seems to exist?" Erin paced the floor.

"Are you sure you're not just trying to make something out of nothing?"

"Well, do you have any ideas?"

"Mom and Dad died in a plane accident when we were babies. I don't know what else there is to say." He picked up the ball and left the room, closing the door with magic. Magic that they both were given only last summer when they decided to wander into the cottage uninvited. And now it felt like a common accessory.

But why couldn't Bain see it too? Maybe he didn't want to. Maybe it was too hard for him to change the only story he had known all his life. Even if he was easygoing, it hadn't been easy growing up without a mom and dad.

"Oh, Pulsar," she said, even though he was not close by. The dragon was too big to fit through the staircase leading out of the magical forest and into the cottage. She hadn't talked to him in days, and she hated it. "One more day. I'm gonna see you tomorrow. Finally."

She thought she would enjoy being at home so much more than she did. Even though they had only been away for three months, an entire lifetime seemed to have passed by since the last time she had seen her room. She had not only officially transformed into an elf at a kingdom in Iceland—a kingom that she could have never guessed existed before last summer—but she had also ridden a dragon, rescued her brother from an army of imps, and met the most amazing guy.

She couldn't help but be annoyed that every time she was alone, her thoughts were on Joel. She wasn't supposed to miss him. But she did. She barely even knew him, but that didn't stop the visions of his face from parading through her thoughts. Why did she have to like him so much?

She tried to convince herself that the reason she wanted to return to the kingdom was to spend time with her dragon, but somewhere in her mind, she knew that wasn't entirely true. She really wanted to see Joel again. But she could rationalize even that. Maybe Joel represented the new life she began as an älva: magic, swords, and Pulsar.

She let herself sink into her bed. Thanksgiving had been nice, but now she was ready to go back. Maybe she didn't really belong here anymore, at least not yet. Somehow everything that was comfortable and familiar was now stifling. She wanted to ride Pulsar and use magic. She didn't want to pretend she was the same Erin who grew up here. Her world was already too big to chain herself to the limitations of being just human.

She watched through her window as the stars beamed through the darkness. She hadn't bothered turning on the light, and her room reflected the night.

A soft knock sounded on her door.

"Come in," she called.

The door opened, and Bain let himself in. He came halfway

into the room before turning and directing the door to shut. He pulled up the chair from her desk and took a seat across from her in the dark room.

Erin could only make out his silhouette as he sat there in the dark silence.

"Erin, I'm sorry," he finally said.

She let another pause of silence fill the gap.

"It's just that I don't think I'm ready to change history. Do you realize how complicated things get when you change Mom into an elf?" he said.

"Maybe I know even more than you," she answered.

"What do you mean?"

She wished she could see his face, but it was too dark. "There are some things I learned while you were in Black Rain." The place Bain was held captive for over a month. She hated even bringing it up.

Bain dropped his head in his hands.

"Are you okay?" she asked.

"When you said Black Rain, I could feel the headache. It's still hard trying to fit all the pieces together. You're not making this any easier."

"Sorry."

"I know. Keep going though. What were you going to say?"

She didn't really want to say it. Bain was only barely coming around to reality anyway, the new reality of the elf world. One more thing might push him over the edge. "Are you sure you want to hear?"

"No. I don't know. Go on, what do you have?"

Erin let out a long sigh. "If Mom really was an älva, then she couldn't have died in an airplane crash."

"What are you talking about?"

"Joel said that elves can only die from magic. I don't think an airplane crash counts as magical."

"You think Mom's still alive?"

"I don't know. I've been trying to figure it out. If she didn't die, why would she just leave us alone? And if she did die, how?"

"That's a lot of ifs." Bain picked up his wand, and light pierced the darkness as the diamond tip shone.

Erin watched Bain in the light cast from his wand. She couldn't see his white aura. In the dark she couldn't see anyone's aura. Sometimes she liked the night for that reason. She could pretend she was the same girl she had been before stepping through that fateful door of the cottage that began her path to becoming an elf.

She wasn't human anymore, but she really didn't feel like an älva either. Sitting in her quiet room at home, the kingdom felt more like a dream than a reality. From here it would almost be possible to convince herself that none of it was real—learning that she could use some kinds of magic, crossing the bridge that would forever make her and Bain immortal elves, becoming friends with fairies and a dragon. So many things. How could it all be real? All because she and Bain couldn't resist going into a cottage they found in the woods last summer.

She could blame it all on Bain. He was the one who insisted on snooping around the secluded cabin. Then they found a magical door in the basement, and everything changed. She changed. But she chose it too. She could have left it all behind, but there was something about the world of elves that drew her in. And now there was no going back. But sitting here in her bedroom, all of those things felt distant and impossible.

She laughed aloud at her own thoughts. How could she think that anything was impossible? Her brother only proved it by creating light from his wand. He was the one who had the right to question everything. It was he who spent a month held hostage by an evil sorcerer.

"What's so funny?" Bain asked. He was waving the wand in figure eights, letting the light follow so it imprinted the pattern in the dark.

She sat up on her bed. "Nothing. It's late, and tomorrow's school."

He looked up at her with a confused expression. "School?"

"Yeah, remember, we were accepted to a special program in Iceland, full tuition scholarships and everything." She knew her voice dripped with sarcasm, but Bain smiled. "Like that would ever happen. Well, at least not with your grades. I don't think they even have Thanksgiving in Iceland. We're lucky Grandpa didn't think of that."

Bain stopped his wand. "I can't believe it's only been three months."

"I know. It seems like it's been a whole lifetime. How did you do that? Your wand . . . who taught you that?"

Bain examined the glow from the end of his wand. "I don't know. I was just thinking it was dark in here and," Bain touched the bright lighted end, "I just did it."

"Maybe I should get a wand."

"Nah, you have Pulsar. You don't need a wand. He could just light a tree on fire or something."

"Yeah. That sounds practical."

Bain walked to the door and turned around. "Erin, don't think about Mom too much. There really isn't anything we can do about it." He blew the hair away from his eyebrows. "I just don't want to see you get hurt digging through this. You might never find your answers."

He pointed his wand at the door, which opened at his bidding. "Good night, little sister."

"Only by ten minutes," she answered, but he was already gone.

3

Here and There

It had been way too long since Erin felt the air lashing through her hair as the sky wrapped around her and the dragon. The twins said good-bye to Grandpa Jessie the next morning and met Pulsar. Finally. Erin had missed the dragon's warm scales and suede wings. With their bags tied to the saddle, Pulsar flew over the forest to their new home.

She spoke again to the dragon through her mind, loving the fact that he could read her thoughts when she let him. *Pulsar, I'm not coming through the cottage anymore. I'm not going anywhere without you again.*

I couldn't agree more, little one.

Erin smiled at the words. He still called her little one, and probably always would. Next to him, she would always be little. Erin gripped the butterscotch-colored saddle, watching the world below rush by. She closed her eyes and reached out to the hot golden scales. Pulsar was a constant source of magic, like electricity to a light bulb. And the reality of it all hit her with force.

It had only been a couple of months since the miracle of becoming an elf. Pulsar shared his magic with her even longer ago than that. She reached up to feel her ears. At least they were still pointed at the ends, proof that all of it could not be a dream.

Where are we? she asked Pulsar. She had only just noticed that he had left her to her thoughts.

Soon you will see the lights of Iceland burning through the night, and then we will be home.

And then she wondered if the dragon had cast a spell over her mind. He projected scenes back to her from her own memory: Bain and her sitting on the patio in the summer watching the fireflies, Adarae and the other fairies darting through the sky in the Living Garden, and the pegasi dancing through the clouds in the Door of Vines; everything jumbled together in her mind and wove her old world in with her new one. Magic flooded through her mind. It had always been there. All of it. The old and the new, she just didn't know.

"Erin?"

She knew she was on the verge of waking up, but she was too asleep to commit to opening her eyes.

"Erin Fireborn, come on! I have missed those emerald eyes. Please don't make me wait to see them again."

That voice . . . Joel! Realization crashed through her and she blinked against the light. It was already morning. They made it back to the castle last night. It was late when Pulsar dropped them off on the balcony of her room.

"I was wondering how long you would sleep. The queen insisted that you wake. I told her I could kiss you, like you were Sleeping Beauty, but she didn't agree to it."

Erin stared at Joel's face, trying to lock it into her mind. Even though she had seen him only a couple weeks ago, she was sure that her memory was incapable of doing Joel justice. His hazel brown eyes twinkled as he leaned over her.

Joel smiled the crooked smile that always melted her. "Welcome back, Erin Fireborn. I hope you'll stay a while."

She sat up, trying to figure out what time it was. Iceland and Pennsylvania time zones were so different.

"What do you want for dinner, my lady?"

She couldn't stop a giggle from escaping but then chastised herself as her cheeks burned.

What do you want for dinner, Fireborn?

She gasped as Pulsar's voice boomed through her mind. Joel laughed; of course, he could hear the dragon too. He opened the balcony doors so that the dragon could be seen outside.

"Dinner for three?" she asked.

"Make that four." Bain sauntered in and flopped onto an over-stuffed chair.

Her stomach growled loud enough to be heard even without an elf's supersonic hearing. "Where's Ella?" Ella was Erin's Fairy Godmother, not that Erin ever could get used to that title. Even though Erin hadn't seen her godmother in a while, her dreams of the woman were vivid. Just last night, Ella seemed to really be there, talking with her. It seemed too real to be a dream.

A flash of pain crossed Joel's face before fading into a false smile. "Why do you ask?"

"I saw her in a dream last night. She was trapped somewhere. It was strange, though. It was like we were both dreaming at the same time, but we knew it. Does that make any sense?"

Joel shook his head. "I'm not the one to ask about dreams." He glanced at the door before continuing. "But no one's seen Ella for over a week."

"In my dream, she was trying to tell me something. It was confusing, though. What do you know about Whispering Winds?"

Joel stood. "I think it's high time we brought you some dinner."

Erin shook her head, trying to figure Joel out. The look on his face when she said "Whispering Winds" made her wonder if there was something he wasn't saying. And why didn't he want to talk about it?

"I want some grilled salmon," Bain added.

"What's going on, Joel?" Erin asked.

Joel put his hand up to silence her. "The Whispering Winds are in the hands of the älvor. I really don't know that much about it. I wonder why Ella would try to explain that to *you*."

Something about the way he said this made Erin's skin crawl. He made it sound like a complicated secret that she shouldn't know about, but why? She watched Joel leave the room and wondered when she would see Ella again. There was still so much she didn't understand. Bain winked at her from across the room. Embarrassed to be caught watching Joel, she sighed and sunk back into the pillows.

What are the Whispering Winds, Pulsar? she asked.

I'm sorry I don't know more, Fireborn. I think Joel is right. That mystery lies within the realm of the älvor. Secrets of fairies are not known even to most elves.

"What's going on?" Bain asked.

She grabbed her clothes and headed into the bathroom. "Tell Joel I'll be back. I'm going with Pulsar for some fresh air."

"Fresh air?"

"Come on, Bain. I'll be fine." Fresh air was a terrible excuse. What she really needed was some time to adjust to the shock of being back. As much as she loved staring into Joel's perfect face, she couldn't make herself feel at home here. Too many terrifying memories crowded to the surface. It was going to take some time to sort through them all. No one could save her from the memory of screaming men as shattered glass rained down on them because of her magic. Maybe she wasn't ready to be an elf.

The balcony opened to the yard where Pulsar stretched out. "I'm not leaving you again, Pulsar. Besides, I bet you know where we can find a few butterfly fairies." She climbed up his golden scales, the warm magic shocking through her with every touch. Being near the dragon made her feel powerful and invincible, a feeling she would never get used to or get enough of.

We are two of a kind, Fireborn. With that, he beat his enormous wings, thrusting them skyward.

4
Whispering Winds

THERE WAS SOMETHING TO BE SAID ABOUT THE LAND RUSHING below them and the wind in her hair. The sky offered more security than the ground. Up here, nothing could touch her. Erin thought about the last few days. Compared with the craziness of the last six months, she supposed it wasn't so unusual.

She would have to call Grandpa, let him know that they made it to Iceland. It was too hard living in both worlds. Riding Pulsar in the sky, she could pretend dragons were normal, elves were an everyday occasion, and that butterfly-winged fairies should be your best friends. That was the life she lived now; whether she could ever let Grandpa Jessie into that reality was a whole different question.

Are you up for a hunt? Pulsar's strong voice entered her mind.

"I wouldn't want you to drop out of the sky from hunger. Just don't make me watch you eat, and I'll be fine." She gripped the saddle as he tucked his wings and dove through the clouds. Trees covered the ground below, and it amazed her when she spotted deer running on the ground far below. Someday she might take it for granted, but it still took her breath away to see so much detail.

The hunt wasn't what she wanted to see, even though she knew what to expect. He would single out a deer before using his magic to close down its mind, rendering the animal unconscious. Then, with another wave of magic, Pulsar would stop its heart. The thought of killing something seared her. After the fall of Black Rain, she wondered how many deaths were on her hands. The image of the shattering city still haunted her. She'd saved Bain, but it had come with a heavy price.

Some part of her mind was aware of the deer that Pulsar had scooped in his thick talons. His wings beat heavily against the air, and they rose once more above the clouds.

"You're not bringing that back to the castle, are you?" The thought of Pulsar eating a deer on the pristine lawn made her laugh before an angry growl escaped her stomach. She was hungry too.

I can share, he said.

That did nothing to quell the nauseating ache. "Cooking a slab of venison over a campfire brings back too many memories." She wasn't running away this time. Not like last time when she thought Bain had taken off without her, leaving her alone in the foreign world of elves. The abandonment had almost crushed her. When she figured out that he had been captured, nothing could stop her from rescuing him. Not even an army of imps.

I'm taking you back to the palace.

She felt his mind wind through her thoughts. If Pulsar had been with her at Black Rain, things would have turned out so much differently. Maybe she would not have been responsible for collapsing an entire city on itself, sending shards of crystal-like daggers onto the people below. She wasn't sure if she felt sorry for the imps there so much as the cooks, the only humans in the entire city. They were the ones she worried about.

War has victims of every kind. Pulsar glided down to the green expanse of lawn, releasing the deer before touching down. *Sometimes the things that are required of us are difficult. Not everything has a simple answer. You did what you had to at the time. It was enough. You must free yourself from this guilt. You did not serve the first offense. You did the only thing you could. Even then, it was quite miraculous. They are in your deepest debt.*

"But the cooks weren't at war." She slid off of his smooth side and landed on the grass.

They will live with the consequences of their own choices. No one forced them to work there. They must have known to some degree the nature of the person they served.

She looked at the lump of a deer lying on the grass. "I think I'm going inside now. There's no way I'm watching you eat that." If a dragon could laugh, that's what Pulsar did.

She wandered the halls of the castle. Somewhere in this massive palace, there was an aviary, a place that made her feel hope. For a while, the only way she ever kept from getting lost was having Joel as a guide or using Pulsar's perfect memory. She wondered if all dragons had a gift for remembering land, layout, and anything to do with directions. A loud growl escaped her stomach, making her feel conspicuous.

"There you are!" Joel's voice startled her.

She sighed as Joel appeared instantly in front of her. "Do you really think it was necessary to be invisible?"

"I was following the sound of your stomach. I could hear you clear upstairs."

"So much for stealth. Is that a Caesar salad?" She grabbed the food from his hands. "Mmm, chicken . . ." Nothing had ever tasted so good.

"Can you eat and walk at the same time?"

She nodded and let Joel guide her down the hall. This time she was too absorbed with the salad to bother feeling embarrassed at his chivalry. It was as if he had read her thoughts as the doorway to the enormous aviary opened. Inside, the popping water fountain surrounded with teacup flowers filled the air with its sweet fragrance.

She set her salad down and filled a flower with the carbonated water.

"Bain told me you went for a ride," Joel said.

With her mouth full of another bite, she could only nod.

He laughed.

The sound flooded her mind with the many moments they had shared. As if in response to the memories, her heart raced and her cheeks burned. All she could hope was that he hadn't noticed. It was nice sitting next to Joel. He made her feel so much better, like all of the craziness she was trying to get used to was simple everyday normal. She didn't have to try.

She dug her fork into the salad. "Why won't you tell me about the Whispering Winds? And why hasn't anyone seen Ella?"

His smile faded. "I don't know who can tell you about Ella." He looked around as if to see if anyone was watching them. His voice dropped to a low whisper. "Ella doesn't do this. She can come and go so easily that we see her all the time. Something's going on, but I don't know what it is."

"What about the Whispering Winds?"

He blew a long sigh out and leaned back on his elbows. "That's not really my place to say."

At least Erin knew he was telling the truth. The brilliant aura around him hadn't faltered for even a moment.

He finally said, "How do you think she instantly travels?" He raised his eyebrow in expectation.

"It's the Whispering Winds?" Finally she was getting to the bottom of this. The dream had been so confusing. The words Ella spoke were a different language. None of it made sense.

"I shouldn't talk about it. Are you done with your salad?"

She looked at her empty plate. No amount of magic could change the evidence. "Dessert?" It was the only thing she could think of to put off the inevitable.

Joel stood and offered his arm, reminding her of an old-fashioned ballroom dancer. She wished that Joel hadn't found her. What she really needed was time alone. Maybe no one blamed her for the disaster she left in Black Rain, but she could hardly stand the guilt. One evening in silence probably wouldn't offer the release she longed for, but it might help. With Joel there, she could do nothing other than feel the heat of his gaze on her face.

But she was powerless when Joel was this nice. She let him take her arm and lead her once again down the never-ending halls, pretending that she belonged in this surreal world.

5
Calling from Dublin

SOMEHOW SHE MADE IT THROUGH THE FIRST DAY OF THE PALACE, but now there was nothing that could keep her indoors. With Pulsar's heat, any weather was manageable, and added to that was her ability to create a magical ward that could hold a stable air density and temperature. Erin breathed in the thrill of flying over a thousand feet above the ground. They hadn't decided on a particular destination as they glided on air currents above the clouds.

"What do you think Ella wants?" The dream about Ella had worn through her thoughts. As much as she tried to decipher the strange language her godmother had spoken, it was locked from her understanding.

I think time will tell. Patience is the key to unraveling many mysteries.

"Pulsar, I think you're too noble for your own good. People aren't as patient as dragons."

You're not just a person, Fireborn. You are an älva.

"All that means is that now I have pointy ears, immortality, and magic. Trust me; it doesn't have anything to do with patience. I've had the dream twice now, and I still don't get it. Why couldn't she just say it in English?"

Pulsar didn't answer. Instead, he tucked his wings and dropped into a freefall, rocketing them toward land. The rush of wind streaming at her cleared her mind of Ella, only to be replaced with thoughts of Joel. Pulsar twisted out of the dive and blazed fire into the heavens. Erin hadn't seen him breathe fire in a long time.

Had it been since they stayed in the forest? She must have been too depressed to be rightfully impressed with the sheer horror and miracle it was that he could create such a terrifying flame.

You don't want to forget your training. There may come a time when you wish to call upon it.

"That's the other problem, Pulsar. I think you picked the wrong girl. You should have found someone who was ready for a fight. I'm a run-and-hide kind of girl, not a warrior. I love you, Pulsar, but I'm a wimp."

He straightened out his flight so they were gliding smoothly again. *You were born with fire in you. Perhaps you cannot see it yourself, but I can feel the flame that lights you. It is your gentle heart that tempers your passion. If you were cornered, I know your fire would win. In time, you will be matchless.*

One thing she had learned in the last few months was that she couldn't beat the dragon. No matter how many things she thought of, he could always counter it. Instead, she watched the landscape below, her thoughts drifting back to Joel. Even here in the sky, miles away from him, she felt warmth spread through her chest at the thought of him.

Turbulent air assaulted their flight in spite of the clear weather. The abrupt wind clouded her vision, and she held tightly to the saddle as they convulsed through the tumultuous current. She searched through Pulsar's thoughts as panic gripped her with ice, but all she could find was his steady effort to avoid damage to his wings as they were torn into by the violent wind. A metallic ring shrilled in her mind before the air grew still and silent.

"What was that?" Her breathing came in quick gasps as Pulsar glided over the green land. They were much closer to the ground than they had been only seconds before. The grass had a distinctly different hue than before. "Pulsar, I don't think this is Iceland."

She was aware of the invisibility shield that he warded them both with as he touched down. "What happened?" Even the sounds of the land had changed, along with its smell. "Where are we?"

She jumped off Pulsar and covered the ground with unnatural

speed. Sheep and farmhouses came into view along with a small town. As she continued on, older structures mingled with highways and modern buildings. As hard as it was to believe, realization forced itself into her mind. This was Dublin, Ireland.

Did you do this? she asked Pulsar as he flew well above her in complete invisibility.

There was another force involved, something magic. You too felt the angry wind and heard the sonic blast as we defied the speed of sound.

She stopped running. *We should go back.* What would Bain think of their sudden disappearance? The last couple of months had been hard enough without adding another dimension of drama to his life. And why, since elves had the most advanced technology of all mankind, did she still not own a cell phone? She fingered the changing brooch she got when she became an elf. A piece of magic that could transform into anything as long as it was small and inanimate, but what good would it do to turn it into a phone if Bain and Joel didn't have one? She could call Grandpa.

It seemed like a crazy idea, but the thought reached tangibly through her. Of all the gifts she could have been given, why did she end up with one that told her the truth of things? It wasn't very convenient, especially when she didn't understand why some things were right. Even so, experience had proven itself. If she ignored the truth, there would be consequences.

She unlatched the golden leaf pin and held it in her hand. A familiar warm buzz surged through her fingers as she transformed her changing brooch into a sleek, silver phone. Smiling at the results, she flipped the phone open and dialed Grandpa Jessie's cell phone number.

She waited while it rang, hoping that maybe, just maybe, he wouldn't answer.

"Hello?" he said in his business tone.

"Hi, Grandpa." She couldn't help but smile at the sound of his voice.

"Hello, love. I miss you."

Erin bit the inside of her cheek, trying to decide what she would say.

"You should hang up and let me call you back. This is probably costing you a fortune."

"It's okay, Grandpa." She wondered what the caller ID said on his cell phone. "I'm doing a report on Dublin, Ireland. Do you know anyone who lives there? Maybe someone I could talk to about it." It wasn't a very good lie, but it was all she could think of.

"Dublin?"

The sound in his voice was sad and distant. And that's when she remembered. How could she forget? Her parents had been killed on an airplane on their way to Ireland. She held her breath while a lead weight settled into her stomach. They had been coming to Ireland to visit family.

"Grandpa? I'm sorry. Don't worry about it. I can just look something up on the Internet."

He cleared his throat. "Lyndera. That's all I know. Your mom was on her way to see someone named Lyndera. I don't even know her last name."

"It's okay, Grandpa. I'll figure something out." Silence ensued as she stood there trying to think of something else to say. "I miss you, Grandpa. Are you getting along okay?"

"You know Mrs. Hammel. She does her best to keep me stocked with baked goods. I'm doing fine. You'll have to come home again for Christmas. I might be able to hold out until then."

"Christmas. You got it. I guess I better go. I love you."

"I love you too, angel."

A click on the line indicated he had hung up. She stared at the silver phone.

"How am I going to find Lyndera?" she asked Pulsar. She knew he could hear everything even as he flew above the city.

Is she human?

"If you think we're looking for an elf, I'm never going to find her."

You're giving up so easily?

"I don't know, Pulsar. How am I supposed to find a complete stranger?"

Do you not think there is a reason we are here? What was the force that brought us? Don't you want to discover the meaning behind it?

She sighed. "What do you suggest we do?"

It had been hours. Not that it helped. Even the phone books offered no answers. "I'm sure that someone back at Álfheim will be able to help us with all their fancy computer and satellite equipment. You never know," she said, holding onto the saddle horn. Pulsar had not wanted to give up on their search, but as the light faded into dusk, he finally consented on returning to Iceland. It wasn't that she was happy to be right this time. The thought of Lyndera burned in her mind. Maybe it was a link to her past.

As they flew over the deep blue ocean, she laughed at the fluid sensation of weightlessness. Nothing could beat flying. It might have had something to do with not wanting the moment to end. As soon as she touched down in Álfheim, Bain and Joel would be there to interrogate her about her latest absence. At least this time she was with Pulsar and hadn't been kidnapped by an evil elf. How bad could it be?

6
Invisible

She hadn't expected it to be so late. Everyone in the palace was sleeping, or so it seemed by the dead silence. Erin breathed in the familiarity of her old room. Pulsar perched on the enormous balcony that opened up from the oversized suite.

"Are you going back to the cave?" she asked. He had found an abandoned cave not far from here and had called it his room since they had come to Iceland. She still hadn't seen it but wasn't in a hurry to. Thoughts of old bones from his previous meals kept her from wanting to explore that side of him.

I'll see you in the morning, Fireborn, unless you wish to accompany me on a midnight hunt.

Sometimes she forgot that he could hear her thoughts. Whoever thought dragons didn't have a sense of humor had never met Pulsar. "I think I'll pass, just this once." She watched him fly into the night sky and turned back to the empty room.

It felt like a lifetime ago that she won and lost everything in the world right here in this room. She couldn't help looking in the wardrobe to see if the deep green gown was still there. The day she wore it was the day that changed everything forever. The day she would never be a human again. The day she became an älva.

Maybe there was something magical about those clothes. It was probably superstitious, but maybe the fairies would recognize her better wearing something familiar. Tonight she was going to get some answers. Dressed in the green gown and topped with a simple gold tiara, Erin left her room. The halls stretched out in every direction with staircases leading to endless rooms. There was a time when all the space scared her. But Joel had changed that. Now, instead of worrying about getting lost, she let the halls lead her as she followed her instincts. It wasn't until she finally found it that she realized what she had been searching for.

The trees stretched to the ceiling in the glass room. It was here that she met the queen for the first time. In the dark, it didn't seem as big as it had that day. She took in the forest of trees and bushes before settling on a bench. No one had ever said if she was allowed to come in this room on her own. No boundaries had ever been set. A quick smile flashed as she noticed the small metal box on the wall by the door. The queen had pushed a button on the metal plate summoning Joel. Even that first day, Erin knew she had been hooked. It was impossible not to like the tall, easygoing boy. Or was he a man?

But the reason she had come was not to reminisce. She cleared her throat and wondered if the älvor were asleep. "I respectfully wish to speak to any friends of Adarae." It was the best she could do. Bain always had a way with the fairies. When he called to Adarae the first time, she was sure he said something like that, and it had worked.

She waited on the bench, glad no one was there to be an audience to her rejection. What did she expect? Having a friendship with the älvor was rare, and in her case, it only extended to Adarae's colony. The scent from the surrounding plants calmed her, sending her into another senseless decision.

"Ella has visited me twice now, in my dreams," she began, talking to the open air. "Ella tried to tell me something. I know it is important, but I couldn't understand a word she said.

"Then it happened again. All I know is that this time, Ella finally said everything she wanted to say. Then she disappeared. The only phrase that made any sense was 'Whispering Winds.' Everything else was a different language. It was beautiful, almost like a song."

She closed her eyes and tried to remember. "*Ala moriana sey. Klandton frestion blantesfre sulianton trestonde.*" The words slipped away from her almost as fast as she said them, as if Ella's echo had only played through her mind. She shook her head and waited.

There was a soft brush barely crossing her arm. She opened her eyes to find an älvor with bright purple wings dotted with black. The tiny fairy wore a gown of purple silk that shimmered even in the dim light of the stars. Her hair reflected silver in the moonlight as she kissed her fingers and touched Erin's hand.

Erin held her breath and waited.

"Friend of Adarae and friend of Ella, you speak the ancient tongue of our kind. I am Carish of the queen's house. Do you know the danger you are in?"

"Danger?" How did she manage to find danger right in the middle of the safest city in the world? Erin watched the brilliant eyes of Carish and waited.

"You speak of a spell that only the queen of all the älvor has in full, with just one exception."

"What spell?"

The purple wings blurred as Carish fluttered eye level with Erin. "Whispering Winds, child. And your friend Ella is the keeper of this secret. Why would she choose to share it with you?" Even with the musical tones of the älvor's voice, jealousy bled through.

"What is Whispering Winds?" Everything in her burned and twisted as she waited for the answer. Her gift of truth told her that Carish had that answer. Erin's blood threatened to burst through her veins as she waited.

"It is the ability to be wherever you wish on the wings of light."

Why did she think she was going to understand this? Wings of light? What was that, a new kind of fairy? She realized her jaw was hanging slack and forced her chin up. "Wings of light?"

"Yes, of course. It is how Ella travels so fast. Wings of light."

Carish flitted quickly into the air, and Erin knew it was only a matter of seconds before the conversation was over. "Sorry, but are you saying that Ella has wings?"

The blur of purple darted up into the branches of the nearest tree. "Wings of light," she called in her tinkling voice that sounded like wind chimes.

Erin watched the fairy fly higher into the tree. "Wait! What danger?" But the purple wings were already out of sight. She looked through the glass ceiling at the glowing moon. The stars broke through the sky like diamonds spread on black velvet. She had seen Ella many times and never once noticed wings.

"Can more than one person have wings of light?" she asked the darkness. Just to be sure, she felt her shoulder blades for any protruding wings. She shook her head at her own gesture. Of course she didn't have wings. "What does Whispering Wind have to do with wings of light?"

Erin left the oversized greenhouse and wandered again through the halls. Why couldn't Carish at least explain the danger? Her thoughts reached out to Pulsar, but he slept. There was no one left to ask tonight.

The only sign that she had slept late was the position of the sun as light streamed through the window. She pulled the covers over her head, but she couldn't ignore the low growl that reverberated through the bedroom.

I thought you were going to sleep all day. Pulsar waited on the balcony.

"What time is it?" Erin asked.

Almost noon, Fireborn. Are you coming with me, or shall I come back for you later?

"You go on. I need a shower. Don't worry, I won't get into any trouble while you're gone."

Tendrils of flame escaped Pulsar's mouth before he shot out into the sky.

She hurried to ready herself. After ditching him for a whole day, Bain was probably furious. A knock came at the door before she managed to escape. She took a deep breath and opened the door.

"Nice of you to join us, little sister." Bain was holding a plate of fruit and bread. He walked in and set it on a table. "Where have you been?"

"How did you know I was back?" she countered.

"Pulsar." He sat down and picked out a large, pink fruit. "You never answered my question."

She sighed. "Ireland. But don't ask me how."

"Do you think Pulsar can take me there too?"

"Bain, do you ever feel like we're being irresponsible? We haven't even graduated from high school. Grandpa Jessie thinks we're foreign exchange students and really we're hanging out at a castle in Iceland. It seems wrong, doesn't it?"

"Only when you put it that way. The way I see it, right now we probably know more physical science than our teachers and way more botany than most of the planet."

"Maybe." She picked up a roll from the tray and sat down. The warm bread reminded her of Mrs. Hammel, their next-door neighbor back home. "I'm just saying; I don't really know what we're supposed to be doing."

"So, Ireland. That sounds interesting. What did you do there?"

"You would have to ask." The change of subject didn't escape her, but she explained her day, leaving out the conversation with Carish. Bain had finished off most of the food by the time her story ended.

"I think I can help you." Joel flickered into view.

"How long have you been here?" Erin asked. Her heart was stuck somewhere in her throat and her mind was quickly calculating the conversation she had with Bain to see if there was anything she should worry about Joel overhearing.

"Gotcha," Bain said with a smirk. "He came in with me."

"You've been here the whole time?" Heat flushed her cheeks. *The nerve.* Of course Bain would be able to see him even if he were invisible. Seeing magical auras definitely had its advantages.

"The whole time," Joel said unapologetically. "But what I really want to know is why you would seek an audience with the queen's colony."

"The queen's colony? What are you talking about?"

"Last night, you entered the queen's greenhouse and talked to Carish."

"How did you know?" Her heart pounded as she waited for his response. She would know if he was telling the truth. His aura would give him away.

"I followed you," he said.

7
Answers in the Amazon

THE TREE LINE OF THE FOREST WASN'T FAR AWAY. IF SHE KEPT running at this speed, she would end up in the middle of the forest in a couple minutes. Then she would *have* to call Pulsar just to find her way out. The thought made her slow to a simple walk. "Why do boys have to be so stupid?" Then another thought made her heart clamp down. What if Joel had followed her again?

If he did, she hoped he heard her. She sat on the grass, wondering what on earth could have persuaded her to wear the light blue gown she found hanging in the wardrobe. Today was a jeans kind of day.

She wrapped her arms around her legs as she stared at the dying grass. It felt good to be alone. An abrupt metallic clang screeched through the air as the wind suddenly whipped into a fury. The gale took her by surprise, but she recovered enough to put up a touch ward. But the wind would not be repelled. Before she could think of a better solution, the sound was gone and the air had settled. All around her were walls.

Pulsar! she screamed in her mind. But it was too late. Somehow she knew she couldn't reach him, even though she couldn't fathom where she was or exactly how she got there. "Why me?" she asked the empty room. She pulled the changing brooch from her dress and transformed it into a satellite tracking unit. *There's more than one way,* she thought.

The little black device blinked while it traced a map. South America. The Amazon River.

That made no sense. She transformed the brooch back. Maybe she didn't know enough about magic to make a GPS that worked. She couldn't be in South America. And wherever this place was, it was empty.

She opened the door and found a narrow hallway. It wasn't the palace. Ignoring the thought, she followed the hall of doors, listening for any sign of life. Curiosity overruled logic, and she decided to open a door.

Her breath was lost, and even though she wanted to scream out, she couldn't exhale. The beautiful Ella was sleeping on a metal-framed cot. Instantly, Erin was at her side, softly shaking her arms to wake her, but the älva would not stir. "Ella!" Erin cried, gently pulling Ella's shoulders up. "What happened to you?"

Ella's head lolled back as Erin lifted her from the cot. Erin's heart raced as she carried Ella from the room. Something was very wrong with this place. It had to be. The feeling of Black Rain's castle pierced her as she navigated the hallway carrying the elf. The sight of a stairwell gave her hope of escape, and she descended quickly. Sounds echoed up the stairs like a lost memory. It couldn't be.

Warded with invisibility, Erin made her way into the open kitchen. In spite of herself, she smiled at the banter and listened as the men jeered and teased each other. They were the same cooks from Black Rain. Even though she was still carrying the unconscious Ella, a weight lifted from Erin's shoulders. She hadn't killed the cooks after all. Her lungs felt as though there was more room for air. After all that had happened, somehow Xavene and Carbonell, the blackest elves to live, had managed to save them from the destruction. It seemed impossible.

Erin carefully maneuvered around the cooks, leaving the kitchen behind. There were too many similarities and too many memories she didn't want to revisit. The next door she found opened to sultry hot humidity and lush green plants. Maybe her GPS was right. It felt like the middle of a rainforest. She stared back at the building. It had the modesty of a conservative mansion, unlike the gaping castle of Black Rain. And it wasn't black.

Erin turned, taking in the jungle of trees that spread before her. This is where Bain would have been really helpful. If a barrier ward surrounded the area, she was never going to get out. The last time was a fluke; a combined effort of her twin and herself that no one could fully explain. Their escape had been an emergency. Hundreds of imps were chasing them, but Bain could see the magical wall that would have otherwise paralyzed them. Erin wasn't willing to risk running into an invisible wall that could hold her and Ella captive indefinitely.

She sat on a stump in front of the mansion not far from the front door. In Egypt a magical barrier had surrounded the castle that paralyzed anything that touched it. It was impossible to know how far out she could go before maybe hitting a magical wall. Ella didn't stir as Erin carefully laid her down on the ground.

"You missed us, didn't you?" a voice said behind her.

Lightning fast, Erin was at Ella's side, creating a touch ward around them both. Invisibility wasn't enough to hide from Carbonell—she never understood why—but a touch ward would still work.

"Stay a moment. You can't leave anyway." Carbonell made himself comfortable on the same stump Erin had been sitting on. He folded his arms and casually looked at her.

Ice pulsed through her veins as Erin tried to maintain the wards. His eyes stayed on hers, never once flickering to Ella's. Maybe he couldn't see the unconscious godmother.

"I like it better here, don't you?" Carbonell asked conversationally. "I got tired of all the sand. I don't know why he chose Egypt in the first place."

Erin carefully lifted Ella and backed away from Carbonell.

"I can still see you, Erin. You know you can't leave. If you like, I could force you to stay."

Her arms felt like lead under Ella's weight. She didn't want to undergo a torture spell, and she knew Carbonell was capable of terrible things. A soft sob escaped her throat as she sunk to the ground, Ella resting in her arms. Hopefully Ella was invisible to Carbonell.

"That's more like it." He sat on the grass next to her. "Now, where should I begin? There are so many things to tell you."

Erin watched the black swirling aura around him. Wisps of white wove through like highlights in the darkness. She had never seen an aura do that before.

"I'd like to thank you for creating a reason for us to relocate. Egypt was desolate. I never wish to return. But this," he spread his hand out to the mansion, "is somewhere I could live." He rested his elbows on his knees before continuing. "Some things in our world are really not much different than the human world. Most of the time, wars are waged by the decisions of very few. Power and influence. It's all politics."

She bit her lip as the white wisps of his aura flashed around Carbonell.

"I doubt you realize your own relationship to Black Rain. *Your* very existence is the reason for *its* existence," he continued.

The thought burned in her mind, and she almost spoke the question. *How?*

"The royal family," he said simply.

Now she was lost. Her lack of knowledge about the älvin society glared at her in her mind.

"Yes, the king and queen and their three children were perfectly happy for many, many years. Or so everyone thought. The eldest son, who was destined for the throne, chose his wife. But you see, Erin, the one he chose did not choose him back. She was headstrong and left Álfheim. But that was not enough to keep the prince from her. It took years but he finally caught up to her. By then she had married a *human*. The prince went into a rage. If he couldn't have her, no one would. He eliminated her husband, but of course, that did not win her heart. And, with murder on his hands, the prince transformed into an imp."

The white wisps of light penetrated the darkness of his aura until Carbonell's skin took on a brighter tone. His words caused a lump to form in Erin's throat, and she waited for him to continue.

"But the prince could not be stopped. There were other ways of becoming king over the elves. He collected followers, some of them powerful old friends. It is only a matter of time now before he wins. All of Álfheim will be under his rule and then the world.

The humans are too weak to prevent it, and the elves are too proud to accept his potential. Things are already in place."

Erin watched him carefully, still wondering if Carbonell could see Ella. He hadn't so much as glanced her way. Surely he would have said something by now if he knew her godmother was there.

"It is a wonder indeed that all of Ālfheim has not discovered the truth behind you and your brother. Your very face should be evidence enough."

Erin shook her head. "But what do you want with Bain? And me? What are we to you?" The worst heartache she had ever endured had come at this man's hands. First he stole her brother and then he stole her. She looked down at Ella's sleeping face and wondered why the beautiful dark-haired elf was next.

"It is not about what I want. The prince is in charge, and his orders are always carried through."

Erin tried to fit the puzzle together, but the story had too many empty spaces. Xavene was an elf, not an imp. "What about you? Why did you choose to follow him?"

Carbonell stood and circled the stump. "That is a fair question—one that I have been giving much thought to." He stopped pacing and faced Erin. "From here I have the advantage of knowing all the angles. If it appears that I am following both leaders, then there is little that escapes me. The real question is, who does my heart follow? In the end, whose side will I be on?"

Erin watched as his aura clouded, the white mixing with the black until a smoky gray outlined his form. The color was less intimidating than the black she had always seen around him. She couldn't help but wonder why he had confided so much information. The story was heart wrenching and left her with chills. He spoke as though he expected her to understand where she fit into the picture, but it all felt too foreign.

"Why do you say that all of Ālfheim should know me?" The burning in her blood witnessed that this was the key. She held her breath as she waited for his response.

His stare pierced through her soul. "The prince, the heir to Ālfheim, was in love with your mother."

"No!" she cried, but his words spoke truth into her very soul. Her gift would not allow her to reject the truth. Something inside her felt as though it was tearing a hole in her chest, widening where she thought there was no room for more pain.

"But one like your mother is worth going to the ends of the earth to find. She was a rare älva, beautiful beyond comparison. Like you."

She looked at him in anger that he could talk about her mother after all that had happened. But he wasn't looking at her.

Carbonell stared at the mansion. "Have you ever considered that there is more than one right answer?" He blew out a long sigh, stood, and then offered his arm to her, the way Joel always did.

The gesture made Erin's heart speed up before it sank down even further into the black abyss.

"Please join me for dinner. You must be famished," he said with a sincere look of concern.

Erin looked back down at Ella still sleeping on her lap. What else could she do? If she tried to escape, Carbonell would stop her. Maybe if she went along with Carbonell for a little while, she could work out a plan and escape with Ella. It was a big maybe. What were the chances of anything working out? It hadn't been easy rescuing Bain. Ella probably wouldn't be much different. But maybe—maybe she would think of something.

"Don't be shy. I've got the most wonderful chefs. They would be delighted to prepare anything your heart desires."

She carefully settled Ella onto the ground and stood. Carbonell's eyes never left hers. He must not be able to see her, but why? Dinner. It was already too late to wonder what the worst thing that could happen might be. She just needed to buy some time.

"See? That's more like it." Carbonell stepped closer, offering his arm again.

Her chest tightened with anxiety. She stepped cautiously to Carbonell, earning a broad smile from him. Reluctantly, she let her touch ward drop and laced her arm through his. She looked back up at him timidly as he led her into the mansion, relieved that he never once glanced back at the sleeping form of Ella.

8
Three Questions, Almost

THE FOOD WAS TANTALIZING, FILLING THE ROOM WITH SUCCU-
lent flavors. "All right," she conceded. Erin didn't want to let
Carbonell win, but she was starving. It was worth keeping up the
charade of pleasing him if she could protect Ella. Even if Carbonell
was in sight, someone else could just as easily find the sleeping elf
outside the door. If this place was anything like Black Rain in
Egypt, there were sure to be imps around.

The skill of projecting an invisibility ward over someone without touching them was something Erin had never tried before.
Pulsar managed it without any effort, but his magic was so different than hers. And she didn't know if she was even succeeding. All
she could do was hope that the magic she tried to project would
reach Ella. She made it into an obsession, allowing the current of
thoughts to flood over the taste of the food or the grandeur of the
formal dining room.

"It's good, isn't it?" Carbonell asked casually.

She nodded and took another bite.

"I have to say, you have taken to everything much better than
I expected."

Silence lapsed as she concentrated on Ella's invisibility. At
least she didn't have to try to ward herself at the same time.

"I'm surprised you don't have more questions. I would have
thought . . ." He stared out blankly before tearing a piece of bread.

The food Erin had swallowed now stuck in her throat. Of
course she had questions. But how was she supposed to help Ella

and learn the mysteries of the universe at the same time?

Carbonell surprised her with a genuine smile as he saw her look of concern.

"I knew it," he said. "Tell you what. I'll let you ask me three questions. Anything you want. I even promise to tell the truth." His aura confirmed his promise, and Erin's mind buzzed, trying to compile thoughts.

"How come you can see me when I'm shielded with an invisibility ward?" Almost as soon as she asked, she regretted the question. To waste a question on herself when the mystery of her mother was still to be revealed was irresponsible. But her mind was still consumed with the invisibility ward she was desperately projecting over the sleeping älva outside.

He caught her off guard as he set his fork down and cleared his throat in a nervous cough.

"I shouldn't have underestimated you," he started. "But I am an älv of my word. I will answer your question." He leaned back in his chair and stared at the wall behind her. "I was Ormond's best friend."

She had to stop herself before the words slipped through her mouth. Ormond? It wasn't a question she could afford to waste.

"Julia lived next door to me all my life. As children, we played, learned magic, and went to school together. I never told her how much I adored her, but I did. Just seeing her face was as good as the sun coming up in the morning. When Ormond decided that she was to be his bride, it took all my hope from me. Julia never knew I loved her, and Ormond would not be swayed. She was the most beautiful woman in the kingdom, and he would have her at any price.

"I chose to step back and let him court her. It hurt to see them together, but I loved them both, and true friends sacrifice for each other. I could be a true friend. It wasn't until then that I realized that I had a gift. The ones I love could not be hidden from me. Even with invisibility wards, I could still see their faces. So I watched Julia, often following her. When she left the kingdom, I did as well."

Erin shook her head, trying to follow the story. Her mother's name was Julia. Ormond must have been the prince. "But you still haven't answered my question."

His eyes brimmed with tears as he looked back at her. "I have known you your whole life, Erin. From the day you and your brother were born, I was there. And I have loved you and watched you grow into a stunning replica of the most perfect lady to walk the earth." Tears spilled onto his cheeks, and he made no attempt to brush them away. "Erin, I can see the faces of the ones I love. Invisibility wards only cover you from the neck down."

The aura around Carbonell spun white around him, making his skin glow even brighter. She felt her own well of tears threatening to spill over. How could he have betrayed Bain and her if he loved them so much?

Carbonell left the table and came back with a box of tissues. The sight of him blowing his nose made her smile. It was so odd seeing the glimmer of white around him where darkness had always been.

"I think you've got two more questions. What's it going to be?" He picked up his glass and drained the juice.

Her mind felt like it would explode with the ambush of questions. If he was such a decent guy, why was he bent on destroying the elf kingdom? And how could anyone hurt someone they loved? And what was her mom like? Was she still alive? And if she was, where was she? What did they want with Ella?

"I've got one for you," he said. "How did you find this place?"

Erin tried to hide her panic by shaking her head. "No. I never promised I would answer any questions." But it would be better to keep Carbonell talking. "Do you know if my mom's still alive and where she is?"

Even as she asked the question, her stomach knotted and her body began to tremble. Chills ran up her spine as she waited for his response.

Carbonell stood as if in a daze and then abruptly left the room. She turned to see him disappear under an invisibility ward. Shivers ran up and down her arms as she waited. "Carbonell?"

But only silence answered her. Sitting still was no longer an option. Erin pushed her chair out and bolted through the front door to the sleeping Ella. The invisibility ward enveloped them both as she scooped her godmother into her arms. There was no way to know if Carbonell had followed her, but it didn't matter. She had to get out. Erin held onto the beautiful elf as if the action could save her from the pain that seared her heart.

A whisper of wind surrounded them, but Erin barely noticed the breeze. An echo of tinkling of bells filled the air as though it came on the wind from hundreds of miles away. Erin wiped her eyes and gasped at the change. Where the canopy of trees had hung over her head, now clear sky and a frigid breeze swept over a vast lawn. December was cold in Iceland.

She ran toward the palace, all along shouting for Pulsar in her thoughts. But no answer came. She didn't stop running until she was within the palace walls.

"Joel!" she called. Even though she was sure she could find her own room, she had no idea where anyone else stayed. "Aelflaed! Anyone?" This would be a great time for the healer to happen by.

Ella had not stirred and still lay limp in Erin's arms. Slowly, Erin made her way through the halls toward her own room. At least there she could let Ella rest on a bed. A small fire kindled in her chest as she thought of Joel following her around invisibly. Now, when she needed him, he was nowhere to be found. "I need help! Someone, please!" she cried out. With their supersonic hearing, surely someone would have heard her effort to rouse help.

If nobody came, it was their own fault. She was almost to her room now. Maybe after she settled Ella into her bed, she could go find someone. "Pulsar?" That was the strangest part of all. *Why hasn't Pulsar come by now?*

9
Aunt Lyndera's House

BAIN RAN HIS HANDS THROUGH HIS STREAMING HAIR. HE WAS starting to regret growing it out. If his high school buddies could see him now, they would probably tease him about putting his hair in a ponytail so he could play basketball. Already the thick blond waves were past his chin. He wondered how girls could stand having hair in their eyes. When he got back, he was getting a haircut, pointed ears or not.

But his hair wasn't the biggest regret he was facing. Why had he thought it would be a good idea to look for Erin on Pulsar's back? At least he wasn't the only one worried about her. Joel freaked out when Pulsar told him that Erin was gone.

"Are you sure?" Joel had asked the towering golden dragon.

Whatever the answer had been sent Joel into a fit, but Bain didn't speak dragon. He didn't understand how everyone else seemed to communicate with Pulsar as if the dragon was human. All he knew was that they could somehow hear each other's thoughts.

But not him.

While Joel told the others, Bain asked Pulsar if he would take him to look for Erin. When Pulsar lowered his head to the ground and folded his suede wings tight against his body, Bain took it as a yes.

Although he had ridden the dragon a few times before, it had never been alone. Erin had always been in the driver's seat, if there was such a thing. There was no steering. In fact, Bain had no idea where they were. All he knew was that the ocean had been under them long enough for him to feel queasy, and the longer they flew, the less likely it seemed they would ever find her.

After what felt like forever, Pulsar touched down on land that looked like Iceland, only a little warmer. "Why here?" he asked but felt like an idiot almost immediately. Pulsar would probably explain it to him if Bain had any idea how to listen.

"I'll take a look around." He set off and noticed that Pulsar disappeared. *Good plan,* he thought and warded himself with invisibility as well.

He didn't go very far before a tiny farmhouse came into view. Nothing about it seemed significant, with the glaring exception of the lime green magic aura that surrounded it. Whoever lived there spread enough magic around for the whole house to glow. Usually only elves and fairies glowed, with a few exceptions like the eternal blades and the Book of Knowledge.

Hesitantly, he knocked on the aged pine door. At first, the door opened only a crack, not even wide enough for him to see inside.

"Who is it?" a woman asked.

"Uh, Bain. Bain Farraday." He heard a gasp on the other side of the door and latches loosened.

"I've been waiting sixteen years to see you, I have." The door swung wide open to reveal a petite lady with red hair pulled into a haphazard bun. Her clothes looked old and worn, but her face was filled with energy and she seemed to be in her thirties. "Come in, already then. What are you waiting for, the entire house to feel like the dead of winter?"

He let her usher him in. "I didn't catch your name." He couldn't help but notice her pointed ears.

"Call me Aunt Lyndera. Or Lyndy. My stars, I can't believe how grown up you are. It happened so fast." She bustled into the kitchen where a pot was on the stove. Instantly, the kettle whistled as steam escaped the lid. "Care for a spot of tea? I only drink peppermint."

He nodded his head as he watched her work. "*Aunt* Lyndera?

Does that mean we're related or something?"

She was already back in the kitchen fetching sugar for their cups. "Dear boy, what do you think an aunt is, after all? I'm your mum's sister. Older sister."

"My mom had a sister? I thought her only family was in Ireland."

Her laughter filled the air with high-pitched gurgles interrupted only with small snorts. She wiped her tear-struck eyes. "Where, in the name of all that is green, do you suppose we are? This *is* Ireland, boy. How on earth could you be here and not know it?"

"I was looking for my sister, Erin. Have you seen her?" He wasn't sure if he was ready to explain that he came here on a gigantic dragon and that it happened to be just outside her door.

"I would love to meet your sister. It is a wonder that *you* are here, sitting at me table and all. You're tall, like your mother. You have her smile, you do." She sipped her tea and peered at him over the rim. "Is your sister lost?" she asked with concern coloring her voice.

"I hope not." He wanted to believe that everyone had overreacted. Inside he didn't feel panicked, but like everything was going to work out. "When was the last time you saw my mom?"

She set her cup down and pierced him with her green eyes. They looked the same color as Erin's. "Aye, your mum left the kingdom years ago. After she left, so did I. But she sent me letters and pictures." She flicked her hand, and a book floated to the table.

Scooting her chair next to his, she opened the book.

"That's my dad. And . . ." Bain murmured. All his life, he had only seen side shots of his mother. But here she smiled back at him from the pages. She was extraordinary. He couldn't begin to describe it. His mother could have been a superstar, a model, or someone famous, she was that stunning. In the picture she held hands with his dad, a man he had only known through photographs and stories his grandpa had told. And even though the picture captured but a moment, his parents looked perfectly happy and in love.

She turned the page, and two chubby-cheeked babies smiled out. "It's the two of you. I was supposed to get to meet you, I was. That was before the . . . well, that was before. But you're here now! And where are my manners? You're a growing boy—you must be starving."

He didn't have a chance to answer before she was back in the kitchen clinking dishes together. "So, you haven't seen my mom since I was born?"

"Aye, it has been a while. I'm sorry about that, dear. It must be hard losing your parents."

A lead ball settled in the bottom of his stomach. Why had the news disappointed him all over again? It had only been a couple of weeks since he had tried to convince Erin that their parents were gone. Hearing the words from Lyndera settled it, as if she were passing a sentence. That's when he realized that he had been holding out hope that maybe his mom was still alive. Part of him had listened to Erin, and that part was tearing into pieces. He ate the bread and cheese she set for him without tasting it. For once he wished that he hadn't been right. He was going to have to break the news to Erin. If he could even find her. Missing persons seemed to be a family tradition.

"I suppose I should let you meet Pisces. He's a bit jealous of strangers, he is. It might be best if I take you to him before he beats the house in though. Would you care for a bit of fresh air?" She was already wrapping a shawl around her shoulders.

He followed her outside, surprised that Pulsar's golden glow was nowhere to be seen.

"Best hold your ground, Bain. Pisces doesn't take to frightened younglings very well."

He looked down at the tiny lady as she put two fingers in her mouth and whistled so loud it would have put his track coach to shame.

"He'll be around soon." She pulled her shawl tighter around her.

He watched his aunt squint at the sky in expectation. Following the direction of her gaze, he searched the horizon, and soon a chuckle escaped him as he recognized the white magical aura. He had seen that color before. As the creature approached, he caught his breath. The pegasus wasn't pure white like the herd in the Door of Vines. This one was a paint with brunette splotches covering white fur as though chocolate pudding had been spilled onto its coat. The stallion's wingspan defied the size of the other pegasi. If Eakann had been impressive, Pisces had him beat by double the size. He was enormous and wild. The horse shook his brown and white mane and looked at Bain with one blue eye and one brown eye.

This would have been a great time to know how to speak pegasus.

"Pisces, this is Bain. Bain, this is Pisces," Lyndera said.

The stallion brayed loudly and shook his head.

"He's family, Pisces. Family." She turned and walked toward the farmhouse.

Bain stood facing the enormous horse. He wasn't sure what he was supposed to do now. "You probably met Pulsar, I'm guessing. He's nice, and my sister's crazy about dragons, so go easy on him."

The pegasus turned and took a mouthful of grass.

"Okay, well, it was good to meet you. Thanks for watching out for my aunt. She seems like a nice lady." He waved his hand halfheartedly before turning back to the house. He couldn't help but think that this would be a perfect opportunity for Pisces to run him over, or whatever horses did. The pegasi in the Door of Vines were different. They seemed so much tamer than Pisces, with the quick movements and flash of anger he shot at Bain.

He heard the sound of hooves galloping behind him. A quick look over his shoulder confirmed that the horse was headed straight for him. With a smirk, Bain bolted into a full sprint.

The horse kept pace with him, nearly catching up at times. The race led them along the cliff lines that capped the ocean-front. The constant rhythm of the hooves beating on the ground felt like a drum in his chest. He loved running and hadn't had a chance to lose himself in it for a long time. A laugh escaped him as he charged down the cliff side toward the ocean. The rocks became steeper, and Bain found himself leaping over much of the terrain.

The sound of feathers cutting into the wind filled the air as Pisces took flight. The horse shot high into the sky while Bain ran along the narrow beach. Pisces was quite the view with the white magical glow surrounding the broad brown and white patches. His wingspan had to be more than a full ten feet on each side. Bain smiled as he watched the magnificent creature.

"You win," he called. "Maybe one of these days you'll let me ride you. I'm not that bad, you know."

Pisces circled in the sky once before beating his wings against the air current and flying back over the land.

"All right, Pulsar, I know you're here somewhere." He started the climb back up the rock cliff, his mind trying to wrap itself around the fact that his tiny little aunt was friends with such a huge beast. He laughed at the thought. Maybe it ran in the family. After all, Erin was in love with a dragon.

Erin, the lost sister he still had failed to find, even with the help of a dragon. Pulsar was wrong. Whatever the dragon had been trying to tell him by bringing him here, it didn't end in finding her. Wherever Erin was, it wasn't Ireland. But he was going to figure out where she had disappeared to. She had done the same for him.

10
Jeans and Heartbreak

ERIN SETTLED THE SLEEPING ELLA ONTO HER BED. "IT LOOKS like it's just the two of us."

A soft knock came on the door, startling her. Overreacting to her pounding heart, she made it to the door instantaneously. Her heart leaped into her throat as she saw Joel standing there.

"Come in." She pulled the door open wide and looked over at the bed. "It's Ella. I found her."

He nodded with an expression that gave no sign of surprise. She held back the questions that flooded in. Had he heard them come to the palace? Why didn't anyone answer when she called?

"I think we should have Aelflaed take a look at her." He sat next to Ella.

Erin stood, nodding dumbly. "She's been out since I found her." There wasn't really anything more to add.

A mix of emotions welled up as she watched him touch Ella's face. Something pierced her chest, stinging unexpectedly. She tried to brush the feeling aside. Joel had never belonged to her, but it was still hard to watch him look at Ella with such gentleness, maybe even love.

She couldn't watch any longer. "Do you need me to get Aelflaed? Maybe if you know where she is, you could tell me." Her words stuck in her throat as she watched Joel scoop Ella into his arms, his tender affection more than obvious.

Erin couldn't think of a single thing to say. It had never before occurred to her that Joel might be in love with Ella. Erin had shared so many moments, and he had talked with her with such fondness, even protectiveness. She must not have been listening.

As he stepped out into the hall, Joel turned back around. "Are you coming?"

The question tore a hole in her emotional battle. She shook her head, tears threatening to find their way to the surface. Words refused to be led from her mind as she watched him disappear into the hallway.

She shut the door and stared at the beautiful room. Everything about this place was bittersweet. It was her fault for not realizing that she never meant anything to Joel all this time. He was the first one to offer his arm to her, and even though it was just on her hand, he was the first boy to kiss her.

But the thoughts only made the pain worse. She had to get out of here. Pulsar would know what to say. If nothing else, he could put some space between her and the too handsome Joel.

She looked down at her princess dress. Placing an invisibility ward around her, she slipped out into the hall. There were no poor among the älvin society. With their banking ability and stock market skills, Älfheim had enough money for everyone and all were encouraged to share the wealth they accumulated. She found the computer lab where they kept the money, grabbed a handful of Icelandic currency, and made her way outside.

On her way to civilization, she had called for Pulsar several times, but there was still no response. Maybe he had gone deep into the forest for some serious hunting. There, animals of enormous size were readily available. The thought of him ripping into his dinner made her glad she wasn't with him.

Soon asphalt roads and modern buildings greeted her. It felt strange to venture into the city alone. Although she and Pulsar had visited the airport, it had only been a mission to find Bain, not the local department store. In town she managed to discover a suitable shop, but she had to take a deep breath as she lifted the invisibility ward that had protected her from the inevitable stares. Wearing an elf gown in December on a weekday afternoon couldn't be normal.

As she picked through the jeans, a sales lady approached her.

"Are you working on the Christmas play, dear?"

Erin smiled, relieved. "Dress rehearsal."

The lady nodded. "Is there anything I can help you find?"

"Jeans and a sweater would be great." It felt weird to lie to the sales lady about being in a play, even though it was the perfect way out of an awkward conversation.

"I know just the thing," the lady said and pulled some pants from the racks and quickly filled her arms with an array of sweaters. "Would you like a fitting room?"

"Yes. Thanks." Erin followed her to the fitting room, where the lady filled up the walls with clothes.

"What about shoes?" the lady asked, eyeing the heels Erin had found in the wardrobe.

Erin nodded.

"I'll be right back."

The heels of her new boots clicked on the sidewalk, sounding like music in her ears. Jeans were the clothes of the truly blessed. She smiled as she realized that she wasn't invisible and no one was staring at her.

A butterfly flitted down between the buildings. Her first thought was how cold it was outside for butterflies to still be around—they should have migrated by now. But as she watched the light blue wings, realization dawned.

She kept her pace as if she hadn't noticed the älvor. Had Joel sent a spy? It seemed possible. If he couldn't be there to personally follow her around, he could send someone else to do it. She had yet to meet a fairy in Älfheim who was genuinely friendly to her. None of them were like Adarae and the colony back home. After spending so much time and growing to love them the way she did, it was odd feeling so outside of the älvor's affection.

The butterfly fairy made no attempt at concealment while flitting over Erin's head for nearly a half mile.

"Okay, you win." She looked up at the tiny, blue fairy.

"Erin Fireborn," the fairy spoke with a voice like bells, "Joel has requested you come to the palace at once."

The bubbling lava rumbled in Erin's chest. He sent a fairy to fetch her? She didn't have time to respond before the älvor darted into the sky.

Why did he have to go and ruin a perfect moment? Just when she was beginning to forget his burning hazel eyes, his wavy light brown hair, and the smile that sent her into Utopia, he had to send a fairy to tell her to come back. Maybe she wouldn't. Who was *he* to send for her? He was just another good-looking elf with a charming smile that melted her heart. And he happened to be in love with Ella. Not her.

11
Dancing and Other Disasters

ERIN WANDERED SLOWLY TOWARD THE KINGDOM. EVEN ICELAND seemed to recognize the significance of the land where the elves lived. It was sanctioned as enchanted land owned by the fairies. How they knew this, she couldn't understand. Maybe the people in Iceland were more aware of their surroundings than the rest of the world.

The sales lady at the store hadn't mentioned Erin's large, almond-shaped eyes that defied normal human proportions. But then, maybe Erin wasn't the first elf the lady had met. The thought was as comforting as it was disturbing.

She crossed the wall that separated Álfheim from the rest of Iceland. But she wasn't going back to the palace because Joel sent for her. In truth, she didn't know where else to go. Nowhere felt like home. Grandpa Jessie would have taken her back in a heartbeat, but going there didn't feel right either.

And then there was the dragon. Pulsar was the only thing that made anywhere feel right.

Fireborn! His voice resonated through her thoughts.

It just occurred to her that she had been so preoccupied that she had been blocking him from her mind.

His golden scales glinted in the sunlight as he touched down beside her.

"Hey! I've been looking all over for you." Bain unlashed his legs from the saddle and jumped down from the dragon.

Erin watched, stunned into silence. Bain had been with

Pulsar? That was two betrayals in a row. First Joel, and now her own brother takes off with Pulsar. He didn't even like flying.

Her throat tightened. *How could you?* she asked Pulsar. *And all this time I've been wondering what happened to you. I thought you were hunting or something. You took Bain?*

She didn't want to be mad at Pulsar, but emotions raged through her, eating at her logic. If Pulsar would leave her and take Bain, then she really didn't belong to him either. She was a nobody again. Pulsar didn't have to care about her any more than Joel did. And why should they? There wasn't anything special she had to offer, anyway.

"Erin? Are you okay?" Bain asked. "Where were you? I came out here to look for you and you were gone. Pulsar didn't know where you were either." He smiled crookedly as he looked up at the towering dragon. "But he was nice enough to let me come with him to look for you."

Erin stared at him. So much had happened that the day felt like it had taken a week.

"I met our aunt," Bain continued. "She lives in Ireland."

She finally found her voice. "What are you talking about?"

"Pulsar flew us there. I still don't know why, but can you believe it? We have an aunt. And," he shook his head, "you were right. She's an älva. Our mom was an elf, just like you said."

Erin covered her face with her hands. This was information overload. Emotional overload. First Carbonell, then Joel, now Bain. She was starting to see a pattern: guys, boys, men. She wasn't entirely sure she could group Pulsar into that equation, even though he was male too.

Bain touched her back and spoke softly. "Erin, I think our mom . . . she's gone. Aunt Lyndera hasn't seen her since before the accident. I'm sorry."

Whatever hole it was that had been ripping open in her heart was now torn beyond help. The anger was dissolving into a puddle of hurt. She looked at Bain and saw the sincerity in his eyes and his own sadness. Any resolve she had for being angry with him disappeared.

He took her into a hug before pushing her away again. "I'm going inside." He looked meaningfully at Pulsar and then back to her. "We'll talk later. I'm starving."

She didn't have a chance to answer before he disappeared. *What's going on?* she asked Pulsar. At least if she kept the conversation in her head, no one could overhear them.

Silence lapsed between them. Her pulse slowed down and she realized her own infraction. She had attacked him with an accusation and now she owed him an apology.

"I'm sorry, Pulsar." She didn't care anymore who could hear her. It didn't matter. The golden scales lured her in, and she reached out to their warmth. The familiar surge of magic filled her as she wrapped her arms around him.

Where have you been, Fireborn?

The best part of talking to a dragon was the effortlessness. All she had to do was remember all that had happened, and he could hear it and see it. She saved her own questions and feelings, giving him only the series of events. It was hard hiding the emotions Joel raised in her. The memory of him carrying Ella out of the room stabbed her.

"I know. I shouldn't care. I'm working on it," she offered as Pulsar followed her feelings that weaved through her memories.

You haven't shared any of this with the queen. I think you need to explain your findings. The whole of Álfheim could be affected by this. Fireborn, it is your duty to put your people first.

She leaned on Pulsar's massive body. "You're right. But does that mean I have to talk to Joel?"

Pulsar didn't respond but he beat his suede wings against the air, forcing her to move as he hefted into the sky.

"Thanks. I guess that means I'm on my own."

I will still be with you in thought.

"Perfect." Could this day get any better? She picked up her shopping bags and headed for her bedroom suite. If she had to confront Joel, at least she got to do it in jeans.

It occurred to her soon after searching the halls that she again had no idea where anyone was. If Joel wanted to see her, he was going to have to do better than this. She walked into the open aviary where the popping water sprayed from a large fountain in the middle of the tree-strewn room. This was where she met Joel. This was where he took her breath away for the first time.

She dipped an orange flower into the bubbling water and drank in the mango cream soda. The last time she had been in this room, Bain had been missing and it was up to her to figure out why. Today things couldn't be more different.

Carbonell had been a surprise. She remembered the lullaby he whistled on the helicopter ride to Black Rain. That song. She knew she had heard it before. And maybe that's why his story fell in step with her changing opinion about him.

Was he really the bad guy? When he said that he could see the ones he loved, his aura blazed the truth around him. He loved her. He was like family. But it was so confusing. She couldn't make the puzzle fit together. If he loved them, then why did he kidnap Bain and her?

"Erin Fireborn," a deep, majestic voice boomed behind her, making her spill the soda from the flower she was holding. "If you will please follow me."

Erin nodded and followed the tall älv through the labyrinth of halls. She didn't have the guts to ask why Joel would send for her, or why Anjasa would be the one to find her. It was all so formal. And it was making her nervous.

Anjasa stopped at a double door entrance and bowed to her slightly.

Erin watched, confused by the gesture. Was she supposed to bow back? Was she that rusty with elf culture? *All that and more*, she thought as she used her magic to open the door.

"Thank you." She tried a small curtsy and immediately felt like an idiot.

"Erin!" Joel said.

She didn't even have time to step inside the room before Joel was at her side. When he wrapped her arm in his and led her into the room, her heart melted all over again. It was impossible to stay mad when his earth sweet aroma and warm skin was so close.

Ella sat in a chair as elegant as the first time Erin had seen her. Erin couldn't help but notice Queen Āldera's appraisal of her as she entered the room. It was all Erin could do to not shield herself with an invisibility ward. She couldn't have felt more out of place or out-dressed.

"How nice of you to join us, Erin Fireborn," the queen said. "Please," she motioned to the surrounding furniture, "have a seat."

Joel led her to a love seat, where he sat next to her. Erin tried not to look surprised or confused, but why would Joel do that? Especially with Ella sitting just across from them in her gorgeous red and gold gown and her silky brown hair. No wonder Joel was in love with Ella.

"I wish to thank you," the queen continued.

Erin realized she had been staring at Ella, and that only made her cheeks flare up again. She looked over to the queen.

"You have retrieved one of my greatest treasures, and for that I am in your debt," the queen said.

"And I too wish to thank you. You and I have a lot to talk about." Ella gave her a wink.

Erin nodded and looked back at the queen, still confused by her words. "You're most welcome, your majesty." She couldn't think of what to say, having no clue what elves were supposed to do in these circumstances. It probably involved bowing or kissing hands or something. If she ever decided to completely forgive Joel, she was going to make him give her elf etiquette pointers.

Joel squeezed her hand, and she glanced at him in time to catch a wide smile.

Erin tried to breathe normally and ignore the flutter in her stomach. "I'm glad to see you're feeling better," she said to Ella. It was true. Ella looked as though nothing had happened.

Ella nodded with a smile.

Erin stared at the grain on her blue jeans. Dork of the year.

That's what today would mark. She had to go and buy jeans so that she would end up wearing them in a room with the queen. Of course.

"I am holding a meeting with the counsel this afternoon. I would like you to come and tell us everything that transpired as you rescued Ella."

Erin nodded. "I can do that."

The queen smiled. "There is one other item of business. The Winter Solstice Ball is coming up in just two weeks. I would like to have you, Erin Fireborn, be our Guest of Honor."

That brought Erin's eyes up.

"Do you accept the invitation?" the queen asked.

Erin nodded. "Yes. Thanks. I mean, thank you, your majesty."

"Very well, I shall have my tailor fashion a gown for you." The queen stood and left the room.

"I suppose that means you're going to need an escort." Joel squeezed her hand.

Erin had nearly forgotten Joel sitting next to her.

Ella interrupted. "Erin, I'm so happy for you. The Guest of Honor. It's perfect." Then the godmother disappeared.

"Joel?" Erin said softly, turning to him. It was hard getting used to seeing people disappear and not know for sure if they might still be in the room. "Does that mean I'm going to have to dance?"

He tipped her chin so that she had to face him. "Yes, Erin Fireborn. You are going to have to dance."

Heat zapped through her where Joel touched, but it did nothing for the ice that flushed through her chest.

"What's wrong?" he asked in the most perfect tone of concern. "You look like you just lost your changing brooch."

Her hand went automatically to where the brooch was still pinned to her sweater.

"It's just an expression. What's wrong?"

His hazel eyes were making her head swim.

She shook her head. She might be able to hear the buzzing of a fly in the next room or see the petals of the flower that grew in the field beyond the palace, but nothing had changed one thing about who she was.

"I can't dance," she muttered. It was like admitting that she didn't have an arm. Didn't all girls know how to dance? Probably all elf girls, anyway. This was going to be a disaster.

"I can teach you," Joel said.

He stood and pulled her from the seat.

She smiled, wishing she could be invisible.

He wrapped his arm around her back and twirled her around.

"I don't think I can do this." It wasn't just the dancing—it was everything. How was she supposed to go to a ball with Joel, knowing he would have his eye on someone so much lovelier? She would never be able to compete with Ella. And she had always liked Ella. Now what was she supposed to do?

He only smiled and spun her around again. "You're doing great."

She groaned inwardly. Learning how to use a sword was easier and a lot less humiliating. "So . . . Ella is one of the queen's greatest treasures?"

Joel spun her around. "An älva always is."

12
Be Careful What You Wish For

ERIN TRIED TO COME UP WITH THE SMOOTHEST WAY OF ASKING Joel. She just had to know. "Do you love her?"

Joel guided her down the hall with her arm wrapped around his. "What?" he asked with a genuine tone of bewilderment.

She blew her breath out, taking up courage. "Ella. Do you love her?"

He laughed. "Of course. Why do you ask?"

Her heart crunched in as though a steel ball swung at it. "I was just wondering." What was she doing walking down the hall with Joel if he loved Ella? Shouldn't he be spending his time with her? It made her heart shrivel a little smaller.

Any other girl would see straight into Joel's heart and know from the beginning that it didn't belong to her. Not Erin. No. She only had the power to detect truth, and from the brilliant white aura that surrounded Joel, he was telling it. He really did love Ella.

Her heels clicking on the stone floor was the only sound in the hallway.

"I will walk you to the counsel meeting in one hour, if it pleases you." He let her arm drop from his and bowed slightly.

She nodded. They were already to her bedroom door.

"I guess I'll change then." Even though he was in love with someone else, she couldn't help adoring him. It drove her crazy.

She shut the door behind her. "I can't do this," she said to the empty room.

"Sure you can." Bain materialized in a chair. He flipped his wand and directed her shopping bags to the wardrobe. "Do what?"

She sighed and found herself rattling off the events, relieved to be able to finally tell him. They used to share everything.

"I still can't believe you found Ella. How did you get there in the first place?"

"I don't know. Do you remember when I was asking Joel about Whispering Winds?"

Bain shrugged.

"Well, I asked an älvor. She said that Ella is the only one besides the Fairy Queen who knows the spell. She said Ella has wings of light."

"You mean, like real wings?"

"I know. It sounds stupid. Ella doesn't have wings."

He looked thoughtfully at his wand. "Do you think she gave you some of her power?"

"I guess. Maybe she was trying to get me to come save her. But that still doesn't explain how I ended up in Ireland the other day."

Bain lit the end of his wand and made it turn different colors. "Maybe she wanted you to find our aunt."

"I don't know." She shook her head. "Look, the queen wants me to go to a counsel meeting in an hour. You want to come?"

"No." He directed a pillow to levitate in the air.

She stared at him. "Please?"

The pillow dropped back onto the bed. "Okay."

"Good, now get out." She pulled him out of the chair. "I have to change."

"What's wrong with what you've got on?"

She noticed that he was wearing a long sleeve shirt, jeans, and tennis shoes. The exact same thing he would have worn if he was in Pennsylvania. "You wouldn't understand," she said, taking a gown from the wardrobe.

"It must be a girl thing."

Erin directed the door to open and pointed to it.

"Fine. I'll be back in a few."

When the door shut behind him, she tossed the gown on the

bed and went to the window. She didn't feel like going to a meeting. Or seeing Joel. Or walking down the hall again with her arm wrapped in his, knowing that he was in love with another girl.

"Pulsar," she called out to the lawn. "I know you're here somewhere."

She backed up as he landed on the dragon-sized balcony.

"I'm not going to get out of this, am I?"

No, little one, but you could spare a few minutes first. Bain is not the best companion. His head is like a brick.

"Be fair. That's only because *you* can't talk to him." But she smiled in spite of herself. She leaped onto his back and tied her legs to the saddle even as he lifted into the air.

Home. That's all it could be called. In the air with Pulsar, nothing could touch her. Everything that tied itself in a complicated knot stayed on the ground while they flew through the effortless sky.

She thought of the flight home from Egypt and how it had been one of the best moments of her life. The sea and sky—both seemed like an endless vast blue, and she loved it. Closing her eyes, she pictured not land below them, but a never-ending ocean somewhere far away from Joel. Far away from everything.

Suddenly howling wind swarmed around them as a metallic clang sounded in her ears. She couldn't see past the wind or hear anything but the deafening ring. At least this time she didn't panic. They had done this before.

When the air cleared, Erin gasped. Just as she had imagined, an endless ocean stretched for miles in every direction. There was nothing to see but blue.

"Woohoo!" she yelled. *Freedom.*

Where . . . are . . . we? Pulsar asked.

Her mind was suddenly filled with Pulsar's thoughts. He was not thrilled to be thrust in the center of the ocean. "I don't know where we are. Does it matter?" Visions of the counsel meeting were projected into her mind. Yes, it mattered. "How do we get back?"

How did we arrive, Fireborn?

She wasn't completely sure. Even so, she didn't want to go back—not yet.

Their shadow against the calm, blue water was the only break in the view. No ships, no land, no people. No complicated problems to figure out. No broken hearts. No betrayals. Below, the sea darkened to a shade of blue that reminded her of Bain's eyes.

Dark clouds gathered around them as they flew over the endless water. A blinding light filled the air with heat and electricity, striking so near that she could smell burning flesh. And then they were falling. Pulsar had been hit by lightning! She tried to reach inside his thoughts, but red pain filled her mind. Lightning flashed again across the sky as the ocean seemed to rise to meet them. He couldn't fly.

Too late to do anything else, she put a ward around them. There was no way to know if her touch ward would have saved him from lightning. She had never tested it against anything that powerful. Time measured in heartbeats. Bubump. The blue water coming at a furious speed. Bubump. Thermal manipulations. Touch ward. Did she know anything that would keep them from drowning? Bubump. She held onto his golden neck. He was right. They shouldn't be here. They needed land. Dry land. Something safe. The fourth heartbeat was lost. She couldn't hear it over the crashing sound of water.

13

Lost a Sweater, Gained a Friend

THEY SUBMERGED BELOW THE WATER. INSTINCTIVELY, ERIN HELD her breath, but the flood of water never came. All around her the ocean swirled, but she was dry. The touch ward was waterproof.

"We did it!" she screamed to Pulsar.

Silence.

"Pulsar?" She reached out to him, but his mind was stone.

They bobbed to the surface inside the bubble.

"Pulsar!" she screamed.

No answer.

He might just be blocking her out. He could do that so well. She untied her legs from the saddle and crawled over to inspect his damaged wing.

Deep crimson blood stained the torn golden suede. Nearly half of the wing was shredded. If only she had learned something about healing from Aelflaed. In all the time she spent in the Door of Vines, not once had Erin asked a question about healing. Bile rose in her throat as she pieced the wing together. There was no way to make the pieces stay, and no way to stop the bleeding.

"I'm so sorry." Tears rolled down her cheeks as she looked for an artery she could put pressure on. She couldn't let him bleed to death. She pulled her sweater off and held it to the largest wound.

"We're going to make it," she reassured him.

Something broke the swirling sound of the water. She looked up to see a giant set of jaws attacking the ward. Another shark and another circled around them. Soon the water flurried with savage bites, as if the sharks could eat their way through the barrier.

Nausea and cold fear gripped Erin as she realized that Pulsar's blood was calling to every shark for miles around. They could smell it even through the ward.

Again, the massive jaw lunged at them. And then another. Sharks of all sizes attacked with ferocity, seeming undeterred by the competition they were giving each other.

She wrapped her arms around Pulsar's neck, abandoning the bloody sweater. It was more important to maintain the ward. The sweater slipped off his body and dropped right through the ward. Several sharks darted for it at once, ripping it to shreds before eating it. Her new green sweater was ingested by no less than three sharks. But they were still hungry, and even more sharks were now butting their jaws against the barrier.

Erin closed her eyes against the horror that surrounded her. With the short-sleeved T-shirt on, she was cold. She thought about thermal control, but it would be too much magic. She shivered. How long could she keep the ward going? How long before fatigue and hunger sapped her ability to sustain the ward? There were limits.

"Do you remember the first day we met?" she whispered. "You were just a tiny thing then. Not even big enough to kill a Saepard. Now look at you. If you were awake, you could kill every shark around us with a mere thought. Then you'd be eating seafood until you couldn't eat anymore. Imagine that, Pulsar. Enough fish to last you for a week."

The flurry of sound around them increased.

"Not today, huh? Maybe we'll come back here another time and you can catch all the fish you want. Do you swim?" She realized she didn't know, having never asked before.

"Oh well. What do you say we get out of here? Somewhere nice. Somewhere with all-you-can-eat steak, or maybe they'll just give you the whole cow."

She tightened her grip around his neck and thought about the palace. "We have to get there! We have to get back. The palace." It wasn't working. "The palace!" she screamed.

Tears streamed down her cheeks. The sharks were still swarming around them. Maybe if she lifted the ward, she would have enough magic to get them back. But the truth was obvious. Once she lifted the touch ward, they would both be eaten in seconds. Or maybe just the dragon would be.

In her mind, a picture was forming, and she began to understand. A ward would always be there to protect her. It would happen even if she didn't choose it. It was elf instinct. Self-preservation magic. That's why elves couldn't die from anything nonmagical. Magic was infused in her very cells. It would protect her even if she didn't consciously choose it.

Another truth. Why did she have to figure that out now? Why, in the middle of the ocean surrounded by hundreds of sharks?

The answer rained down on her: because it was her choice to bring Pulsar here, and he would die if she didn't protect him.

"The palace!" she screamed again. But she knew she didn't have enough magic to ward them both and transport them at the same time. "Then how?" she asked. But only the sharks could hear. Pulsar was still unconscious.

She didn't know how long they floated in the ocean. Time slipped away. Clouds came and went. But the sharks stayed. It must have been too promising of a meal for them. Even though their attempts to penetrate the ward failed, they kept trying.

Pulsar never roused. They drifted for hours in a bubble. Erin longed for home with all her heart, but it didn't work. Pulsar was too big for her to ward and still have any magic left over.

But she kept up her trance. "Back home. The palace. We're gonna make it." She said it to herself as much as to Pulsar.

Her stomach growled, sending a jolt through her. If she lost her strength, she would lose her magic. Not completely, but enough. Enough to get Pulsar killed. The gnawing hunger pains awakened her senses. She would not let the dragon die.

"We're going to make it. We are. We're going back."

The sharks circled around her. Maybe they knew it was only a matter of time before the game was up.

She gave up trying to transport them and focused on the ward. That much she could do. It was hard. Her stomach hurt. Magic was using up her resources.

At first she thought she was dreaming, but her death grip on Pulsar's neck and the swarming sharks assured her that she was still awake. That sound. She couldn't place it. It was coming from above.

The sun settled on the horizon, giving everything an unnatural hue. Across the sky, a huge insect-looking craft loomed, steadily making its way to her. A large, army-sized, black helicopter with two rotating propellers cut through the air.

When the craft hovered directly over them, a net landed in the water surrounding her bubble. Someone was climbing down from the net. At first, it was too hard to tell who it was, but as he dove into the water and latched the net around her ward, she saw him.

Carbonell smiled at her as the helicopter lifted the three of them out of the ocean. He clung to the outside of the net as the water sped underneath them.

She watched him, confused. His aura was shining in the dimly lit sky. It was impossible not to trust him. He nodded to her as if understanding and then looked off in the direction they were traveling. When he started whistling the same tune from their first helicopter ride, she allowed a small smile. It was a lilting lullaby, something that haunted the crevices of her mind. A song from her past.

He stayed there, hanging onto the net with a breeze blowing through his hair until land came into sight.

14
Question Number Three

THE HELICOPTER LANDED ON THE SANDY BEACH. ALREADY, THE sun had dropped below the horizon and the moon had taken its spot in the sky. Erin clung to Pulsar's neck. The dragon's heat had diminished enough for his golden scales to feel cold.

Carbonell released the net and returned it to the craft. She watched him. Nightfall made it hard. She couldn't see auras in the dark.

Carbonell came back. "Do you want me to take a look at him?" He stood a safe distance away on the beach.

Erin never lowered the ward.

"I've got some leaves that would help his wing." He pulled a wrapped package from his backpack.

She recognized the broad, dark green leaves. Last summer, Agnar used it to heal Bain's ankle. "Okay."

She dropped the ward and knelt by Pulsar's injured wing. Carbonell fit the torn pieces together and placed leaves over the edges.

"Is he going to be okay?" The drop in Pulsar's temperature worried her more than anything else. Heat was how he stored magic.

"There's too much damage. He's going to need a healer." He continued to pack the wing with leaves until his supply was out. "But time can do wonders." He whistled as he headed back to the monstrous helicopter.

"Oh no." For the first time, she realized that they probably weren't alone. Someone had to be piloting the craft. And the helicopter was big enough to fit fifty soldiers in it. If it had been much smaller, she doubted it could have handled Pulsar's weight. Why didn't she think of it before? Carbonell probably had imps with him. There was a whole army of imps at Black Rain. Who else would be willing to work with him after he had been branded a traitor?

Again, she wrapped her arms around Pulsar. She didn't know if she had enough magic to transport them, but now there were no sharks. All she had to do was get them home. Back to the castle. Back to Bain. This time, she had to make it.

But no wind surged around them; no clang filled the air. The hot night air circled her as the stars poked out of their hiding places.

Carbonell was back. He arranged a pile of wood and started a fire before emptying out a pack filled with food. In moments, the smell of cooking meat filled the air.

Erin smiled. Maybe he was trying to wake up Pulsar with the succulent smell.

Carbonell sat on a rock and watched the fire. The yellow light sparked, allowing Erin to catch glimpses of his aura.

"Who was flying the helicopter?" she asked.

He raised his eyebrow at her. "Is that your third question?"

She had forgotten their deal. "No. You don't have to answer that. But you never answered my last question, so I still have two left."

He laughed heartily. "Erin, you are just like your mom. My crew can take care of themselves. Don't you worry about them."

"So I still have two questions left? Or are you going to tell me what happened to my mom?"

He rubbed his forehead with his fingers. "Let's just skip that one. How about a different question for number two?"

She wanted to ask him how he found her in the middle of the ocean and why he saved her, but a heavy feeling told her there was something more important at stake.

"Who is Xavene?" Pain ripped into her chest and took her

breath away. It was harder than asking about her mom. Xavene was the only other elf in Black Rain, and he was evil. He was the one who wanted Bain and her kidnapped, and for all appearances, it seemed like he was the one calling all the shots. In spite of the warmth radiating from the campfire, her arms trembled and goose bumps raised the hair on her arms.

"Fair enough, Erin. You can have that one." He used magic to turn the meat on the spit over the fire. "Xavene isn't his original name."

He looked at her as if he expected her to fill in the blank. She stared back and shook her head.

"When Ormond killed your dad, he lost his status as prince and his life as an älv."

"He turned into an imp," she finished.

He nodded and stared into the fire. "Most imps run off and hide from the world for the rest of their lives. Not Ormond. He wasn't willing to give up what was rightfully his. So he called on some old friends, borrowed magic from a few of them, and changed his name to Xavene."

The campfire's smoke drifted into the sky, and Carbonell's aura flickered in the dim light. Maybe he was telling the truth, but it was hard to tell. She had seen Xavene, the älv in Black Rain, and he defied the possibility of being an imp.

"You're saying that Xavene is really a prince who turned into an imp." It wasn't a question, but it did seem impossible.

"That's the nuts and bolts of it." He directed the meat from the fire and cut it into pieces before handing her a plate.

"I don't believe you."

He took a big bite of the meat and leaned back. "Can't say I blame you. He's not the same person I grew up with. Ormond's changed a lot."

"I thought you said Ormond was an imp. I think you skipped a step. How can he still be an älv if he became an imp?"

"Is that your final question?" he asked casually.

"No. If you don't want to explain yourself, then I won't make you. You just have a lot of holes in your story."

"All right, Miss Erin, I will tell you this one for free. Xavene learned how to change himself back into an älv. Well, temporarily, anyway."

She lifted her eyebrows at him, urging him to continue.

He blew out his breath and leaned forward as though he were telling a secret. "He can only be an elf when he is surrounded by a barrier of magic. Like the one in Egypt. He had that thing big enough to surround the entire city. Pretty impressive, if you ask me. As long as he's inside the barrier, he looks just like an älv. But if he leaves or," he gestured to her, "if someone goes and shatters it, he turns back into an imp."

"You're working for an imp?" It was at the heart of all of her questions. Why was he loyal to Xavene?

"I like to think of him as my friend. I've known him all my life. Ormond, Xavene, or mountain lion—he's still the same guy."

It felt like someone had punched her in the gut. Her insides hurt, and her throat felt suddenly swollen. *Mountain lion?* The pieces snapped into place. Xavene was the prince who fell in love with her mom, and he was the monster who killed her dad. In her dreams, Erin had seen the falling plane and heard her mother scream Dad's name. It was as if she had been there to witness the crime.

"And you said you loved us." There wasn't any more she could say. Her mom and dad were gone because of Xavene. He had taken them away from her forever.

Beyond the sound of the crackling fire and the gentle waves, another sound pierced the night—a sob. Erin looked up to see a tear drop before Carbonell covered his face.

After a while, he wiped his face on his sleeve and looked up at her. Even though his aura was diminished in the night's darkness, she could see the light sparkling in his wet eyes. "It's because of question number two."

15
Answers in the Fire

LIGHT BROKE THROUGH THE SHEER CURTAIN DRAPED OVER THE enormous window. Bain couldn't believe she was still gone. That was three times in one week. Erin, his straight-A, never-been-tardy sister, was missing again. This time, he was going to talk to Joel about it.

Yesterday when he came back to her room, she wasn't there. Bain went with Joel to the counsel meeting and did his best to explain to the queen what he knew about Black Rain, which wasn't much. All he had was that Erin found Ella and Carbonell somewhere in the Amazon. The order of events escaped him as much as the exact location. He felt like an idiot. National security, and all he had was a story his sister told him.

He closed the door of Erin's room and started down the hall-way. The best part of seeing everyone's magical aura was that he could find anyone he wanted. Each person's color was different enough that he could tell who it was from a long way off. And it didn't matter if they were using an invisibility ward, he could still see their magic. No one could hide from him.

"Bain!" Joel called.

Bain turned around to see Joel already caught up to him.

"Have you seen Erin yet?" Joel asked.

"No. I checked her room. She's still not there."

"She's not anywhere. Pulsar's gone too. At least they're together."

"Yeah. Any idea where they are?"

"Got me. Do you think they went to your aunt's house?"

Bain shook his head. His aunt would have tipped someone off if Erin was going to be there overnight. Wouldn't she?

"Listen, Ella wants to talk to you. Do you have a minute?"

"She wants to talk to *me*?" The gorgeous elf had talked to him plenty of times before, usually to tell him the rules. As his godmother, she filled them in on things last summer, even gave him a wand, but she always made Bain nervous. It was worse than talking to a movie star. She had magical powers.

"Come on. You'll be fine." Joel smiled. "You don't have anything to worry about."

Bain followed him to an open room where trees sprouted out of the floor. There, in the center of the room, stood Ella. Her red gown swept the floor around her, and she smiled as she waited for them to come to her. He swallowed and tried to look confident as he stood before the beautiful dark-haired älva.

"Thank you so much for coming, Bain," she said.

"Sure," Bain answered.

She walked between the trees, weaving around the tall trunks slowly. He followed her, trying not to stare. She turned and faced him, the full strength of her beauty shining on him. "I need to explain what has happened to your sister," she said.

Relief. If Ella knew where Erin was, then he could stop worrying.

She started walking again. "For days, I was Xavene's prisoner," she started. "All my magic was leeched from me, or so they assumed. I thought that all was lost. And then Erin came into view."

He stopped walking and let her walk alone. None of this made any sense yet.

"At first I thought that she had come for me, but then I realized she has the ability to dream real-time. She can transport her thoughts while she sleeps."

"Oh." He was still lost. He glanced over to Joel, who was inspecting the trunk of a tree.

"I decided to share Whispering Wind with her in hopes that

she could come for me," Ella continued as though she hadn't noticed his reaction. "If it worked, I would be free."

"So you gave her your power? Is that how Erin got to Ireland and the Amazon? You brought her there?" Bain asked.

"Yes, and no. Once I transferred the spell to her, I tried to call her. She didn't seem to hear me. It took longer than I thought, but at last, she found me. For that I am in her debt."

Bain nodded and turned away. Ella was in Erin's debt. He didn't know exactly what that meant.

"I thought there would be time for me to teach her the ways of the Whispering Wind. I planned to help her learn how to use the gift, but now she's gone. She doesn't understand her limitations, how to control it, or what it can do."

"But you know where she is, right?" She had to know. Ella could do anything.

His heart beat faster as Ella held him by his shoulders and looked deeply into his eyes—into his soul.

"I'm afraid I don't, Bain. She is wherever the winds have taken her."

He swallowed. "The winds?"

She dropped her hands and turned away. "The Whispering Winds can be powerful. I didn't realize Erin would learn how to use it before I showed her. I was counting on having more control. I thought she would be more like me."

"She's nothing like you," Joel spoke up.

Bain looked over to see Joel watching them. He couldn't decipher the look Joel was giving her. Was it anger?

"What do we do now?" Bain asked. That's all that mattered. Now that Erin was gone, how would they get her back?

Erin watched Carbonell steel himself in the flickering light.

"Question number two?" she asked. "Are you going to tell me?"

Carbonell rubbed his arms and sat up straighter on the

boulder. Squaring his shoulders, he made the firelight dance.

Erin watched as the flames took shape and the story unfolded. Carbonell's voice melted into the crackling fire, making it all seem like one sound. The forms flickered on the stage of wood.

It was her mom's plane. The engines caught fire, and the plane dove into the ocean. The intense fire burned so hot that by the time it hit the ocean, the only one alive was her mom.

Erin had seen this all before.

Before the silence could be broken, another image leaped from the fire. It was Xavene. He stood over the bed of her sleeping mother. She lay motionless under his spell. The image changed again, and Xavene was replaced by Carbonell. He reached out and touched the sleeping face. Xavene came in with a sword. They fought, but even in the firelight, Erin could tell that Carbonell didn't try to win. Instead, he left.

The scene broke into flames.

"What happened to her?" Erin asked. It seemed like even the waves were waiting for his answer.

"I don't know. That was the last time I saw her. I decided to help him build Black Rain. It was the only way I could get to her, or at least that's what I thought. I've been working for Ormond for fifteen years now, and I still haven't found her." He rubbed his hands together as if warming them. "But I'm not giving up. One of these days, I'll figure it out. I'll find her, and I'll take her away from him."

Erin wasn't sure when she stopped breathing. When she drew her next breath, it came in jagged, as if her lungs had forgotten how to work. "She's still alive?"

"She has to be. I would know if she wasn't."

"What do you mean? I thought you haven't seen her for fifteen years."

Carbonell poked a stick into the fire and stirred the coals. "You asked me how I found you."

She watched him, wishing it wasn't dark outside. If she could just see his aura, she would know.

"I can feel it when the ones I love are in danger. Just like I can see your face, I can feel it when your magic is compromised. You came pretty close to losing it out there today."

She looked over at Pulsar, who was still out. Carbonell was right. It was a miracle they were here. "But how did you find me?"

"I've got friends too, Erin. You're not the only one who talks to the fairies, you know."

"The älvor told you where I was? How did they know?" Now she really wished she could see his aura. There were no fairies in the middle of the ocean.

"Friends on the land, friends in the sea. If you don't mind, I think I'll keep that one to myself. You did get three questions."

The crackling fire and soft waves filled the moment.

"My mom's alive." It was hard getting used to the idea that her mom could still be around. She had always wanted it to be true, but now it seemed impossible.

"She has to be." Carbonell stared into the flames.

16
Wrong Again

PULSAR LOOKED LIKE A GOLDEN STATUE LYING ON THE BEACH. THE morning rays sparkled off his scales, reflecting light in every direction. Erin spent the night under Pulsar's good wing. She knelt by his head and touched his eyelids. "I'm gonna get us home today." She closed her eyes and focused on the lawn outside of the palace, allowing nothing else into her thoughts. But the wind never rushed around them, and the steady beat of the waves was the only sound.

"You ready to go?" Carbonell called.

Erin gasped and spun around. She hadn't seen him all morning. "Go where?"

"We need to take you two back home." He pointed to the black helicopter. "We need to get a move on."

She stood and brushed the sand from her jeans. Her boots had been abandoned as soon as they landed on the hot beach. "If you're taking us to Xavene, we won't go."

He laughed, and his aura was a clean white. "Of course not, love. I'm taking you two back to where you came from."

The nickname caught her off guard. Only Grandpa Jessie called her "love." "You're taking us back to the kingdom?"

"Only if you don't take all day about it. Do you want to help me move the dragon to the helicopter? I think he'll be more comfortable inside than hanging from a net."

Erin watched his aura carefully, but it never faltered. When was she ever going to figure him out? "Okay. What do you want me to do?"

"Material manipulation. You can do it. Just think of him as a really big basketball."

How did he know? She and Bain used to play basketball without their hands in their backyard, alone. At least, she always thought they were alone.

"You ready?" He faced the damaged side of Pulsar.

She nodded.

Together, they lifted the dragon and directed him to the opening of the helicopter. She was right—it was big enough to hold fifty soldiers, but the entire craft was empty.

Carbonell latched the holding door from the outside. "That's it, then. Time to go."

She followed him to the cockpit and strapped herself into the seat next to his. Soon the rotating propellers roared, and she watched the ground sink below them. Carbonell whistled in spite of the noise, and when she glanced over at him, he nodded and looked back out the windshield.

"What did you do with the imps who were flying the helicopter yesterday?" she couldn't help asking. The thought had crossed her mind a hundred times since he brought her to the beach. It was another reason she'd slept under Pulsar's wing. She didn't want to meet up with one of those monsters in the middle of the night.

Carbonell looked at her for a moment before turning back to the windshield. "You ask a lot of questions, you know."

She waited, giving him her best innocent look.

He glanced at her and laughed. "Just like your mom." He laughed again. "Okay then. I only had one guy with me, and I let him go. He didn't want to work for Xavene anymore, anyway. It was a convenient arrangement."

She stared out at the ocean spread underneath them. "Does Xavene know you rescued me?"

He cleared his throat. "Not exactly. He thinks I'm recruiting more imps."

She imagined the hold filling up with monsters of every kind. "You're not going to tell him about me, are you?"

He didn't answer. Instead, he looked as if he were considering something.

Her heart sped up as she waited. "You're not, are you?"

He laughed. "You're just as much fun to tease as your mom. If I was planning on turning you over to Xavene, you'd already be there."

At least he was telling the truth.

The sprawling brown lawn in front of the palace was a welcome sight.

Carbonell cut the engine and opened the door. "This ought to be interesting." He hopped out and opened the hold where the dragon was still unconscious. "It was good to spend some time with you, Erin." He kissed her hand. "I need to go now. I'm sure you'll understand." He glanced at the palace.

"Thank you." She didn't know where the urge came from but didn't try to figure it out. Impulsively, she threw her arms around his neck and hugged him. It was strange how new and natural it felt at the same time. He smelled like fresh cut wood.

"You're most welcome," he answered, patting her on the back before pulling away. "I'll see you again. Sometime."

"Okay." His aura made him look like a completely different person than the one she met a couple months ago. He seemed happier. She watched him walk back to the helicopter.

A stream of light shot over the lawn and hit Carbonell in the back. He stopped suddenly, midstride, and didn't move.

Erin looked around, confused. Then she saw Joel standing across the lawn, holding up his hand, his face furious. "Carbonell!" But he didn't move.

Joel was already there beside them. "Don't worry. He won't hurt you anymore."

"What did you do?" She didn't try to keep the anger out of her voice.

"He's fine. I'm sure there are a few people who would be

most interested in talking to him."

He lifted Carbonell's frozen body and floated him toward the palace.

"You can't do that!" It was cruel. Carbonell looked like a mannequin hanging from a fishing line as he crossed the lawn. "Let him go. At least give him the chance to talk to you."

"Let him go? You, of all people, should understand who he is."

"He's different now. I thought I knew him too, but I was wrong."

Joel didn't look at Erin as he directed the palace doors open. "There's a good chance that you're still wrong, Erin Fireborn. How else would you explain the dragon?"

She looked at his lifeless golden body slumped on the grass and back to Carbonell.

Joel may have been right about Erin making mistakes, but that didn't excuse him from treating Carbonell so harshly.

17
On Trial

ERIN FELT TORN. SHE COULDN'T LEAVE PULSAR OUTSIDE ALONE, but she couldn't let Joel treat Carbonell like a prisoner. It wasn't fair. But in the end, Pulsar won.

She sat next to the unconscious dragon and waited. Someone would come out of the palace and help them as soon as Joel spread the word. It was only a matter of time. She reached out and touched the cold scales. Pulsar's heat was completely gone. Panic shot through her. Maybe it was too late for him.

"Let me take a look," a soft voice said.

Erin turned, relieved to see Aelflaed. "He was hit by lightning."

Aelflaed knelt by Pulsar and touched his side. "Oh." Her voice was overcast with concern.

"What?" Erin asked. She knew it was bad but had no idea how bad.

"I think we should bring him into the palace. There's a room that would be perfect for him."

"Is he going to be okay?"

Aelflaed rested her hand on Erin's shoulder and looked her in the eyes. "We'll see."

Erin followed Aelflaed as they walked around the palace. An enormous windowpane opened up from the ceiling of a room, and they lowered Pulsar in.

"If you don't mind, I will send for you as soon as we have examined him thoroughly," Aelflaed said.

Erin nodded, but not because she agreed. She wanted to be

there with him to touch his scales and to tell him that everything would be fine. Instead, her feet slowly carried her past doors and food courts.

"I can't prove anything." Carbonell's voice echoed down the hall.

There was more talking, but this time several voices blended, making it hard to decipher the words. Erin found herself running toward the sound, as if her feet were in charge instead of her head.

The door was open. Carbonell sat in the middle of the room where several elves were seated behind a large mahogany table. Carbonell winked at Erin. All eyes followed his gaze. With the stares of the elves pressing on her, she felt like she was the one on trial. A small part of her brain registered that she was standing there barefoot, wearing a bloodstained T-shirt and pair of jeans. Her hair had to be a disaster, and she knew she needed a shower in a bad way.

Carbonell's smile widened.

"Is there something you would like to address the counsel with at this time, Erin Fireborn?" the queen asked.

Erin's thoughts couldn't catch up with the moment. She was too overwhelmed by the room of dignified elves to think of something to say.

Silence lapsed as everyone watched her expectantly.

"I just wanted to make sure Carbonell was okay." Erin looked at Carbonell, who was still smiling.

"Indeed," the queen answered. "It seems you have brought us another long lost citizen." She looked back at Carbonell. "If there is nothing further, we shall proceed."

A white upholstered chair floated over the heads of the seated elves and landed next to Erin. Why did it have to be white? She felt like disappearing but instead sat on the chair already feeling bad that she was going to get it dirty.

"Carbonell, explain to the counsel why you feel they should grant you any lenience after your association with Black Rain and the kidnapping of Bain and Erin Fireborn."

Erin didn't know the name of the dark-haired älv that spoke, but his words sank into her mind. She hadn't considered that they would attempt to imprison Carbonell. It would probably be done with the same spells Xavene used to keep Ella hostage.

"I know Julia is out there somewhere. I want to help Bain and Erin find their mother," Carbonell answered. There was only confidence in his voice.

"This is outrageous," one of the members said. "How dare you hang that over their heads. Julia is gone."

Erin's heart sank. But she stared at Carbonell's aura glowing white.

"She's still alive. I know it. If you let me take the twins, they can help me find her," Carbonell continued, his tone smooth and unruffled by the accusation.

Joel stood. "Do you think you can petition the counsel to steal Bain and Erin Fireborn? You have already had them under your control, and you didn't produce their mother then. How can you imagine we would let you take them again into your lair? We won't be swayed by your lies!" His face was flushed with anger.

Carbonell looked at Erin as he spoke. "I do not wish the counsel's approval, only Bain and Erin's. If they want to help me look for Julia, then I will take them." He looked back at Joel. "Without them, without their gifts, their mother will be lost forever. Only they have the power to find her."

Warmth surged through Erin's chest, radiating to her limbs. It was electric and magic. It was her gift telling her the truth of Carbonell's words. The white aura glowed around him, but even greater was the tingling inside her, making it impossible to deny. If Bain came too, they would find their mom. Carbonell was right. Her mom was still alive. She knew it just as much as Carbonell did.

"No," Joel said flatly. He sat back down and stared at Carbonell. "I will not allow it."

Erin watched, confused at the authority Joel assumed.

"Is the counsel ready for a vote?" the queen asked. The elves around the table nodded in agreement. "Those in favor of sentencing Carbonell to one hundred years of imprisonment for the traitorous act of kidnapping and assisting a known enemy, raise your hands."

"Wait!" Erin bolted out of her seat and ran to Carbonell. "You can't do this. Carbonell's right. My mom is still alive. I know it. If you don't let Bain and me help him look for her, we're never going to find her."

"How can you be sure, Erin Fireborn?" Queen Āldera asked.

Erin looked at the queen's soft expression. There was no anger in her face, only concern. "I can see the truth in Carbonell's aura, and I can feel it. With every cell in my body, I know he's right. If you take Carbonell away, you have sentenced Bain and me to wait another hundred years to meet our mother. By then, who knows if she will still be alive or what else Xavene will have done to her." The confidence with which she spoke surprised even her. But it was all true.

"I see," the queen said. "All in favor of proceeding with Carbonell's sentence, raise your hand."

Erin watched in shock as Joel's hand went into the air.

"Those in favor of granting Carbonell freedom, raise your hand," the queen said.

One by one, the hands lifted from the counsel.

"Erin Fireborn, you have taken Carbonell on as your own personal risk. If you choose to accompany him, I cannot guarantee your safety." Queen Āldera stood. "As for you, Carbonell, you have let your alliances lie on the side of treachery. If it is, as you say, a way to gain back Julia, you have but to prove yourself. We will not tolerate another infraction toward the kingdom on this matter. You must leave and return to Ālfheim with Julia or not at all."

The queen turned to the members at her sides. "Thank you all for attending on such short notice. This meeting is closed."

Erin held her breath as the elves filed out of the room, leaving her alone with Carbonell and Joel.

"Joel," she said.

Joel stood and shook his head. "You are in too deep, Erin Fireborn." He turned and left the room too.

Erin's heart plunged into her stomach. Why did she have to choose between Carbonell and Joel? It didn't make sense. She hardly knew Carbonell, but then, she only thought she knew Joel.

18
The Healer's Art

Erin sat on a bench next to Pulsar and stared through the trees out the tall windows. Even though she was indoors, it looked like a forest here. Her mind felt numb. Nothing seemed to get past words. Carbonell took his helicopter and left. She wanted to go with him, but she couldn't just leave Pulsar, and her twin would never forgive her. Bain was somewhere in the palace, but she didn't know where.

She pulled the changing brooch out of her pocket and turned it into an iPod. Music pulsed through the ear buds, erasing the pain from her mind. There was nothing she could do now.

Pulsar was still unconscious. The healers had come and cast their best spells. Aelflaed administered with plants and elixirs. None of it did any good. Apparently the lightning had hit more than just his wing. His face had caught a large share of it, and even though his scales protected him from the heat, the voltage that shot through his system must have been too much for him to handle.

No elf had ever seen a dragon hit by lightning, and no one knew what would happen next. She pulled her eternal blade out and touched the forever tear. "I wish this could work," she told Pulsar. She touched the tiny diamond to his scales. Nothing happened.

"You're just too big. Maybe if I had hundreds of älvor tears." She smiled. "Make that thousands. Pulsar, you've got to stop growing."

She tucked the blade back in the sheath. "I miss them—Adarae and the colony. It's been too long."

Erin lapsed back into silence. Pulsar couldn't hear her anyway. The music changed, and visions of her house in Pennsylvania flashed in her mind. There it was simple—just school, Grandpa Jessie, and Bain. Nothing there had ever stretched her to the brink of her ability to cope until that day they found the cottage. Was it a good thing? She could have been a regular high school student this year.

"I could come back later, if you want," someone said behind her.

She turned to see one of the healers that had been in earlier with the dragon. He was the youngest one—he didn't even look eighteen—but looks didn't mean a lot in the world of elves. For all she knew, he could be eighty years old.

"It's okay," she said. At least her voice was strong, not giving away her overwhelming hopelessness. Reluctantly, she moved away from Pulsar and stood by the windows.

The älv knelt by Pulsar, and Erin turned away.

"Are you okay?" he asked.

She tugged on the earpieces and changed her iPod into a brace-let. How was she supposed to answer that? She was tired of lying. But how could she tell a stranger that everything in her world had turned upside down? "How's Pulsar?" she asked instead.

"The same," he answered. "But there is so much we don't know about dragons. He is the first one to choose a human in many centuries. Most of what we know about them is found in books, not in our heads. You never know what's going to happen."

"Why did he choose me?" It was a question that tormented her. Pulsar chose his own death when he chose her. She was the one who brought them into the eye of a storm. He shared his magic with her, taught her how to use a blade against an opponent of fire, and sounded reason in her mind every time things went wrong. Though it had only been half a year, it felt like he was most of who she was. And yet it had been the biggest mistake of the dragon's life.

"You must know," he said.

She sat on the bench and stared at the bracelet instead of looking at the elf. To her surprise, the healer sat next to her on the bench.

"Legend says that when a dragon meets the right person, the magic inside of him—or her—yearns to be free." He looked at her with a raised eyebrow.

She met his gaze with indifference. "Pulsar still chose wrong."

He shook his head and continued. "Finding the right person rarely happens. Most dragons live out their lives in the wild. It isn't until they share their magic with a human that their tendencies become what you might think of as civilized. Without a human to share magic with, dragons live like other animals. They maintain no association with any kind of people."

It was more than she had heard about dragons so far. There was still so much she didn't know about Pulsar.

He continued, staring at the golden scales reflecting the half-lit sunlight. "It was just as much your doing as his that you share this bond. You can't blame it all on him."

"What do you mean? I didn't do anything." She thought of that day in the forest when he had subdued the pack of saepards with his magic. He was so small, then. Pulsar gave her his magic without even asking her first. It wasn't her decision.

The healer turned to her. "You simply are the right person. It's you—your life, your talents, your personality, tendencies, abilities, and quirks. All of it. Pulsar couldn't *not* choose you."

She stared at him, still confused. Maybe this was some kind of ancient elf wisdom, something she was never going to get.

"You really should feel grateful. Anyone in the entire kingdom would gladly trade you places. It's ironic, isn't it? You don't even understand what you have."

She couldn't answer. He was probably right. "You know, when I first met him, he was controlling a pack of saepards." She looked at Pulsar's mended wing. It was whole again, free from any sign of the lightning. "He told me that dragons heal fast."

"They do," the healer said.

"Then why hasn't he healed yet?"

"Do you have any idea how much voltage is in a lightning bolt?"

She shook her head.

"Between 10 and 120 million volts. The electricity reacted with his magic until it magnified in proportion." He looked at her as though he knew she still didn't understand. "It's like pouring gasoline onto a fire. Pulsar is in a coma. The biggest threat now is that a blood clot will stop his heart or cause a stroke. He must have been hit in a vulnerable spot for the lightning not to deflect off of his scales."

"Can't you give him something that will keep his blood from clotting? Blood thinners or something?"

"We have tried that. We're still waiting to see how it works out. But there's also the possibility that the lightning caused brain damage. Time will tell."

She sunk back into silence and watched the light reflect off his scales, casting eerie beams all over the room. It was hard getting used to the limited daylight in Iceland.

The healer patted her leg. "I'll come back in a little while."

Pulsar couldn't have brain damage. He would be okay. He had to be.

"Can I talk to you for a minute?" Ella's voice sounded behind her.

Erin turned to see Ella standing beside her. "Sure." But she wasn't in the mood for talking. She wanted to sit here and wait for Pulsar to wake up and be better.

Ella sat down on the bench where the healer had just been. "I can't be your Fairy Godmother anymore."

Erin pulled her eyebrows together as she looked at Ella. Of all the things Ella could have said, she didn't see that coming.

"Erin Fireborn, I want to apologize for giving you the Whispering Wind. It was reckless of me. I thought I would be able to teach you how to use it after I called you to me, but things didn't work out the way I had hoped." She stared at the sleeping dragon.

"This is my fault," Ella continued. "I should have insisted on talking to you about it the first moment I could."

"It's not your fault, Ella. I was the one who thought of a blue ocean. I kind of wanted us to disappear like that. It was me. I was trying to get away."

"That's just it. You're the first one who has been able to use the Whispering Winds without being trained. You were only supposed to be able to rescue me. At least, that was what I was counting on. Your traveling by thought alone brings on a whole new dimension. You only thought about the ocean?"

"Well, I pictured it in my head. I wanted to be far away." Erin sighed. "It was pretty selfish. I was thinking about how nice it was when we were alone over the ocean, and I wanted to do that again. I didn't realize how dangerous it was."

"Whispering Winds is a gift created by the queen of the älvor. I was the only one she ever shared it with. I spent hours training to control it. It required practice and sheer determination for me to choose my destinations and arrive with accuracy. I expected to take you through the same training when I had the chance." She stood and walked around the golden mound. "It's the dragon magic." Ella looked up at Erin. "That must be what it is. Your magic is different than mine. Why didn't I think of it sooner?"

Erin watched her, still a little lost. Nothing about her magic had been different from everyone else's so far.

"Erin Fireborn, I don't even know how to train you. It seems you have changed all the rules."

"But I tried to bring Pulsar back here after he was struck by lightning, and I couldn't. I tried so many times, but I never could get us home." It was hard confessing this weakness on top of her decision to take them out in the middle of the ocean in the first place. Maybe the counsel would want to deliberate on incarcerating her now.

Ella put her hand to her chin. "But Pulsar was already out. Probably his magic combined with yours allowed him to travel with you in the first place. He is rather large for Whispering Winds to carry. There are limitations. Once his magic was sapped, you were on your own."

Ella stood in front of Erin, her tall, slender frame towering over her. "You could have come back by yourself, though. Did you try?"

Erin craned her neck to look up at Ella. She dropped her eyes again and stared at the floor. "I couldn't leave him. Where would I go without him?"

"I see." Ella walked the floor, her heels clicking on the tile. "Since I gave you Whispering Winds, you can no longer call to me. I cannot sense you. That is why I cannot be your Fairy Godmother. You should also realize that Whispering Winds requires magic and that the more you use, the more it will take out of you physically. When you transported me halfway across the world, for example, I doubt you would have been able to maintain much of a ward once you arrived."

"I didn't even try," Erin mumbled.

"You would have either failed to ward or perhaps collapsed." She stopped walking suddenly. "But there's Pulsar," she said excitedly.

Erin looked at her, confused.

Ella pointed at the unconscious dragon. "He could ward you even if you couldn't ward yourself. You can use his magic." She laughed. "He can use his magic on you without you even agreeing. This could be very good."

"Except that he's in a coma." Erin didn't like talking about Pulsar as if he wasn't there, especially since he was nearly lifeless.

"I'm sorry, Erin Fireborn. But don't you see? With him, everything about Whispering Winds changes."

Erin didn't answer and stared out the window instead. December had drained the vibrant colors from the grass and trees. The sun was gone most of the day. It matched how she felt.

"Mere humans survive lightning strikes," Ella said. "I think Pulsar's going to pull through."

Erin wanted to believe her.

19
Broken Things to Fix

BAIN HEARD THE HELICOPTER, AND SOMEONE SAID IT WAS
Carbonell. He didn't even go to the window to look. If there was
one person he never wanted to see again, it would be Carbonell.
Last summer he was duped into believing that Carbonell was a
friend. And then Black Rain turned Carbonell into the enemy.

It had only been a few weeks. Being back at the palace made
believing in magic so much easier. That, and riding on a dragon.
He was almost getting used to the idea.

"There you are. I've been looking all over for you," Joel said.
"Your sister's here. And Pulsar."

Bain followed Joel as he slowly walked toward the door. "I
take it you're not in a hurry to see them," Bain said. Joel never
walked this slowly.

"Not especially."

Bain stopped. "What's going on, Joel?"

Joel turned. "Your sister almost killed Pulsar."

"What?" Bain couldn't believe it. Erin could barely kill a
mosquito. She would never purposely hurt Pulsar, and it seemed
impossible that she could be powerful enough to accidentally do
much either.

"And she cleared Carbonell's name with the counsel. We
almost had him in our hands, but now he's free, thanks to your
sister."

"I don't believe you." Bain watched Joel's face, but there was
only anger there.

"Then maybe you should come see for yourself," Joel said and disappeared.

Bain followed the orange aura down the corridors. "What happened?" he asked the orange light.

"Your sister thinks that you and Carbonell are going to go find your mother."

"You've totally lost me." Bain wondered why Joel bothered to do an invisibility ward.

"Carbonell claims that your mom's still alive and that the three of you are going to find her." The cloud of orange paused. "And she believes him."

This was a disaster. Erin already had too much false hope. After all, Aunt Lyndera had all but confirmed that their mom was dead. What more did they need? "What about Pulsar?" Bain asked. "What aren't you telling me?"

"You're going to have to see for yourself," Joel answered.

Bain followed Joel as he silently wound through the halls. "Joel?"

The orange glow didn't answer.

Bain continued anyway. "Does that mean Carbonell is still here?"

"No, he left," Joel answered.

That was a relief. At least he wouldn't be forced to confront the traitor. "Do *you* think my mom's still alive?"

The orange glow moved on silently. Even though Bain could see where Joel was, it was hard talking to his aura. "I take that as a no."

Silence filled the halls until Joel flickered into view.

"They're in here," Joel said, motioning at the door.

"Aren't you coming?"

Joel shook his head and took off down the hall, his orange glow giving away his speed under the invisibility ward.

Bain opened the door to the large tree-filled room. He wondered if the palace had so many tree-filled sanctuaries to make up for the limited winter sunlight. But this room didn't shine as if it were midday like all the others. In here, the windows let the tall trees cast long, dark shadows as the early setting sun bled through the windows.

He followed the trees until he saw his sister on a bench in front of the large, golden dragon. Maybe Joel had been right. Pulsar wasn't moving.

"Hey," he said, not wanting to startle her.

Erin didn't look up. He closed the distance and sat on the bench next to her. "What happened to Pulsar?"

She looked at him with her red-rimmed eyes. "He was struck by lightning."

"Oh." That made more sense. But why would Joel blame her for that? He wrapped his arm around her, and she immediately curled into him and started sobbing.

He held her as she cried against his chest. "It's going to be okay."

He noticed the blood stains on her shirt and pants and saw that her feet were bare. As he pulled her hair away from her face, he felt sand fall from her locks. It would have been a lot more helpful if Joel had told him what had really happened. If Joel cared about her half as much as Bain did, he would have tried to comfort Erin instead of accuse her.

After a while, Erin's shoulders stopped shaking. The room was silent. She hadn't lifted her head from his chest, and it felt good to be the protector. Even though she had a dragon, maybe she still needed her brother. "I'm taking you to your room. You need a hot bath. I don't think there's anything more you can do here right now." Bain looked up to see the trees lit with the glow of the älvor's magic. "If I may humbly request, could you please send a messenger if the dragon awakes?"

A tiny, dusky plum-winged fairy flitted down from a tree. "It is well, little one."

Bain nodded and scooped Erin into his arms. She didn't resist and laid her head against his chest as he walked out of the room. He never realized how light she was, or maybe how strong he had become.

He directed the door to her room open and laid her on the

bed while he filled the tub with water. "You need to take care of yourself, Erin. Don't make me send Aelflaed in here." He had never seen her so despondent. He kissed her on the forehead. "I'll come back and check on you in an hour. You better smell a lot better by then."

He closed the door behind him and stared out at the corridors. How was he going to fix this? There had to be something he could do. He ran, letting the doors fly by him until he made it to the dimly lit room. Shivers ran up his arm as he touched Pulsar's icy scales. How could he be so cold and still be alive?

A thought flashed through his mind as he looked up at the tiny lights of the fairies.

20

A Drop in the Bucket

BAIN ENTERED THE SPARRING ARENA, LOOKING FOR THE SAGE-green glow. Agnar was almost always here giving lessons. He smiled as Agnar waved at him from across the room.

"Are you ready for some more, Master Bain?" Agnar teased.

"Actually, I need a favor." It didn't take long for Bain to unload his story and give his request.

Agnar nodded, offering no comment.

"Am I right? Is there a shortcut to the cottage?" Bain could see in Agnar's easy smile that he had hit it right on. "Will you show me?"

Agnar looked around at the empty room and scratched his chin. "Well, I suppose it is for a good cause."

"Absolutely."

"And you *are* one of my best students."

Bain smiled in response.

"I don't think it would hurt anything. This one's on your shoulders, though. If anyone finds out, tell them you found it on your own,"

"Whatever you say, Swordmaster." This was too easy. He followed Agnar outside of the building, where they stopped at a gray brick structure that looked like an oversized well.

Agnar turned the handle, raising an enormous bucket out of the depths. "You climb in and hold on. It will take you to the cellar of the cottage."

"How do I get back?"

"Same way. You climb in, and it will reel you up. There's nothing to it, really."

Bain grabbed the tall barrel and looked at Agnar. "You're sure about this?"

"I've done it plenty of times. You'll be fine."

Bain climbed up the brick wall of the well and stepped in. He grabbed the wooden sides of the barrel with both hands as it plummeted into the darkness.

His stomach was somewhere in his throat, and it felt like his blood was circulating backwards. It was a deep well. There was nothing to see in the blackness as the air rushed by him. How long was he going to fall? He looked up to see if there was any light, but Ālfheim was already pretty dark when he left. There was nothing to see as he fell, sucked into the earth in a bucket. He pulled his wand out and lit the end. The sight of the gray bricks speeding upwards only made his stomach turn. He put the light out and chose a touch ward instead. Agnar hadn't promised an easy landing.

All at once, there was silence. It was still dark, but the bucket wasn't dropping anymore. Bain lit his wand and climbed out. At least he didn't have to find his way in the dark. He ended up wandering for a while before he recognized the hall that led to the stairs: forty-nine granite steps.

As he popped the trapdoor open, he looked at the empty kitchen table. Good times. It was tempting to check the old fridge to see if there was still cold soda in there. He took a deep breath and opened the front door. It was freezing. At least six inches of snow covered the ground. And it was bright. Unlike the short daylight of Iceland, Pennsylvania was blindingly light. But no colorful glows came from the snow-laden trees. The älvor were probably tucked away in their garden for the winter.

He jogged to the Living Garden, whistling as he went. Normally, vines and flowers hid the entrance to the garden, but today, everything was withered away and covered with snow. He pushed the dead plants aside and stepped through the thick layers of bare stems as he opened the gate.

"No way," he said. The temperature had to be in the high seventies. The fountain of popping water gurgled, and the teacup flowers grew on bright green stems right next to it.

"Bain, how nice of you to visit."

He knew that tinkling voice anywhere. "Adarae!" He watched the tiny blue fairy dart around. "This place is great! It's so warm."

"Thermal control," she answered. "It helps the plants grow."

Bain looked around at the tiny berry bushes and fruit trees. "Do you hide out until it warms up out there?"

Adarae landed on a branch in front of him. "Bain, we heard about Pulsar and your sister."

He sat down in front of the small tree Adarae was perched on. "I have an idea—you know, to help Pulsar. The diamond tear that Loden gave Erin—I know älvor tears can heal. I was wondering if you could come to the kingdom to help Pulsar."

"I see," Adarae said. She lifted off the branch and floated over the garden. "It would take many tears for a creature as mighty as Pulsar."

"But it would work, wouldn't it?"

"If we left the garden, we would take our magic with us. Everything would turn to winter, and our garden would die. Without the food, we would be forced to relocate. The Faerie dragons wouldn't be able to survive here either."

Why did he think this would be such an easy idea? Suddenly, his whole plan felt stupid. He thought he would just waltz in here and expect the whole colony of fairies to come back to Älfheim with him. What was he thinking? "I'm sorry. I didn't know. I wouldn't ask you to do that." He got up and headed for the gate.

"I never got a chance to thank you for what you did for me in Black Rain," he said without turning around. "I saw you there. Even though Carbonell kept telling me I was crazy, I knew you were real. I know how hard it must have been to be stuck in that horrid place for so long."

The black walls surrounded by a sea of sand flashed through his mind. It was hot, dry, and void of happiness. The fairies must have been tough to endure a place as evil as that for so long. He shook his head, trying to clear the memory of the hellish place.

"I've got to get back to Erin." He pushed the gate open, and snow fell from the trees.

At least he knew he had tried. The cold wrapped around him as he headed back to the cottage. He thought of Grandpa Jessie and Mrs. Hammel. They would probably freak if they saw him. It wasn't even Christmas yet, and plane tickets were expensive. But nobody would have to see him.

He smiled. If there was anything that could help a bad day, it was seeing his home again. One quick look around couldn't hurt anything. Erin wouldn't even know he had been gone. It was so convenient having an invisibility ward at his disposal. He found the spare key and went in the back door. No matter how grand the palace was, nothing could compete with the feeling of his house. He grabbed a drink and headed upstairs to his room.

As he passed Erin's room, he remembered her bloody clothes. She would love him forever for this. He pulled her old duffle bag out and filled it with what she had left in her closet. There wasn't much. He went into his own room and surveyed the too-short jeans. That stupid elf magic had somehow put six inches on his height in a couple hours. He didn't have any pants that fit that Carbonell didn't buy for him. It was a hard truth to acknowledge that the clothes he wore every day came from the enemy.

He shut the door to his room and went back downstairs, locking the door and returning the spare key. The basketball sat there on the court filled with snow. He couldn't help it. He lifted the ball with magic and made a perfect basket. "I've still got it."

He sprinted until the houses were out of view and then slowed and dropped the invisibility ward. Going back without a cure for Pulsar did not make him want to hurry. He breathed in the frigid air. One nice thing about the immortal transformation was the immunity to extreme weather. He could feel that it was cold outside, but he wasn't freezing like he should have been. In fact, he wasn't cold at all.

Out of habit, he dug his hands into his pockets. The duffle bag was slung over his shoulder like a backpack. What was he going to do about Pulsar? There had to be an answer.

The silence of the forest broke with the sound of uneven pounding. At first he thought of the mountain lion, but the rhythm was wrong. He pulled out his wand and cast an invisibility ward while he watched the woods in the direction of the sound. It was coming closer. When a screaming whinny sliced through the air, his heart skipped a beat. It couldn't be.

21
Giving It Away

As he watched the trees, the enormous paint galloped toward him, but he wasn't alone. On Pisces's back was the traitor—the one who had kidnapped not only him, but also his sister and even the powerful Ella.

Bain stood his ground as the giant pegasus stopped in front of him. The horse whinnied again and threw his head but never looked directly at him. Carbonell jumped off the tall horse. It was creepy how Carbonell locked eyes on him. He shouldn't have been able to see him.

"It doesn't work, you know," Carbonell said. "You're not invisible."

Bain lowered his wand and let the ward drop. "What are you doing here?" If he couldn't hide or outrun Carbonell, he didn't have much choice but to talk to him.

"I thought you might be here," Carbonell continued casually. "I've always loved Pennsylvania in the winter."

"But I thought . . ." Last summer Carbonell said that he was new to the area. He believed a lot of things Carbonell told him, but that didn't make any of it true. "What do you want from me?"

"I want to talk to you about your mom."

A fire burned in Bain's mind. "How many lies do you expect me to listen to? Just because you can fool my sister doesn't mean I'm in. I've got other things to worry about." Bain turned and walked to the cottage. He couldn't believe the nerve of Carbonell, after all he had done to him.

"Your mom's still alive, Bain. You can help me find her."
Carbonell spoke with an almost convincing warmth and concern.

It felt like a hot blade twisting in his heart. Why was Carbonell
doing this? Why couldn't he just leave them alone? "Give me one
reason why I should believe you. One reason." Bain's anger flowed
into his words.

Carbonell patted the massive head of Pisces. "It's simple, Bain.
If you don't try to help me, she's never going to be found."

"She's dead." Bain walked to the door of the cottage. Before
opening it, he turned back to the pegasus. "You're a traitor, Pisces."
He shut the door behind him as the sound of hooves charged at
the cottage. The spells would keep them out. No one could enter
the enchanted cabin besides Erin, the masters, and him.

He ran down the forty-nine steps and wove through the halls
until he found the one that took him to the bucket. Why did
Carbonell think he could lie to him? It was probably the only way
Carbonell thought he could get Bain on his side. It was cruelty.
The fact that Erin seemed to believe it too made it even more
dangerous. She might go with Carbonell willingly. If he lost her
again . . . he just couldn't.

He leaped into the barrel and as soon as his feet touched
the bottom, it lurched skyward. Maybe it was Carbonell—or
the barrel ride—but Bain was sure he was going to be sick. He
climbed out of the Jacuzzi-sized well and looked around the
already dark landscape. If it weren't for the bright rooms in the
palace, he would likely hate living where there was sunlight only
a few hours a day. How did the Icelanders do it? He made his way
to the palace doors, contemplating where he could find something
to settle his stomach.

After knocking lightly on Erin's door, he opened it to find her
sleeping on the bed. Her hair was still wet, but her clothes were
clean. He set the duffle bag down by the wardrobe and closed the
door quietly behind him. She was probably exhausted. It was more
than ironic that she would manage to find herself in the middle of
a disaster while he was practicing swordplay with Agnar. Why did
she get to have all the fun?

He went to the room where Pulsar slept and knelt down by the cold dragon. Pulsar's glow had faded so much that only a hint of gold shimmered off his scales in the dark room. "What good was all that training if I don't even know how to help you?" He doubted Pulsar could hear him, but he didn't care. "It's not fair, is it? One minute you're a perfectly healthy dragon, the next you're a big lump of gold."

The thought knocked through his head. One minute he was a popular basketball star with decent enough grades, and the next he was a too-tall-for-his-jeans elf with no friends and some freaky bad guys trying to convince him that he was crazy or that his mom was really alive. And if that wasn't bad enough, he was the one who had tried to convince Erin that they should go through with it and become elves. At the time he really did believe it was the right thing to do, but now? It was already too late. It didn't matter if he changed his mind—he was already immortal.

"Let that be a lesson for you, Pulsar. You stick with us and you get burned." Now if Bain only knew how to unburn. He rolled his wand in his hands, the bright silver metal glowing in the darkened room. There were so many things he still didn't know about magic—things he never wondered about until now. He touched the end of his wand on the dragon's side and called the magic from inside to flow through his wand. It wasn't like heating something up or turning invisible: he was releasing his magic and giving it to Pulsar. The dragon needed it more than he did.

The electric surge flushed through his arm and out the tip of his wand. Maybe it was just his imagination, but it seemed like Pulsar's aura grew a little brighter. It had to be working. He willed the magic to flow out of his wand and watched the golden glow burn brighter around the sleeping dragon. The room began to spin in the darkness, but the golden glow of the dragon was steadily increasing as he forced the magic out of his wand. He wasn't sure when his arms and legs went numb, but soon it felt like something was constricting his body like a python. It didn't hurt, exactly, but his strength siphoned from him, squeezing his very breath away.

Reality faded into a golden glow from the dragon. It was all he could feel, all he could think of.

Little points of light gathered around him before something zapped him, forcing his hand to drop the wand. He wanted to see what it was, but his brain turned everything off. Lights still floated around him, but even they washed into blackness as all awareness ceased.

22
Confession

ERIN STRETCHED HER ARMS BEFORE OPENING HER EYES. IT FELT so good. Beds weren't this perfect anywhere else. All at once, her mind caught up, and she remembered Pulsar. How could she have left him like that? She threw her covers and was almost off the bed when she saw Joel sitting on a chair in the corner. Her heart beat erratically, and she didn't know if she was angry or flattered that he was waiting for her to wake up.

"I hope you slept well," Joel said.

Erin's hands went automatically to her hair. She remembered how wet it was when she collapsed on the bed. There was no alternative—it had to be a mess.

"What time is it?" she asked.

"It's almost noon. You've been asleep since yesterday."

She watched his sincere expression haloed by his honey-colored hair. It was getting harder to stay mad at him.

"Are you hungry?" he asked. "I have breakfast waiting for you." He went to the door and retrieved a tray. "You should eat." He set the tray on the bed and sat on the other side of it.

She took a strawberry and bit into the tart fruit. Her stomach growled as the smell of bread filled the air. She hadn't realized how hungry she was.

Joel smiled and took a piece of bread off the tray. "Eat up. You need it. How are you feeling?"

She looked at him with her mouth full of food and nodded.

He poured a glass of juice and handed it to her. "I guess you're eager to get back to Pulsar."

"How's he doing?" she asked.

"I think you'll be pleased."

She tried to decipher the strange smile, like he was hiding something. *Pulsar?* she asked in her mind. If he was conscious, he would hear her.

Fireborn.

Erin jumped off the bed, her heart racing. "Where are you?" she shouted. "I have to see you!"

I haven't gone anywhere.

"We have to go," she said to Joel. "Now!"

"Don't you want to finish your breakfast?"

She pulled his arm until he stood. "Come on!"

"Don't you need to freshen up, or something?"

"Who cares what I look like? Pulsar's awake." She didn't wait for him to respond as she sprinted to the door. She would find that room if she had to do it by herself. He was okay! Everything was going to be better.

Joel easily caught up to her and grabbed her hand. She almost looked at him but restrained the instinct. It felt like electricity surging from his hand to hers, and she didn't want to ruin the moment, not now when everything was so good. He guided her to the room filled with the noon sun. "Pulsar?" she called.

The dragon emerged from the trees.

"You're okay!" She ran to him. His heat wasn't the blistering heat that it should have been—just barely above cool. At least he didn't feel like an ice sculpture anymore.

I'm doing much better, little one.

"How? What happened?"

Instead of telling her, he showed the magic flowing into him and then opening his eyes to a room full of fairies. Bain was there, sleeping on the floor, his wand next to him. The fairies circled around Bain and, one by one, the älvor lighted on her brother. She could see their tiny tears drop onto his skin until his eyelids fluttered open. As the fairies flew away, he slowly pulled himself off the floor.

"Your brother saved Pulsar's life, that's what happened," Joel said next to her.

She had forgotten Joel was in the room. "How?"

Joel walked slowly toward her and the dragon. "He was foolish. He could have killed himself. Probably would have if the älvor hadn't stopped him."

"I don't understand," she said.

"Bain gave Pulsar his magic."

"You can do that?"

"It's insane, irresponsible, and dangerous, but possible."

And I am in his debt, Pulsar added.

"That's all it took? Why didn't anyone tell me? I could have given my magic to him a lot sooner." If she had known, they wouldn't have spent a day in shark-infested waters, a night on the beach with Carbonell, and endless hours of torment.

"Giving your magic away is suicide. You remember when I told you that elves could only be killed with magic? Giving your magic away is a one-way ticket to ending things. No one does it. We didn't predict that Bain would even think to try it."

"It should have been me." If it weren't for her irresponsibility, Pulsar would never have been hurt in the first place.

"Bain was lucky. If it weren't for the älvor . . ." Joel didn't finish. "Promise me you'll never try it. I can't lose you."

His last words hung in the air. Why did he care what she did? She was nothing to him.

Promise not to transport us to the middle of a hurricane and you'll never have to, Pulsar said.

"Where's Bain?" she asked.

"In his room," Joel answered.

She had to see him. She couldn't even imagine what his night had been like after a near-death experience. "Are you going to be okay here?" she asked Pulsar.

I'm not going anywhere. Go on and find your brother.

She wrapped her arms around the dragon, but the usual magic flow wasn't there. "You're still weak, aren't you?"

I'll be blazing fire before winter solstice.

She shrugged, not exactly sure when that was. "I'll come right back, I promise." She ran to the door only to find Joel at her side.

"I'm coming with you," he said as he took her hand once again.

"You don't have to." It was so confusing. One minute he was infuriatingly arrogant, and the next he was bringing her breakfast in bed and holding her hand. "What would Ella think?"

He shot her a strange look. "What would Ella think about what?"

"This." She held their hands up. "Don't you think she might have a problem with us?" It was painful saying it out loud. So much of her wanted to keep pretending that it was okay for Joel to be so sweet, but it wasn't fair. It was understandable why Joel loved the Fairy Godmother. Ella outranked Erin in every way. If Erin lived another five hundred years, she would still never be able to compete with Ella's beauty and grace. But then, maybe Ella was five hundred years older already. Immortality was such a strange thing.

"Erin Fireborn Farraday, what are you talking about?"

She didn't want to meet his perfect hazel eyes, so she stared at the floor. "You said you loved her, Joel."

He broke into a laugh. "You think I love Ella?"

Erin nodded. Boys were so confusing.

"Oh, Erin. I love Ella, but I'm not *in* love with her. Do you see the difference?"

Erin waited, unsure what to say.

He pulled her hands up to his lips and kissed her fingers. Electricity shot through her arms, and her knees began to tremble.

"Ella is my sister," he said. "I'll always love her, but she is not the one I think about every day. It's you."

Erin's heart pounded. "She's your sister?"

He nodded, keeping her fingers close to his lips.

She shook her head. How could she be so stupid? Did every-one know except for her? "Why didn't you tell me?"

"You never asked."

"Unbelievable. Is there anything else I should know about you?"

His smile was mischievous. "Absolutely, but I wouldn't want

to ruin the fun. You're going to have to ask the right questions."

She blew out her breath. "How will I know when I've asked the right questions?"

"Oh, you'll know. I have no doubt." He led her silently through the halls to Bain's room.

She couldn't bring herself to break the spell. Holding his hand made something bloom in her that felt a lot like magic. Any more of his secrets could wait. It was enough to know that he wasn't in love with Ella, even if she still hadn't figured out how to change his mind about Carbonell.

23
Up for Visitors

Erin sat on a chair across from Bain. Joel had insisted on leaving the two of them alone to discuss things. He thought they needed their privacy, and Erin was grateful. It was hard to think straight with Joel in the room, and she could tell Bain needed her right now. He looked somber, so unlike his normal adventurous self.

"I didn't know what I was doing, Erin. Honest. I would never purposely try to kill myself. I just figured that no one else could do anything for Pulsar, and if my magic could help him, then that's what I wanted to do." Bain sunk his head into his hands. "I didn't know."

"It's okay. Neither one of us knew. If someone would have told me, I would have tried to do the same thing."

"Don't say that." He pulled his face out of his hands.

All she could do was shake her head. She was lucky that the älvor had been there to save him; she didn't think she could survive it if he died.

"I saw Carbonell," Bain said.

"You did? When?"

"It's a long story. He thinks Mom's still alive and that we have to find her. It's ridiculous. How does he expect me to believe anything he says?"

"That's what I thought too, but he's right," she answered.

"Right about what?"

"When I heard him say that Mom was out there and that he

could only get to her with our help, I just knew it was true." She hesitated. "It's my gift."

"How do you know you're not wrong? What if you just want it to be true?" His ocean blue eyes pierced hers.

"Do you want to stay in this palace forever? Have you ever wondered what it would be like to go out on your own, on your own terms?" She pulled her changing brooch and transformed it into a passport.

"What are you saying?"

"I'm saying, why not find out what Carbonell has to offer? Maybe if we're together, we'll be stronger. Remember the barrier? If we can take down a whole city, I think we could manage him. Don't you want to know if any of it's true?"

He seemed lost in thought. "Would you bring the dragon?"

Relief washed through her. He was going to do it. This was just the kind of thing he needed to pull him out of his depressed mood. "I don't think Pulsar's ready yet. I don't want to be responsible for any more disasters."

"Do you think we could just, you know, wink out of here like you did with Pulsar?"

"Probably. It worked with Ella."

A fire lit in his eyes. "I'm in."

"But I don't have a clue where to go."

"I do. Ireland."

The door opened under her command, and she entered the afternoon-lit room. "Pulsar," she walked up to the sparkling mound. "Bain and I—" She stopped herself from explaining. He had been there in her thoughts and already knew. "We're going to be fine, you know."

The golden dragon rested his head on the floor, and his amber eyes blinked at her. *You are growing up, Fireborn. If it weren't for Whispering Winds, I wouldn't be able to let you go without me.*

"It wouldn't be the first time I've been without you."

And it wouldn't be the first time danger has found you. You must be careful, little one.

"But you're okay with us going?" That was the strangest part. It seemed like he should be forbidding it or insisting they wait until he was strong enough to come too.

You and I are not the same. I never considered that my life could ever be so short. I always thought I would live for a thousand years.

"You will," Erin said.

But you have reminded me of our differences. There was a time when you were the fragile one and I was strong, but now immortality has its arm around you and not me. I may live for centuries, but I will not live forever. I am vulnerable where you are invincible.

"That sounds so wrong. Look at you. You're a huge, scary dragon. You could rip any living thing apart without much effort and then burn them to stubble, and that's not even including your gifts with magic. I think you're forgetting that the world is populated mostly with humans and regular animals. You're pretty much the worst thing any of them would have ever seen in their lives."

Thank you, Fireborn. You think I'm scary?

"Yes, absolutely. You would make a grown man hide in a ditch for a week."

What would I do without you?

"Live in a forest alone, hunting animals. It would be a tragic bore."

Indeed.

"Are we taking off while it's still light outside?" Bain looked at his watch. "That's like fifteen more minutes or something. It's almost two already. Daylight's burning."

She noticed his backpack slung over his shoulder. It was just like old times. She reached out to Pulsar and touched his room-temperature scales.

Go ahead, get out of here. Bain needs you more than I do.

"Thanks," she said and tried to hug his massive neck.

"What do we have to do, exactly?" Bain asked.

Erin wrapped her arm around his and tried to picture Ireland the way she saw it last time she was there. A wind warped around them in a sudden gust as she closed her eyes.

"That was wicked! You've got to do that again," Bain said.

Erin opened her eyes to see the same land that greeted her before. "I hope you know where you're going. Last time I got lost in Dublin."

Bain pointed at a little house sitting alone in a field. "There's Aunt Lyndera's house. Too bad Pisces isn't here. You'd probably like him."

"Pisces?"

"Huge pegasus. I don't think he likes me very much."

She smiled. "So are you going to introduce me to our aunt?"

He led her to the tiny house and knocked on the door. "Aunt Lyndera, it's me, Bain. I brought Erin."

The door creaked as locks and latches fell open. "My stars! Look at you. Come in, come in."

Erin stepped into the warm house as the lady shut the door behind them.

"Erin, I can't believe it. So much like your mum. Come, have a seat."

Erin followed her into the kitchen, where four wooden chairs gathered around a small oak table. Already, cups and saucers were floating in front of a kettle of steaming water. Aunt Lyndera seemed to pay it no mind as she sat down beside them.

"Bain, so nice of you to drop in again. To see the two of you together brings a ray of sunshine to my heart, it does." She poured the steaming water into their cups.

"I saw Pisces yesterday," Bain began. "I was wondering if you knew anything about Carbonell."

"Aye. That horse does what he wants. Comes and goes—the usual gallivanting."

"So, you haven't seen Carbonell?" Bain asked.

"Sure, I've seen him. He comes around every now and then for a spot of tea. Nice fellow. Always had a thing for your mum, but she had her mind set on someone else."

"You mean, our dad," Erin said.

Aunt Lyndera smiled. "For a mortal, your dad was a good pick. They don't come any nicer than that."

"Did our mom ever like Carbonell?" Erin asked. It was so hard to imagine Carbonell and her mom together. It was hard enough imagining her mom at all.

"He was a good friend," the red-haired lady said, her eyes sparkling. "The boy next door. Ormond was working so hard to sweep her off her feet that there wasn't enough room to breathe. When she was with your dad, she was the happiest I'd ever seen her. And then she had the two of you. I knew I should have come for a visit. I never would have thought things would end up the way they did."

"But why didn't you come anyway? We never knew we had family. All this time we've been on our own with Grandpa Jessie." Almost immediately Erin felt bad for letting the words burst from her mouth.

"I'm sorry, sweetie. I thought it would be best. I thought your mum would want you to live in the mortal world without the influence of magic. I only did what I thought she would have wanted." Aunt Lyndera looked down at the table as she sipped her tea.

"Well, I guess she forgot to give us the no-magic note. We're in it up to our ears," Bain said.

Erin smiled. It was true. She could still see his pointed ears through his thick blond curls.

A loud knock interrupted their conversation as it reverberated through the tiny house.

"More than two visitors in one day." Aunt Lyndera scooted her chair from the table. Icy wind blew in as she opened the door. "Carbonell! Speak o' the devil."

Erin looked at the man standing in the doorway. His black hair blew in the wind, revealing his pointed ears, but other than that, he looked like a man, not an elf. His jacket was zipped to his chin as if to ward off the cold, and the hiking boots only added to his average appearance. But it was his light aura that gave her a glimmer of hope.

24
Assembling the Forces

CARBONELL STEPPED INTO THE CRAMPED ROOM AND TOOK OFF his jacket. Erin watched Bain's stare harden as Carbonell sat on a chair across from them at the table.

"It's getting brisk out there, Lyndy. You're going to have to break down and put a flame in the old fireplace." Carbonell put down his tea and started on a biscuit. "Nice hair, Erin."

"Uh." Erin's hand went to her hair automatically. She really should have listened to Joel and at least looked in the mirror before she left. "Could I use your bathroom?" she asked her aunt.

Aunt Lyndera furrowed her eyebrows in concentration. Suddenly Erin's hair pulled and parted as if two pairs of hands were demanding control over the thick locks.

"That's better," Aunt Lyndera said. "The bathroom's on the left if you still need it."

Bain barely concealed his smile as Erin felt her newly styled hair. It was pulled into a loose bun in the back of her head, much like her aunt's.

"May I?" Carbonell asked, gesturing at the open hearth.

"Have a go at it already," Lyndera said as she pulled some cookies out of the cupboard.

Carbonell stacked some logs in the fireplace before flames suddenly erupted from the wood. "That's better."

Bain gave Erin a meaningful glance while Carbonell's back was turned. If only she could talk to Bain the way she did with Pulsar. It would have been easier, but a lifetime living with her twin had taught her a few things too. "How do we find our mom?"

Carbonell turned and faced her. His expression was too enthusiastic, as if he had just won a prize. "Does that mean you're coming with me?"

Erin looked over to Bain, who nodded almost imperceptibly. "We're bailing on you at the first sign that you're up to something with Xavene."

"Sounds fair," Carbonell said.

"And I'm not hanging out with imps under any condition," Erin added.

"Anything else?" Carbonell asked.

Erin looked at Bain. His expression was serious.

"How do we know we can trust you?" Bain asked, his eyes finally reaching Carbonell's.

"That's what Erin is for. She'll know if I'm lying, right?" Carbonell asked her.

"Absolutely." She hoped so, anyway. Erin knew they were on to something big. Carbonell's aura hadn't winked darker for even a moment. Whatever he was planning, he must think it was perfect. "Where do we start?"

"That is the tricky part," Carbonell said. "This is where the two of you have to make your choice. The only way I see of finding your mom is to go straight to the heart of the matter."

"Xavene?" Erin asked. Even the name made her stomach twist.

Carbonell nodded. "But we have the element of surprise on our side. Xavene doesn't know I've turned on him. He still thinks I'm out recruiting imps. I should be able to smuggle the two of you in without anyone noticing."

"What about getting out? Anyone can get into prison, but the hard part is getting out." Bain tapped his knuckles on the table.

"But Erin solved that one too. She managed to get out of Black Rain and take Ella with her. That's pretty good insurance if you ask me." Carbonell took his seat and leaned on his elbows. "Even if things get a little shaky, you two can get out. If anyone's neck is on the line, it's mine. Who's going to be there for me if things go bad?"

"How do you even know she's alive?" Bain asked.

"I don't. I mean, I can't prove it, but I just feel like she has to be." Carbonell leaned back and folded his arms. "But does it matter that I'm going on a hunch? Don't you want to find out for yourself?"

"Careful Carbonell. You'll be talking me into it," Aunt Lyndera said from the kitchen.

"No, Lyndy, it's too risky. The twins can get themselves out, but if something happened, you'd be stuck with me," Carbonell answered.

"Would you do it?" Bain asked Lyndera. "You're the only elf family we have."

"Come on, Lyndy. You don't really want to do this," Carbonell said.

"I think you're wrong, Carbonell. Do you see the way those two are giving me the puppy dog eyes? They're practically begging."

"Who says practically?" Erin said. "You have to come. It's the right thing to do, and you know it."

Aunt Lyndera put her hands up. Her eyes danced as she tried to hide her smile. "See, Carbonell, they leave me no choice. Now when do we get on with this horrible journey? Did you bring Pisces back?"

Carbonell rolled his eyes at Erin. "Pisces is outside. I don't know how he's going to feel about carrying the four of us."

"He'll be fine. That horse is bigger than an elephant." Aunt Lyndera pulled her shawl from a hook and stuffed various things into a fat leather purse.

"The four of us?" Bain asked.

"If we stick together, you can't get lost," she answered. "It seems you have a knack for losing each other."

"Can't Erin just wink us there or something?" Bain complained.

"Don't you remember what happened the last time Erin didn't

know exactly where she was headed? She ended up in the middle of the ocean. Unless she figures out where Xavene's new hideout is, chances are, she's not going to find it." Carbonell sat at the table seeming unaffected, as Lyndera fretted around the room, stuffing impossibly large objects into her purse. "Do you really need to bring the kettle, Lyndy?"

She looked up at him and smiled as she dropped the kettle and several mugs into the purse. "You never can be too prepared."

"Does your whole house fit into that bag?" Bain asked.

"I don't know. I've never tried it," she answered.

Carbonell glared at Bain. "Don't be giving her any ideas."

"Do you think I should bring the sofa?" Lyndera asked, looking at the worn, sagging couch.

"I'm sure there will be places to sit where we're going," Carbonell answered.

"But you never can be too careful," Lyndera answered and directed the sofa into the air. She opened her purse wide as the couch rained like sand and the purse swallowed it. "Everybody up!" she ordered as she loaded the table and chairs into her bag as well. "I'll be right back. I just need a few more things."

"She's going to get her bed, isn't she?" Bain asked.

Carbonell reached for his jacket. "You're the one who asked her to come along. I want no complaints out of you."

Bain smiled. "No worries." He turned down the hall and followed the red-haired lady with the bag. "Do you have an extra cot and maybe some pillows? You might need more food. You never know what they'll be serving in Xavene's evil lair."

Carbonell turned and furrowed his eyebrows at Erin.

"Don't look at me," Erin said as Lyndera finished loading her final belongings into the bag. "At least we won't have to sleep on the sand."

25
Water Fight

Aunt Lyndera had been right about Pisces. The massive horse easily lifted off the ground in spite of the four of them clinging to his back. Erin couldn't help comparing Pisces to the other pegasi in the Door of Vines. His massive size made his flight less balletic and more solid. He clearly lacked the maneuverability Pulsar had mastered, but his flight was steady.

"This is going to take forever," Bain said behind her.

He gripped Erin's waist, but she wasn't sure if it was for her safety or his.

"Can't you just tell us what continent we're going to and we'll meet you there?" Bain asked.

Erin waited for Carbonell's answer. Bain was right. Even if Pisces could fly over eighty miles per hour, they could be in flight for a very long time.

"Is Xavene still in the Amazon?" Erin asked.

"How did you know that?" Carbonell asked as he craned his neck, trying to see her.

"Last time I was there I made a GPS," she answered. "Is that still the place?"

"I'm thinking," Carbonell answered as he turned his head back to the front, "I wouldn't want you to go straight to the doorstep. It would be better if we met you somewhere safe. Let me see your GPS."

She pulled her bracelet off and changed it into the GPS before reaching around Carbonell's shoulder to give it to him. After a few beeps, Carbonell held it over his shoulder in front of her.

"Thanks," she said. The GPS now looked like a map. A star marked the end of a red line.

"Can you do it? Can you control the wind enough to go to where I marked?" Carbonell asked.

"I'm not sure. I've never tried it." The clouds below them wisped in the frigid air. Even though she wasn't freezing, she missed the warmth that radiated off Pulsar's scales. He made every day of flight feel like summer.

"Let's do a test run," Carbonell said, reaching his hand over his shoulder again. "Let me see that."

She handed him the electronic map and waited.

"Does that mean we get off the horse soon?" Bain asked.

"Try this one," Carbonell said, handing the GPS back. "Lyndy and I will meet you there. If you don't see us in an hour, you went the wrong way."

"And if we went the wrong way, what do you want us to do?" Erin asked.

"Wait for us. I'll find you eventually," Carbonell answered.

"Be safe, you two," Aunt Lyndera called from her perch near the front of the massive horse.

"We will," Erin and Bain answered at the same time.

Erin looked at the GPS. "Morocco? You're sending us to Africa?"

"It's beautiful this time of year. Just don't go too far into the water. Sharks haven't been your best friend, not to mention the other creatures," Carbonell said over his back.

"Are you ready?" she asked Bain. He squeezed her waist even tighter. "On three then. One," she looked at the tiny screen where the star sat on a line next to the blue water. "Two," she thought of the last time they ended up with the sharks. It had been a nightmare. "Three." The little red star. The little red star. Air swarmed around them in an instant, and the clouds were replaced with white sand.

Bain laughed. "That was so cool. I was hoping you'd land in the water though. I haven't been swimming in forever."

Erin looked out to the ocean, where the waves swelled before cresting into white-capped curls. The air was warm, with the crisp sea aroma drifting over the beach. She watched Bain kick off his shoes and roll up his jeans before splashing into the water. Everything about this solitary place seemed to lift weight from her. Her shoes were off in seconds, and the soft sand seeped between her toes. Pennsylvania didn't have anything like this.

"It's not even cold!" Bain called as he waded deeper into the clear blue water. "You've got to try this."

She walked slowly to the ocean, letting the sand move under her feet. It was so warm and soft, and unlike the sand where she'd camped for the night with Carbonell. The grains of sand were so small that it felt like fragments of silk massaging her feet. A burst of water caught her suddenly from behind, leaking down her shirt.

"Bain!" she yelled. She spun around to find him, but he wasn't there. Another splash of water attacked her legs.

Bain flickered into view. "It feels great. Admit it."

She smiled back at him as she directed the water behind him to rise and catch him behind his knees. His legs buckled, and he fell face-first into the ocean before he disappeared. Slowly, she stepped back away from the water. She could run, but she couldn't hide from Bain.

A stream of water shot out of the ocean at her, but as it hit her touch ward, it cascaded back off.

"That's cheating!" Bain said, coming back into view.

"Hardly," she answered as she reached down and scooped a handful of salty water. It was as warm as a heated swimming pool. "What I wouldn't give for a swimsuit right now."

"Who needs a swimsuit?" Bain said as he kicked a spray of water at her.

She let the ocean water soak her jeans. It seemed impossible for it to be so warm anywhere in December. "I wonder why a beach this pretty isn't packed with people."

She waded deeper into the water, treading against the currents. A swell gathered in a tall hill of water, blocking her view of the rest of the ocean. Before it could wash over her, she launched upward, hoping to clear the mountain of water, but the wave caught her legs and carried her toward the beach.

"I can do better than that!" Bain called, shedding his shirt and diving headfirst into the receding water.

Erin watched as he stroked against the current, becoming a speck in the blue sea. She ran through the shallow current until the water pushed against her waist, before diving in after him. Already another large wave grew until it threatened to encompass her, but she held her breath and ducked through the current as the wave buoyed her high in the water. As she pulled her arms against the opposing force, she broke through the surface, only to realize that the current had sent her farther away from Bain.

For a moment, she let her legs go limp, testing the depth, but her feet never touched the bottom. Finally resorting to a touch ward, she opened her eyes and looked around at the deep crevice of water that surrounded her.

A rush of panic shot through her body, making her stomach sink and her veins fill with ice as she took in the endless sea. Her mind raced. She was being irrational. It was all in her head. Maybe she had developed a phobia of deep water since her last scrape with Pulsar. The water parted around her ward as she burst into the air. She scanned the blue expanse looking for Bain, but he was nowhere to be seen.

"Bain!" she shouted. He was probably invisible. Just another prank, like all the times before. She swam in the direction she had last seen him and called him again. "Bain, come on! Answer me."

The sound of the crashing waves seemed to intensify as she scanned the beach and horizon for him. Maybe he was swimming under the water and couldn't hear her, but the heavy feeling grew like a cancer, and shivers convulsed through her arms and legs. Something was wrong.

"Bain," she called again, but inside she knew that he couldn't hear her. Fighting the growing fear, she swam across the swells, hoping to find an answer. Bain was a good swimmer. There was no reason to worry about him drowning. He was even stronger than he had been when they would go to the pool in the summer. He wasn't really even human anymore.

So why did the dread threaten to overwhelm her senses?

Any moment he would splash the foamy water at her, laughing at his own joke. He would tell her he wished she could have seen her own face.

She let the current drift her across the horizon. In the distance she could still see his T-shirt on the beach. Maybe if she watched the water, she would see some irregularity, something that would give him away.

But the ocean held its secrets. The waves refused to unveil his presence.

"Bain!"

Her words were cut short as something jerked her leg down into the water.

"That's not funny." Without thinking, she created a touch ward that bubbled around her head, but she could still feel the grip tighten on her leg as it pulled her deeper into the water. She tried but couldn't extend the ward beyond her waist.

Master Ulric taught her enough about wards that she could cast one even when she was scared, tired, or panicked. So why wasn't it working now? She pulled her head down into the water to get a better look at Bain. The water boiled around her in bubbles as the speed intensified, making it impossible for her to see.

"Did you catch a ride on a submarine or something?" Erin was sure the words bounced off her ward, never escaping the invisible helmet around her head. Bain was going to give up on this joke. It took all her strength to fight against the heavy water and reach for her leg, but when she finally tucked herself into a ball, the sight made her stomach turn, and she was sure she was going to puke or faint.

It wasn't Bain's hand wrapped around her lower calf. It was some kind of monster. Something with hands that shouldn't have hands. Rows of teeth glinted from the silver snout of its enormous head. The shark's webbed fingers wrapped around her leg as it drug her easily through the depths.

26

In Too Deep

SHE FORCED HER MAGIC TO STRETCH AROUND HER AS SHE screamed. It wasn't working. "Get off me." The shark swam on, indifferent to her kicks and punching fists. Another hand wrapped around her other leg, flipping her backwards as the shark towed her deeper into the dark water.

She kicked again but uselessly against the swimming beast. Her sword. Unsheathing it, she pulled herself against the pressing water and stabbed her blade into the silver hand grasping her leg. The blade sliced easily through the fish skin. Deep red flowed from the wound, streaking the water with crimson clouds. Blood. Even in the ward, she could smell it.

Her stomach tightened as she pulled the blade across the arm severing the webbed hand from the beast. She was free. Before she could inhale, she saw it. Through the red water, jaws gaped at her. Lunging at her was the open mouth filled with razor teeth. The ward. But it refused to come.

I'm dead. It felt like time slowed. The three rows of white triangle teeth tilted inward to the gaping mouth. Pink ridges lined the back of the open jaws as if the shark had nothing to offer but teeth and throat.

"Bain," she whispered as the monster approached. It felt like she was watching from a distance. It seemed possible that her life was going to end, yet fear transformed into contentment. She couldn't feel anything. No water, no cold, no sense of doom.

The eternal blade glinted in the muted light. Let the shark

swallow her. Let it try to rip her with its teeth. It would fail, and she would triumph. It wasn't a question. The seconds closed in, and she sensed the jaws widen. At precisely the right moment, she dove into its mouth. The ward around her held as she took in the view of the shark's silver and red mouth. Almost as soon as she cleared the gaping jaws, they snapped shut.

She curled up with barely enough room to move. She couldn't let the creature swallow her. Light shed through the opening as the shark's jaw dropped again. But she was ready. Holding the sword in both hands, she thrust the blade through the roof of its mouth. Immediately the animal thrashed back and forth as she held onto the blade as an anchor. The jaws fell open and went slack. She jerked the blade from its victim and pushed out into the water.

She tried to orient herself in the water as she kicked away from the bleeding shark. How was she ever going to find Bain?

The sun burned in the sky, and her eyes fought to adjust to the brightness as she broke the surface. She was farther out than she could have guessed. The beach looked like a sliver of white as she stroked toward it. Was there more than one shark in these waters? Had Bain faced the same kind of demon? She let the salty water splash into her mouth as she paddled her feet and propelled her arms.

Maybe it was an imp. Sharks didn't have arms. Below her, a shadow caught her eye. Something was swimming under her, keeping its speed parallel to hers. Then another form came into view and another. Her heart froze as the numbers grew below her. She had defeated one shark, but how would she do with a swarm?

The bubble ward she cast enveloped her, and she ducked below the surface to get a better look at the swimming creatures. The sight made her stop moving. It couldn't be real. All around her were what appeared to be dolphins, but some had the upper bodies of humans. Girls with streaming white and blue hair swam next to long-nosed marine mammals. One of the mermaids smiled at her and winked before diving deeper into the ocean.

Erin popped her head back up out of the water and filled her lungs with fresh air. "No way." Sharks with arms, dolphins swimming with mermaids; this kind of stuff didn't exist. She felt a tap on her arm and turned to see a silver-skinned face with deep blue eyes smiling at her. The mermaid pointed down into the water before disappearing below the surface.

"I must be crazy." Erin took another deep breath of air before plunging back in. The ward allowed her to breathe under water, but the air grew warm and moist, like sleeping under the covers too long. As she kicked deeper into the sea, she saw one of the mermaids holding someone's hand. Slowly, the arm, shoulder, and torso became visible as Bain came into view.

He was smiling and talking to the mermaid as they swam through the currents. Erin stroked deeper into the water, trying to reach him, but Bain didn't notice she was even there. He only had eyes for the blue mermaid that held his hands as they swam.

She caught up to them and reached for Bain's arm. Only then did he reluctantly tear his eyes away from the half-dolphin girl. "Bain, we need to go back."

He looked at her in surprise. "Why?"

His voice carried through the wards and water, giving it a warped sound. Erin noticed his wand and sword sheathed at his waist. At least he hadn't lost those in the swim. "Carbonell's going to be here any minute. We need to go back."

He glanced back over to the mermaid whose hair swirled in a fan of white and blue in the water. "I'll be there in a minute."

Erin blew out a sigh. "Right. One minute." She kicked to the surface and swam to the beach as fast as she could. She almost gets eaten by a shark imp, and Bain finds a mermaid girlfriend. What did she expect?

As she walked the rest of the way out of the ocean, she couldn't help appreciating the burning sun as it baked the sand on the beach. Her clothes were soaked, and she smelled like seaweed and shark blood. It was nauseating. Her hair had fallen out of the bun a long time ago and was dripping down her already wet shirt. So much for the exotic beach. It was December. She should be studying for finals and thinking about Christmas presents, not sitting on a white beach after a near-death experience.

Her life didn't feel real anymore. Who was she? "Pulsar?" She knew it was pointless to call him. He would never find her this far away, but it seemed the longer she was away, the more she questioned her choice to become immortal and the more she wondered what she was supposed to do.

She thought about the smile that stretched across Bain's face as he talked to the mermaid. How devastating that his first crush wasn't even human. But then, he wasn't exactly human either. Joel flashed across her thoughts without warning.

"He's not my boyfriend," she said aloud, but there was no one around to hear her anyway. Why did he have to be so confusing? So infuriating? It was as if he liked her and was annoyed with her at the same time. She couldn't understand it. Sitting here hundreds of miles away didn't help her see him any clearer. Every time she thought about him, her heart raced and her face flushed warm. What was that? Infatuation?

"I'm not that stupid." But maybe she was. She knew she fell for him every time he touched her hand or looked at her with those honey-brown eyes. She was a fool no matter how much she tried not to be. Inside, she melted every time he said something sweet. Every time he tried to protect her.

Part of her wished that he had come too. "Right. How dumb would that be?"

"Do you talk to yourself a lot?" Bain shook his wet hair, spraying water like a sprinkler.

"Thanks for sneaking up on me."

He pulled his fingers through his wavy locks. "It's my specialty." He sat on the sand beside her.

"How was your swim?" She didn't want to accuse him of abandoning her for a mermaid, even if it was how she felt.

A grin spread across his face. "You should meet her. Kelura is amazing."

Erin laughed out loud.

"What?"

"Is that the fish-girl's name?"

"Kelura's not a fish girl. She's a . . ."

"A mermaid." Erin smiled at him sweetly.

"I guess. But she's so much more than that."

"Like beautiful?"

Bain leaned back on the hot sand. "And funny, smart, and easy to talk to."

"You figured all that out in five minutes? Great. My twin is in love with a mermaid."

He pushed her playfully into the sand. "Am not." He was already up and running away as she got to her feet.

But she didn't feel like chasing him. Her legs trembled, and she felt sick. The stomach-wrenching smell only increased in the heat of the sun.

"Erin? Are you okay" He stopped running and walked slowly back to her as if seeing her for the first time.

She hadn't seen it coming and didn't have time to catch herself before her stomach emptied. Its contents splattered on the sand. Her eyes watered, and her throat burned. Maybe she had swallowed too much seawater. Maybe her body was revolting from the shark attack.

Bain's arms caught her before she collapsed onto the beach.

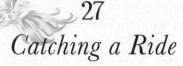

27
Catching a Ride

"IF JOEL COULD SEE ME NOW," ERIN SAID, WIPING HER FACE. SAND
stuck to her chin as she tried to clean herself off.

"I think you need to get out of the sun." Bain lifted her off
the ground and carried her back to where the palm trees offered
shade. "Are you okay?"

She nodded, but her stomach cramped, and her limbs still felt
weak. "I'm such a wimp."

He smoothed the hair away from her forehead and brushed
the sand from her cheeks. "You're a lot of things, Erin, but you're
not a wimp."

She looked up at him, not even able to feel embarrassed that
he was taking care of her. "There was a shark. It tried to eat me."

"A shark? Where?"

"Duh. In the water. But it must have been an imp. It had
arms."

Bain leaned against the tree next to her and rested his elbows
on his knees. "Oh." He shook his head. "So while I'm flirting with
the dolphin girls, you were being attacked by sharks."

She closed her eyes, trying to force her stomach to settle. "One
shark."

"Like you need more sharks in your life." He reached over and
held her hand. "I'm sorry. I should have been there for you."

She kept her eyes closed and listened to the waves crash against
the beach. Even now she couldn't bring herself to blame him. She
should have been smarter.

"Do you think I'll ever see her again?"

"Who?"

"Kelura. I probably won't, huh?"

Silence lapsed again. She wasn't sure when she drifted to sleep, but someone was shaking her arm.

"Time to go kids." It was Carbonell's voice.

She opened her eyes against the bright sunlight. There in front of them stood the massive pegasus with tiny Aunt Lyndera perched atop. Carbonell stood in front of them, offering a hand up.

"You're a mess, Erin. You go swimming with the sharks or something?"

"Don't ask." Bain helped her off the ground.

Carbonell looked them both up and down. "I thought I told you two to stay out of the water."

"You did?" Bain asked.

"This is my own private beach, you know. No humans allowed. The water is filled with all sorts of things, and not all of them are friendly."

Bain stretched his arms above him. "Now you tell us. What took you guys so long?"

"It hasn't been that long," Carbonell said. "You ready to go?" He turned to Erin. "You smell horrible. You don't look so good either."

"Thanks." There was nothing she could do about it. Only Aunt Lyndera had thought to pack before they left. Smart move. Erin had no clean clothes and no shower, and there was no way she was going back into the ocean, not that it could help.

"I've got it. You boys go on." Aunt Lyndera pushed off the giant horse and landed gracefully next to Erin. "I mean it, get lost," she said, eyeing the two.

Carbonell lifted his hands. "Fine, we'll leave. Come on, Bain. You don't mess with Lyndy."

She waited while the two wandered off before opening her leather purse. Erin watched as a bathtub materialized followed by a large shower curtain.

"You can never be too prepared." Lyndera filled the tub with steaming water.

Erin didn't even try to figure out how she managed to do it. All she knew was that she was eternally grateful that her odd aunt could produce miracles in the shape of a bathtub in the middle of nowhere. Maybe being an elf had its advantages. The warm water soothed her, and the spice and floral smell of the soap brought her senses back to life. Aunt Lyndera packed her filthy clothes into the bag and pulled out a fresh set.

This time, she offered Erin a comb and mirror, letting Erin do her own hair. The crisp white button-up shirt fit pretty well. Even the pants worked okay.

By the time Erin finished combing through her hair, the tub was gone and Bain and Carbonell were back.

"You ready?" Carbonell asked. "Bain told me what happened." He swore. "I can't believe that shark idiot would try something like that. He was planning on joining Xavene. Probably thought he had enough magic."

"Magic?" Erin asked. "But imps don't have magic."

"They didn't used to." Carbonell lifted Lyndera onto Pisces before mounting the enormous horse. His tone left no room for further questioning.

Bain copied him and lifted Erin onto the pegasus. She didn't say anything. Here she was a superhuman elf, and her brother still helped her onto a horse. She usually rode a dragon. Maybe he did it because he wanted to take care of her.

The wings beat the air until the ground below them sank. Bain's arms wrapped around her waist as the horse pushed through the sky.

"You never know, Bain. You might see her again." Erin didn't know why she was encouraging him, but part of her understood his ache. Nothing made sense anymore, so why did it matter that he liked a mermaid? How was that different than her mom marrying a human? Maybe her dad and mom were even more different than Bain and Kelura.

"You never know," he answered behind her.

The flight numbed her, and she let her body relax. She was too tired to insist on trying to use Whispering Winds again. And hungry. Her stomach was empty and growling with hunger. Carbonell must have noticed, or maybe Lyndera, because pieces of jerky were being handed back to them. Pretty soon water bottles and crackers followed. But she was still so tired.

She tried not to think of the inside of the shark's mouth and how the blade felt in her hands. How had she known to dive into its mouth? And what did Carbonell mean when he said that imps didn't used to have magic? They could never have magic. That was what made them imps in the first place.

Her stomach settled, and her eyelids drooped. It wasn't worth fighting the fatigue. She was aware of Bain's arms tightening around her waist as she drifted to sleep.

28
S'mores

ERIN DIDN'T MIND SO MUCH THAT CARBONELL AND AUNT Lyndera insisted on sticking together. Pisces wasn't too hard to get used to, and flying never bothered her anyway. She lost track of what day it was a long time ago. Every night they would land and set up camp. Even Carbonell seemed grateful for Lyndera's accessible accommodations. No one went hungry, and the tents were well stocked with blankets and pillows.

Erin still laughed every time Aunt Lyndy pulled the old sofa out of her purse. There was nothing quite like sitting on a couch and roasting marshmallows over a fire.

"Cat got your tongue?" Aunt Lyndy asked her as she blew the orange flames from her burnt marshmallow. "You're missing him again, aren't you?"

Erin's ears burned. How could Lyndy have known that she was thinking about Joel?

"I don't blame you. If I had a dragon, I don't think I would be able to leave him either. It's irony that you landed one. Your mum would have given anything to have a dragon. Not that she could have, I suppose." The white sticky marshmallow oozed over her graham cracker. "I never did get to meet him."

"Yeah. I do miss him." Guilt flooded her as she realized that thoughts of Joel had consumed her more than thoughts of Pulsar. Maybe it was because Pulsar was safe. There was nothing to worry about. But Joel was a mystery, and his face lingered in her thoughts.

The hardest part about being an älva was the lack of easy

communication. Even though the kingdom had an overwhelming amount of technology, they didn't use phones or email. All of the technology in the world, and she couldn't even call. What good was it then? Some of them had cell phones, but not Joel. She didn't even know if they had a postal address. Doubtful. She thought of Pulsar trying to dial a tiny phone with his claws. That made her smile.

The biggest city of elves was right there in Iceland, but it was as if they didn't exist. At least according to most of the world, they didn't. If they couldn't see it, then it wasn't there.

"Do you go to Morocco much?" Bain asked Carbonell.

Erin pulled at the golden brown marshmallow and tried to hide her smile. It was obvious. Bain wanted to see Kelura.

Carbonell unwrapped a piece of chocolate. "Why do you ask?"

"I don't know. Just wondering." Bain glanced her way.

She stuffed the whole marshmallow in her mouth so she wouldn't have a chance to give him away. Bain hadn't told Carbonnell and Lyndy about the mermaid.

"More in the winter than the summer, but I'd say it's beautiful year-round. I like it. It's a good getaway." Carbonell stood and brushed the crumbs off his pants. "I think I'll turn in. Night, you two. Lyndy." He tipped his head and ducked into the tent.

It was late. The stars burned holes in the black sky, and the moon reflected its light in the ocean. Carbonell and Bain shared a tent while Erin and Lyndera got the other one.

Aunt Lyndera stood and directed piles of sand over the fire. "I think we all need to hit the sack. One more day, kids. One more day on poor Pisces, and we'll be there."

"Thank goodness," Bain said. "See you tomorrow."

Erin watched him disappear into the tent. Aunt Lyndy slipped into the other tent, leaving her alone on the couch in the dark. Without the fire, the night blacked out the horizon. Even though the others were only a few feet away, it felt good to be alone for a minute.

Pulsar, I really do miss you. She knew he couldn't hear her. *Campfires are boring without you. And flying. That horse has nothing on you.* It was pointless. Pulsar was hundreds of miles away.

The thought flashed so quickly through her thoughts that she almost dismissed it, but why not? Everyone else might be stuck here in the middle of nowhere, but she wasn't. What good was Whispering Winds if she couldn't take off and come back in an instant? And if Pulsar was better, he could come too. All he needed was enough magic. Even Ella said that it was Pulsar's magic that helped them transport together in the first place.

She pulled the changing brooch off her arm. Lately she had used it as a watch. Now it blinked to life as a GPS. She made it to Morocco just fine. She could leave and come right back. All she had to do was save the location on her device. It would be so easy.

For good measure, she put a sound ward around her while she thought of Álfheim. The warm wind gusted as her surroundings transformed. It shouldn't have surprised her that the room of trees was dark. Iceland was almost always dark in December. She walked through the room, letting her hand brush from tree to tree.

"Pulsar? Are you here?" He was probably sleeping. He could never hear her when he slept.

She crept through the room, looking for any sign of his scales reflecting moonlight, but there was nothing. Why didn't her impeccable sight extend to night vision? Even though she could see so much during the day, her eyes were practically useless at night.

"Pulsar." Her voice carried eerily in the forested room. Here there were no wild animals, no tiny creatures to scurry in the night. It was just another room in the palace.

She wound through the trees aimlessly until she lost track of how many times she crossed the room. He wasn't here. "I tried."

Even though she could have directed the double doors to open, she leaned against them and pushed out into the palace hall. Small candles lit the way, casting shadows along the wide, majestic corridor. Why hadn't she thought of it sooner? She smiled as she raced invisibly through the halls and to her old room.

Aunt Lyndy was nice to share her clothes, but Erin missed having her own things. As she entered her bedroom, she found it meticulously clean, and yet practically undisturbed.

"How did this get here?" She picked up her old duffle bag and found some of her clothes from home. She threw in some more clothes and her bathroom things before zipping it back up. Maybe it was from Bain.

With the bag slung over her shoulder, she made her way back into the hall. The door closed quietly behind her, and she looked at the empty hall, contemplating. If Pulsar wasn't in the palace, he was probably sleeping in his cave. She never did figure out where his hideout was.

It was too bad. She really did want to see him again and hear his voice resonate through her mind. Now she wondered if coming back had been a mistake. She doubted Aunt Lyndera or Carbonell would have approved.

"Funny seeing you here."

Erin gasped at the voice, and she felt a shock surge through her. She couldn't speak.

Joel appeared in front of her. "What are you doing walking around this time of night?"

"Joel, I . . ." Where did she start? How would she explain everything? Why didn't she bother to tell him anything before they left?

"You and Bain went to find your mom."

The weight of the duffle bag suddenly felt heavy on her shoulder. She didn't want to leave him. She didn't want to search the world; she wanted to stay right here in the empty hall with Joel and stare at his insanely beautiful face. Some part of her brain forced her head to bob up and down in agreement.

His expression softened. "I guess I can't blame you."

She waited. What could she even say?

"Pulsar's doing better. He left a couple days ago to hunt. Is that why you came back? To see him?"

She gripped the straps of the duffle bag at her shoulder. Part of her wanted to throw the bag on the ground and forget the wild goose chase. It would be so much easier to stay in Álfheim. "Yeah. I guess I came a little too late." Or maybe she waited a little too long to make the obvious right choice. What good was her gift if she still got things wrong?

He put his hand on her arm as if trying to stop her from leaving. "Can I come with you?"

She shook her head. "You want to come? But Carbonell . . . No one even knows I'm here."

"I already know how it feels to wait here for you. I think I'll take my chances with Carbonell."

Why was her heart racing? Could he hear it? "What about Pulsar?"

He winked at her, and in a flutter had her arm wrapped around his. "May I?"

"May you what?"

He reached over and lifted the bag from her shoulder. "Escort you to my quarters. I think I need to pack."

She wasn't sure if she nodded, but he was leading her through the halls with his hand in hers. Somewhere he had let the formal gesture of taking her arm slip into a comfortable interlocking of fingers, and she found herself easily following him without wondering why.

When they reached his doorway, he vanished as he packed his things in hyperspeed before picking her hand up once again and kissing it. "Ready," he said.

She hoped the shadows hid her blushing cheeks. It wasn't the first time he'd kissed her hand, but it sent her heart flying every time.

"What about Pulsar?" she asked, hoping to sound unaffected by his gesture.

He gave her a mischievous grin. "Follow me."

29
Two More for the Road

THEY RAN THROUGH THE DARK TERRAIN OUTSIDE OF THE PALACE until they were well into the wooded forest that surrounded the city, the same forest she and Pulsar had escaped to when Bain left. Memories of camping for nearly a month flooded her mind.

Joel was leading her up a steep trail where loose rocks trickled down the incline with every step. "We're almost there."

She couldn't see his face as she climbed behind him. How did Joel know where Pulsar slept? The hill leveled off as she followed him through the darkness.

"I was thinking it would be better if you tried to wake him up."

She laughed. The last time she tried to wake up Pulsar she was glad she had the touch ward. She never would have survived. "Where is he?"

He stopped and lifted her hand to the blackness ahead. "Right there."

She couldn't see anything. Why didn't elves carry flashlights? She walked blindly forward, wishing she could see the dragon's form. Her foot hit something hard, and she bent down and picked it up before quickly dropping it again. "A bone." She hoped she didn't sound as freaked out as she felt.

Her feet made almost no sound as she walked slowly forward. It was so dark. "I can't see anything."

She felt him take her hand. "You're almost there."

As they walked, she looked up to see if there were any stars, but nothing broke through the blackness. "Are we in a cave?"

He chuckled softly next to her. "You didn't notice?"

"It's totally dark. Can you see anything?"

"I can see this." He lifted her hand and kissed it.

Even though she was standing right next to him, she still couldn't see him. "You must be able to see in the dark then." Even in the cold night, her hand felt warm where his lips brushed.

He laughed again. "You didn't know?"

"You seriously can? Do you see him, then?"

"Yeah. He's sound asleep."

"Maybe if you get me close enough to his head I'll be able to wake him up."

"Sure."

It was possible that some of the crunching under her feet was more bones. Even though she couldn't see anything, her ability to hear was not diminished. The thought of walking on animal bones gave her the creeps. Even before she could touch Pulsar, the warmth of his scales radiated to her in the freezing air.

"To your left." Joel let go of her hand. "I think I'll wait over here for you."

She would have looked at him, but there was nothing but blackness to see. "Are you afraid?"

"Uh, you know what they say about sleeping dragons."

"No."

"Don't wake a sleeping dragon."

She laughed. She wasn't sure if he was kidding, but the sound of bones crunching under his steps sent flurries through her veins. It didn't matter that she had seen Pulsar hunt and knew what he ate, the remains littering the floor left her stomach unsettled.

Pulsar was definitely sleeping. The loud thrum of his breathing reminded her of all the nights they'd spent together. Sleeping under his wing was the safest place on earth. The heat of his scales met her hand as she traced along his shoulder and to his head. No wonder Joel decided to stand back. Pulsar's head alone was almost as tall as she was. If he woke to an instinctual reaction, he could easily snap a person in two before realizing it.

Even with a touch ward, it couldn't be a very fun experience.

She felt the ridge that led to his ear. "Pulsar. Wake up, it's me."

Still blind from the darkness, she warded herself.

"It's me," she called.

A loud snort filled the air, and a brush of fire lit the tall cavern.

"And Joel."

Fireborn. You're back.

And you're better. Come with me, I can't stand it without you.

"Watch out!" Joel said behind her and took her arm. "I think he needs to stretch."

"He won't hurt me." But she let him lead her back through the crunching floor. "Pulsar, do you think you can come?"

Where are we going?

Does it matter? Just come.

A stream of fire blew overhead, lighting the entrance of the cave. The inferno gave her a glance at his golden scales reflecting in its light. Maybe she should have been terrified, but Pulsar was a part of her now.

"I'll get the saddle." Joel sprinted into the dark.

She waited outside of the cave, where the stars peeked through the sky. "Do you mind if he comes too?"

We're bringing Joel?

She smiled in the darkness and let Pulsar into her thoughts. Joel was already packed, and she didn't have the heart to say no to him.

You like him.

Do not. He's just coming along for the ride.

I know he likes you.

Whatever. But the words made her heart speed up, and it felt like her head was going to float away.

Pulsar's rumble was low and loud. She didn't hear him laugh very often.

"Bain's going to kill me if he realizes I'm gone."

"Don't worry. I'll protect you."

Erin's heart leaped into her throat at the sound of Joel's voice. "How did you get back so soon?"

"Easy. Do you want to do this?" The dragon saddle hung in the air in front of her.

"Um, Pulsar?" It was too dark.

The saddle whooshed away. *Of course, little one. I knew you liked him.*

Stop. She waited, feeling conspicuous. The only person she had ever flown on Pulsar with was her brother. The saddle was big, but not that big. It was going to be a cozy ride. The thought only succeeded in sending a storm of butterflies through her—Joel hugging her waist as they flew through the air, and worse, having Pulsar there to read her every thought.

She pulled the GPS out of her pocket and fiddled with the duffel bag straps.

"Are you ready?" Joel asked.

Erin looked up, but it was still too dark for her to see his expression. "Sure." At least they could use the Whispering Wind. Maybe it wouldn't be so bad if it was a short ride. They climbed up onto the soft saddle, and she strapped her legs into the fenders. Joel sat behind her and wrapped his arms around her waist.

She tried to not think about the warmth spreading through her stomach as she looked at the tiny screen marked with a star. Just go to the star. It can't be that hard.

Don't worry, Fireborn. I will help you focus.

She let his presence into her head as she stared at the red star. For a moment, it felt as if she were alone with Pulsar, but a moment was all she needed before the wind warped around them and the moonlit ocean and beach filled her view.

"I'm going to have to make you take me more often. That was incredible."

"Shh." In the two tents were her aunt, her twin, and Carbonell. Was she supposed to climb into her sleeping bag and pretend everything was normal? Aunt Lyndera would notice if she never came to bed. But what was Joel supposed to do? Sleep outside with the dragon?

At least it was warm here, some country in Africa. As long as he stayed out of the water he should be okay.

Joel's arms moved from her waist as he slipped off Pulsar.

You need to tell them.

I know. It would be better if everyone knew. She unwrapped her legs and jumped off the dragon's tall body, landing in the sand. Between the tents, the campfire blazed. Joel sat there, poking a stick into the flames.

"Sit with me," he said without looking up.

She wasn't sure why she obeyed, but it seemed a lot easier to sit in front of the fire than wake everyone up and tell them they had company. She sat down and watched the flames dance. She loved the smell of campfires.

"Thanks." Joel didn't look up as he stirred the coals with his stick. "I didn't think you'd let me come."

"Are you sure you want to be here?" She wished she could see more of his face than the firelight allowed.

"I don't want to be banished from you anymore."

His answer sent shocks through her. He felt banished from her? "What about Carbonell?"

"I'll take it one step at a time."

"But you're going to play nice, right?"

He turned a log over with his stick. "I'll be nice, but don't expect me to stand by and let you get hurt again."

A lump swelled in her throat. Why did it mean so much to her that he cared? She couldn't answer.

"Hi, Carbonell," Joel said.

She looked up to see Carbonell, his form rigid in the firelight. Had he heard everything?

"Pull up a rock." Joel poked his stick in the fire.

Carbonell disappeared as the flap of the tent zipped down.

"Well, that's one less person you'll have to tell," Joel said.

"I think I'm going to call it a night." She still didn't know what to do with Joel, but he could figure it out for himself. After pulling out her sleeping bag, she made her way to Pulsar. Under his wing was better than any tent, and best of all, it would buy her time. Maybe everyone would see the dragon and Joel before she even woke up.

"You're just going to leave me here alone?" Joel asked. His voice was soft but still carried over the soothing splash of the ocean.

"You're not alone."

He didn't look at her as he stirred the fire.

"Good night, Joel." She couldn't decide if it was a good thing to have Joel here. Maybe he would prove valuable on the search for her mom. But there was always the chance he'd only come to talk her out of it. If that was the case, he was wasting his time. She planned to stick this out to the end. No amount of charm was going to sway her determination.

30

A Sea to Cross

ERIN COULD HEAR THEM TALKING EVEN BEFORE SHE OPENED HER eyes. It had to be morning, but no light penetrated the dragon wing above her. She listened as Carbonell argued with Joel. Joel wasn't invited. If Erin wanted to bring more people along, she should have talked to them first and not barrage them with company in the middle of the night.

"What are you afraid of?" It was Joel's voice. "Was this just another plan to steal them into your corrupt world?"

Carbonell's voice was even louder. "You don't know anything about it. You're just a spoiled little—"

"Knock it off already." It was the first time she heard Bain's voice. "We're not completely helpless. If Erin thought Joel should be here, then let it go."

It was time to face them. Erin wondered what Aunt Lyndera was doing during all this until the smell of bacon registered. "Okay, Pulsar, you can let me out now."

Good morning to you too, Fireborn.

His giant suede wing lifted off the ground like a canopy, and the blinding sun hit her eyes full force. Suddenly she wanted her toothbrush and a shower. For the last few days she had gotten by on the bare essentials, even letting her aunt fix her hair into a sloppy bun, but now?

She warded herself with invisibility and made her way to the cook fire to retrieve her duffle bag from the night before. Maybe they wouldn't notice the bag disappearing with her into the tent.

Carbonell must have gone back into his tent, but Bain and Joel sat in front of the cooking bacon watching Aunt Lyndy work.

"Morning, Erin."

It was Bain. Shoot. How could she forget? Even invisible, he could see her magic aura. She didn't answer as she grabbed her bag and ducked into the tent. At least she could try to make herself look presentable before facing Joel. For once it was annoying to have a brother that could see all things magical.

"Did you get tired of riding Pisces?" Bain asked. Of course he was talking to her.

She wanted to hush him before the pegasus took offense to his comment. Even if they did have Pulsar, they still needed the flying horse. The dragon's saddle only held two people.

"I guess that means Joel's riding with you," Bain pointed out.

As she scrubbed her teeth with her toothbrush, she nearly swallowed the foamy white paste. *With me?* She hadn't even thought about how they would travel. Selfishly enough, she realized she had kind of planned on riding Pulsar alone. She opened the flap of the tent and spit the toothpaste onto the sand before ducking back.

"Gross," Bain said.

Even though she couldn't see them from inside the tent, her face burned. Who cares? So she spit her toothpaste on the ground. Everyone does that when there's no sink. Why didn't she think about the fact that the boy she has been fantasizing about was sitting right there to see the white glop on the hot sand? She pulled her hair into a quick ponytail and looked in a hand mirror.

Being an älva had its advantages. If she overlooked her frizzy messy hair, she didn't look too bad.

"Breakfast is ready," Aunt Lyndera called.

Erin took a deep breath before climbing out of the tent, invisibility ward aside. But she had nothing to worry about. Joel, Bain, and even Carbonell were dishing up the eggs and bacon onto their plates with enthusiasm. She sat back and waited.

"You look beautiful, Erin." Aunt Lyndy handed her a plate and a glass of juice.

"Thanks." Erin could feel Joel's stare burning into her. Instead of acknowledging his attention, she picked up her fork and took a bite of the steaming hot eggs. Green onions, cheese, and the perfect amount of salt and pepper gave it just the right touch. Ever since her ability to taste was enhanced, she wished she knew more about cooking.

"This is so good." Erin pointed her fork to her plate and looked at Aunt Lyndera.

"I'm glad you like them, love," Aunt Lyndera said, winking at her.

The nickname caught Erin off guard, and the thought of Grandpa Jessie flashed through her mind. It was another reminder of the lie she was living—the fact that she still hadn't told him about last summer when she and her brother became elves.

"We need to figure things out," Carbonell said. "We've got five people, a pegasus, a dragon, and an ocean to cover today."

"An ocean?" Erin flipped her changing brooch into a GPS and looked at the map. There was over 1800 miles of sea between them and Brazil. "There's no way we'll make it. Pisces can't carry all of you for that long." She looked at the tiny islands poking through the blue water. Even if they stopped there, the islands had to be nearly a thousand miles away.

"We weren't planning on flying." Carbonell's cold stare bore through her.

She felt the same ice trickle down her spine. The first time she met Carbonell, he had kidnapped her with invisible hands. She stared back at him, watching his aura carefully. Even though it was a cloudy gray and the angry stare refused to budge, she knew he wasn't lying.

"What's the plan then?" Bain asked. "If we're not flying, then what does that leave us with?"

Carbonell didn't lift his heavy gaze from Erin as he spoke. Her heart refused to calm, and defiance boiled inside of her. Who was he to be mad at her for bringing a dragon? What was he afraid of? Or was it Joel? Either way, Carbonell had no right to expect her to leave Pulsar behind.

Carbonell shook his head and looked quickly at Joel as if his presence was a cruel joke.

"What is it?" Aunt Lyndera asked, breaking the tense air. "You don't want to fly, so tell us what we're going to do."

Erin appreciated the spunk her aunt could so easily conjure. If anyone in the group seemed oblivious to Carbonell's temper tantrum, it was her.

"How did you get back to Pennsylvania, Bain? One minute you were in Iceland, and the next, Pennsylvania. Did you take a boat, an airplane? How did you do it?" Carbonell set his empty plate on the ground next to the fire and directed a pitcher to drizzle water over it. The water boiled as it spread over the plate, cleaning it till it shone.

Bain set his plate next to Carbonell's. "The well."

"How did you know about the well?" Joel asked.

It was Bain's turn to shake his head. "Can't tell you that."

Joel looked at Carbonell, who was still staring at the clean plate. "Are you saying you have another well here in Africa?"

A small smile broke on Carbonell's face. "Not entirely. But the concept is close enough."

"Tell us then," Aunt Lyndera said.

Carbonell scratched his chin. "It's right there." He pointed to an outcropping of rocks almost a quarter of a mile into the ocean. "You'll have to swim there, or fly to it. It takes you into the jungle just outside of Xavene's new fortress."

"That sounds easy," Bain said.

"Sure, easy for you, and me and even Pisces, but the dragon?" He shook his head slowly. "The dragon would never fit. You should have asked me before you brought him."

The reality crept into her head. They were all supposed to go to Brazil through the portal. It would have been so easy. They didn't need her Whispering Winds or the extra flying power of Pulsar. And now she would have to watch them all disappear into the ocean and stay behind with Pulsar, or she could go with them and leave the dragon here.

"This can work!" Erin stood up and walked toward the

cresting water. "I'll go through the portal to Brazil, mark it on my map, and then come back here for Pulsar. It's simple."

Bain smiled. "And I'll go with her, just to make sure she gets there . . . unless *you* want to." He looked meaningfully at Joel.

Erin stood frozen against the horizon. Joel? Part of her wished that he would come instead of her brother, but the idea made her stomach flip.

"Whatever is Erin's wish," Joel answered.

Everyone was looking at her expectantly. What was she supposed to say? She couldn't turn down her brother and pick Joel. But she wanted to. No, she didn't. She looked at them, not knowing what to say. Why couldn't she just do it? She had been away from Joel for more than a week. Spending a little time with him would be . . . Would be what? Awkward?

She closed her eyes. *Pulsar, help me out here.*

Leave them both behind, Fireborn. Neither will feel offended.

"Pulsar says I'll be fine alone." She tried to put an authentic smile on her face. "Thanks for offering to be my escort, but Pulsar will provide more than enough protection."

"Okay, sis. If that's what you want." Bain stood and slapped the sides of his jeans. "All right, Carbonell, when do we go?"

Joel didn't approach her as the tents were loaded into Aunt Lyndera's purse. In fact, everyone was unnaturally quiet.

"You ever been to Brazil?" she asked Joel.

He gave her a look that sent a cascade of shivers down her arms. Was he angry? Sad? Disappointed? Before she could figure it out, he turned and headed for the brown and white pegasus.

31
There and Back

CARBONELL INSISTED ON SWIMMING THE DISTANCE TO THE OUT-cropping of rocks. Erin sat on Pisces, sandwiched between her brother and Joel. At least Joel was in front of her instead of stuck behind her with his arms around her waist. She still couldn't figure him out.

Just when she thought she was in love all over again, he would do this. Silence. Or was it brooding? She couldn't tell, but she was glad to have Bain's arms around her instead of Joel's. Bain was harmless, while Joel was a mystery that made her stomach turn inside out.

It didn't take long for Pisces to fly to the rock formation standing conspicuously in the ocean. Erin wondered if they were going to have to get wet after all until she noticed a platform rise up to meet them. Fortunately its breadth easily accommodated the enormous horse. Pisces must have been here before. He landed seamlessly on the flat surface and waited for Carbonell to catch up.

No one dismounted the horse. She was glad. The mood that spread over everyone after Carbonell's speech had lingered until all conversations died, leaving a wake of silence. Carbonell pulled himself onto the platform and put his arm comfortably around Pisces's neck.

The floor fell out from underneath them, and Erin heard herself scream. At least it was dark. They probably thought she was a wimp for screaming, but what did it matter?

Pulsar? Nothing. The portal must have spells preventing

communication. Down. How could they drop in a free fall for so long? Would they end up in the middle of the earth instead of Brazil? This was nothing like flying. Blinded by darkness and falling endlessly opened up a new fear of dark, enclosed places; she needed out. Sunlight. Land. She needed out before her mind imploded.

She was going to be sick. It would be better to jump off the horse than to throw up all over Joel's back. She loosened her grip from Joel's waist and clapped her hand over her mouth. They were still falling in blackness. Vaguely aware of the touch ward, she dove off the side of Pisces and landed on the platform just in time. Her stomach had officially reached its limit, and now her breakfast had found a new home.

She wiped her face, wishing she couldn't smell the partially digested eggs. But it was too late. Her stomach emptied again.

The falling abruptly ended, and light blasted overhead. She could see Carbonell's feet from where she lay curled up on the wooden plank. Her stomach ached.

"If you want to hold on, Pisces will fly you down." She heard Carbonell pat the paint's neck.

Down? Hadn't they been plunging down forever? Wings unfurled above her, and soon Pisces's feet lifted from the platform. Carbonell must have gone with them since his feet disappeared too.

She rolled over onto the vacant platform and stared up into the leaves. This wasn't what she wanted. Maybe she should have stayed with Pulsar after all. There were no guarantees. Her mom. How could she still be alive? Tears leaked from Erin's eyes.

She used her sleeve to wipe the residue from her face. With the hard wood against the back of her head, she pulled the changing brooch out and looked at the tiny GPS screen. Brazil. It looked familiar. The same lines of blue streaked the land. She had been here before.

Why did she come, really? Staring up into the canopy of trees, it didn't seem likely this journey was worth it. *I'm sorry, Pulsar.* But she already knew he couldn't hear her.

Slowly, she sat up, testing her stomach. And that's when she saw him. How long had he been sitting there watching her?

"You okay?" Joel asked.

What was she supposed to say? She was too aware of how disgusting she must have looked. And smelled. And if the toothpaste from this morning grossed him out, she was beyond hope now.

He pulled a handkerchief out of his back pocket and stood up. Then he was gone. The leaves above her shook, and she caught sight of him in the tall branches. She couldn't watch; she was too embarrassed. Maybe she should try an invisibility ward.

He appeared again, kneeling in front of her with the hanky. "May I?" He didn't wait for an answer. The cloth was cool and wet against her face as he washed her. "Better?"

Erin nodded. "Thanks." The softness in his eyes made her want to cry. Why was he being so nice to her? Wasn't he mad at her only an hour ago? It was so confusing.

"You sure you want to go get Pulsar alone? You look kind of pale."

"I always look pale." She tried to smile at her joke, but her stomach still felt weak.

He took her hand and looked at the GPS. "I can't let you go alone. What if something happens?"

She swallowed. She didn't want to go alone. Not really.

"Come here," he said as he stood and pulled on her hand.

They looked out from the platform suspended by magic high off the ground between the branches of the trees. It felt so much better than the underground nightmare portal. "I knew you'd like it," he said.

She looked over at him, realizing for the first time that he was still holding her hand. It felt so natural, like it belonged there.

"Should we go get your dragon?"

She nodded, tightening her grip on his hand. Now she needed the Whispering Winds to take them away. At least she knew where Pulsar waited. Warm air whipped around her before a sandy beach met her feet.

I thought you were coming alone.

I know. I was. But . . . She didn't have to finish. What was there to say?

"I take it you don't care for small, confined spaces," Joel said.

"What?"

"The trip to South America."

Erin shook her head. "Oh, that." Hopefully she would never have to travel by portal again. With Whispering Winds, why should she? "Maybe it was the falling in complete darkness that did me in."

"I saw you jump off Pisces."

She'd completely forgotten that Joel could see in the dark. Just great. He saw everything.

"Do you need to sit down?"

"Sure." She let herself sink into the hot sand. Embarrassment mingled with her doubts. She didn't know what to do. It was hopeless. They were never going to find her mom. Bain could already be in Xavene's mansion surrounded by imps, and it would be her fault. She thought she could tell the right choice based on auras, but what if she was wrong? She had been wrong a lot lately. Part of her wanted to stay here on the African beach forever, forget about the impossible quest to find her mom, and just lay in the sun.

"What are you thinking?" Joel asked.

She didn't open her eyes. It was easier to pretend that he wasn't looking at her. Maybe he wasn't.

He cleared his throat. "*I* was thinking that you and Bain deserve the chance to find your mom."

"Thanks." She took in a long, steady breath, trying to clear her head of emotions. "Is that why you came?"

"Partly."

"What's the other part?"

"To keep an eye on you." There was a touch of teasing in his voice. He drew a long breath. "But I want to find Xavene. This seems like the perfect opportunity to do both."

"Do you think I can do this? Find my mom?" It was a stupid question, but she kept her eyes closed and waited for his answer. Why did she feel so inadequate?

"You faced a whole army of imps and you want to know if I think you're capable?"

She knew a small smile escaped her lips.

"You saved my sister from Xavene by yourself, fought an imp, and stayed with Pulsar for a day in the ocean. Erin Fireborn, you forget who you are."

An unwanted tear escaped her eye, and she hoped he didn't notice. "And who am I?" Her voice cracked at the end, but it was too late. It was a question that hung over her head all the time. Who was she? A sixteen-year-old girl from a tiny village who decided to become immortal. It didn't make her a hero, and it didn't promise that she would find her mom. It made her wonder what the rest of her eternity would be like, immortal in a mortal world.

"You are Erin Fireborn Farraday, and no one can imagine what feats yet await you."

She couldn't stop the tears that streamed down her cheeks.

Fireborn, I know you, and I know you are stronger than this. Who are you to cower? Pulsar projected images in her mind.

He was right. When she saw herself through the dragon's eyes, she wasn't a scared little girl. She was a warrior. All she needed to do was figure out how to summon that courage and keep it in her heart.

You won't be alone, little one.

"Thanks, Pulsar." With a dragon on her side, was there anything she couldn't do?

Joel squeezed her hand.

Oh, yeah. Boys. That's one thing she still hadn't figured out.

The rumble of Pulsar's laugh filled the air.

32
Mixed Messages

BAIN JUMPED OFF PISCES'S BACK, GLAD TO BE FREE OF BOTH flying and falling. The portal had dropped so much farther than the one that took him to Pennsylvania. Maybe it had something to do with the distance. He didn't blame Erin for jumping off the horse. Part of him wished he had done it too, but then, in the complete darkness, he probably would have landed on her. At least Joel had decided to stay with her.

"We're going to walk from here," Carbonell said.

"Aren't we going to wait for Erin?" Bain asked. It seemed odd that Carbonell wanted to take off so quick.

"I'm thinking if we don't clear out of here, we're going to end up underneath a dragon," Carbonell said.

Bain looked around at the wooded area. Bright blue and red macaws flew overhead, their color caught in the glimpses of sunlight that broke through the thick canopy of leaves. This was the kind of place he wouldn't mind spending a lot of time in. There was so much to see. Even the sounds were new. Voices from several creatures floated through the air—birds, frogs, and maybe monkeys. He wanted to spend a month exploring its vast depth of life.

"How far is it?" Bain asked.

"Less than a mile. If you follow the river west, you'll run right into it." Carbonell's voice easily carried through the trees.

Bain looked up to see a monkey leap from a branch into the neighboring tree. He couldn't help it. As long as they were waiting around for Erin, he might as well have a little fun. With a short running start, he jumped at the tree and grabbed the nearest branch. Climbing was easy with the vines and vegetation that grew around the trunk. With an invisibility and sound ward, he crept onto the same branch that a toucan sat on. Its bright yellow beak looked so big on the small black and white body.

As Bain took in the view from the trees, he found numerous creatures. Never before had he seen so many parrots. It was a pet store with no bars or walls. Tiny monkeys chattered as they swung from the branches, looking for fruit.

There were marshes of water below and, thanks to his new elf vision, he could see the eyes of an anaconda poking just above the surface of the water as it waited for its prey. The sight of the enormous snake sent shivers through him. It was hard not to watch the deadly game.

The whir of wings distracted him, and he glanced up just in time to see a humming bird. Its long, blue tail was unlike any hummingbird he had ever seen. The bird hovered, watching him with its tiny black eyes. Or maybe he only thought it was. His invisibility ward should still be working. Before he could decide, the green and blue bird zipped away. The whole forest grew quiet.

Through the trees, a creature resembling a leopard crushed through the underbrush, seemingly unaware of the hush that had settled over the area. Bain watched the beast, whose hind legs stretched too long while its broad chest gave it an apelike appearance. When the animal came up on its hind legs, the memory of the mountain lion from Pennsylvania flashed through his mind. It was an imp.

Bain's breath caught in his throat. Even though he knew he was invisible up in the trees, Carbonell hadn't bothered to ward. And neither had Aunt Lyndera.

Aunt Lyndy clutched her fat leather purse in front of her as if it would protect her from the monster that stood several feet taller than her. Bain wished she would ward invisible. At least then he would know she was safe.

He shook his head. Of course she was safe. She knew more about magic than he did. This imp had no magical aura, and therefore could not be a threat. That didn't stop Bain's heart from pounding in his chest. Every animal in the area silently waited for the aberration to leave.

"Sledjon," Carbonell said, his voice barely hiding disgust.

"Xavene has been waiting for you," the animal spoke through a low growl.

"Yes, of course. Tell him I've brought a friend. I'm sure he would love to see Lyndy again. They've known each other for . . . it's been a long time."

"So be it," the animal said before falling on all fours and distancing itself with its uneven gait.

The chatter from the trees resumed as the creature disappeared from view. Now what were they going to do? Bain stood on the branch and rested against the trunk, allowing his legs to stretch. There went the element of surprise. Now Xavene knew not only Carbonell was there, but also Aunt Lyndera.

He watched his aunt take a pen and paper from her purse and give it to Carbonell. Carbonell nodded and scribbled on the paper before folding it and searching the trees.

With a jolt, Bain realized Carbonell was looking for him. Before Bain could drop the invisibility ward, Carbonell's eyes locked on his with a smile. A paper airplane soared from Carbonell's hand in a perfect shot, whipping around branches and landing in Bain's hands.

He looked at the paper and back down to Carbonell and his aunt. Carbonell waved before taking Aunt Lyndera's arm and walking off in the direction the animal had gone.

They were leaving him. His heart raced as he fumbled to open the paper airplane.

> *Bain,*
> *It looks like they found me. Wait for the others and then follow the river west. It's only a mile. Don't let them see you. Tell Erin I'm sorry, but we can still figure this out.*
> *Carbonell*
> *—And don't worry, Lyndy will be fine*

He folded the note and shoved it into his back pocket. The toucan turned to look at him. Maybe animals could sense him even if they couldn't see him. He tried to force himself to think calmly.

Carbonell should have been more careful. For some reason he looked back down at the anaconda in the water. It was coiled around some small animal and unhinging its jaw to swallow it whole. Bain's stomach tightened, and he looked away.

A plan. He needed to figure out what they were going to do. It had to be completely crazy to walk right into Xavene's lair. There would be guards, at the very least. Bain had invisibility on his side, but even if they did get past the entrance, what did they think they could accomplish? They had no direction, and with Carbonell gone, no leader.

A golden glow filled the clearing before the dragon came into view. Bain took a deep breath before descending the tree. Joel and Erin were already loosening the straps around their legs before he could get to them.

"Hey," Bain called, ignoring the unnatural quiet that fell over the forest. The birds held their songs, and the monkeys hid. Pulsar must have scared every living thing in sight. For a second, he let his mind wander to the anaconda. Too bad Pulsar hadn't been here a little sooner. The thought of the anaconda dangling from the dragon's mouth didn't help.

"Sorry we took so long." Erin freed her legs from the saddle and jumped down.

Joel waited for Erin to clear out of the way before jumping down.

"What's wrong, Bain?" Erin asked.

He knew he couldn't lie to her. She would know. Even without her aura reading, she would still probably figure it out.

"Where's Carbonell?" Joel asked.

"We got caught. An imp found us. I was up in a tree, invisible, but Aunt Lyndera and Carbonell were just standing there, plain as day." Bain handed Erin the wrinkled paper. "They left."

"What do we do?" Erin asked.

"I don't know. What do you think, Joel?" Maybe it was better to ask someone else. Maybe Joel knew more about the situation than they did.

Joel shook his head. "I can't make this call for you. You two are going to have to decide. Either way, I'm coming with you."

Bain nodded. "Erin?"

She ran both of her hands through her hair. "I don't know. We're supposed to follow the river until we get to the mansion? Then what?"

"I know. I've been thinking the same thing. We don't have to do this. We could just go back to the kingdom."

"And leave Aunt Lyndera? How do we know she won't be stuck there as a prisoner?" Erin asked.

The forest rang with quiet. "We can't leave her here," Bain said.

"It doesn't seem right," Erin agreed.

"Okay." Bain looked up at Pulsar. "Does he need to eat or anything before we go? You know what? I don't want to know."

"He said he'll hunt invisibly just for you," Erin said.

"Follow the river west. If it's all the same to you, I would feel better if you rode Pulsar," Bain pointed at the dragon.

At least she didn't argue. She leaped up the dragon's leg as if she'd done it a million times. In a fluid motion, she was in the saddle high on Pulsar's back.

"You want to ride up here too?" Erin called.

It was tempting. Bain looked at Joel. "No, I think we'll walk. Maybe Pulsar can take out any imps we meet along the way. That would make me feel a little better."

Erin smiled from her perch on the dragon. "He says, 'Done.'"

They walked in silence, the golden glow of Pulsar hovering behind him. Bain looked at Joel. "How are we going to do this? Even if we get past the guards . . ." It was daunting.

"I'm still working on that," Joel said.

33
One Ugly Frog

BAIN HID UNDER HIS INVISIBILITY WARD AS THEY APPROACHED THE mansion. Even though lush vegetation surrounded the grounds, the building reminded him of the days spent in Black Rain. Here, flowers and trees replaced desert sand. He wondered how the birds could be oblivious to the dismal feeling that oozed from this building.

"Pulsar's going to stand guard," Erin spoke in his ear. He had been so preoccupied with the mansion that he'd failed to notice his sister's golden aura beside him.

"How did you find me?" Bain asked.

"I've been watching your footprints."

Bain looked down at the muddy forest floor, where obvious footprints tracked for probably the whole mile. "Yeah. I didn't think about that."

Pulsar's golden aura brightened as he erased the tracks from the mud.

"There's no one here." A thrill of fear surged through Bain. With Xavene, nothing was ever simple. If the place looked empty, it was probably just an illusion.

"They're probably inside. The last time I was here, there was no one outside. I guess they don't think there's anything to guard against."

"Let's go," Joel said from the orange glow that kept his place.

Erin's voice broke in. "How am I supposed to know where you guys are? Bain's the only one who can see us. I don't want to get stuck somewhere alone."

"We'll hold hands. Bain, grab her hand, and I'll get the other."

Bain reached for the golden aura. His hand passed through the golden glow.

"Don't worry, no one can see you." Erin held his hand.

Joel must have decided to take the lead. His orange glow headed for the door. Bain took in the view. Xavene must not have had time to furnish the whole mansion. The room they entered was bare and led into a hallway. No barrier or guards secured the grounds. It was too easy walking into this place.

A faint whistle sounded before he felt a dart whiz past his face.

"Duck," Erin called.

They were on their knees as more darts shot out of the walls. Bain held onto her hand and focused on his touch ward. Darts rained through the room and drove into the floor.

"Poisoned darts," Joel said.

"Someone figured out that we're here," Bain said.

"Let's go." Joel pulled them through the flying darts.

Their touch ward held as they crossed the room and made it to the hallway, where stairs offered two directions. Up or down.

"Hang on," Joel said.

Bain watched the orange aura go back. "What are you doing?"

Joel returned, still invisible. "They won't kill you, but they'll put you to sleep for a day or two."

"The darts?" Erin asked.

"Yes. Come on." Joel's orange aura glowed in front as they headed up the stairs.

"Why up?" Bain asked.

"That's where Erin said she found my sister. Upstairs."

Bain didn't answer. A sense of foreboding settled on him as he climbed each step. He wanted to be in front of Erin, not behind.

The sound of scraping and creaking filled the silence. Someone—or something—climbed the steps from the basement.

"Run!" Bain shouted.

They didn't need any more persuading. The three of them cleared the stairs, and Joel led them into an empty bedroom. Bain felt Joel's hand on his arm.

"As long as we're touching, our wards are fused. Your sound ward will still work on the outside, but we all can still hear each other. Do you have your sound ward up?" Joel asked.

"Got it," Erin said.

"Sure," Bain answered.

"Listen, I don't want to be trapped. Our first goal is to find your aunt."

The door burst open, and a wet, green tree frog filled the doorframe. Its webbed hands held a dart gun.

"Lie flat on the floor. Keep all your wards." Joel didn't say more before pulling the other two to the ground.

The frog imp showered the room with darts as Joel scooted across the floor, pulling Bain and Erin with him. Bain imagined how it would feel to sock the flabby giant frog in the face. He wondered if his hand would bounce off it like gelatin.

"I'm going to grab its legs." Joel's aura burned orange as he lashed out at the thick, green legs.

The frog jumped into the room while the orange glow followed.

"Stay here," Bain said to Erin. He picked up a handful of darts and caught the giant frog as it tried to leap out the window. The full weight of the imp landed on Bain. With the green, sticky skin pinning him to the floor, Bain covered his nose and stabbed the darts into the creature. The frog smelled so bad.

The imp sagged immediately, with Bain stuck underneath. "A little help." Bain pushed against the bulging body, the wet skin folding around his hands. It was like trying to move a water bed.

With a strange sloshing sound, the imp rolled off him. There, shining over his head, was the orange and gold glow of his sister and Joel. Bain reached up until their hands found his. "Thanks."

"Frog legs anyone?" Joel asked.

"That's just sick," Bain answered.

"There are a lot of rooms," Erin said. "Do you think we should split up and meet back here?"

Bain looked back at the massive frog lying on the floor. "How about you and Joel take the other side of the hall, and I'll look through this side."

"Okay." Joel took Erin's hand.

"Take some darts with you, just in case," Bain said, scooping some off the wood floor. He watched as the gold and orange glows left the room. His chest filled with dread. All of his life culminated to this point. Did he still have a mom? This whole thing was crazy. At least he could search the rooms quickly. He didn't have to spend very long here, and then the wondering could be over. Maybe he would stay in the rain forest for a while and then go to Africa to look for Kelura.

He stepped out into the empty hallway. One door at a time. With an invisibility ward in place and his wand out, he directed the first door open.

Empty. The room was completely void of any furniture, like an empty hotel room. His heart refused to slow in spite of the quiet. Next door. Nothing. Next door. One after another the doors revealed barren rooms. Only two left. At least he would be able to leave this place and say they tried. Bury his mother all over again.

He stood in front of the door, looking at the black paint. Is this why he decided to become immortal? So he could chase ghosts? He didn't feel like himself anymore. Where were the high school buddies and basketball?

He lifted his wand and pointed at the door. He already knew his aunt wasn't in the room. There was nothing to find here. The door opened, and this time something stood in the center of the otherwise vacant room.

A faint, shimmering, silver glow held his attention. Inside a tall metal cage sat a bird with its wings folded against deep blue feathers. He would have called it a peacock, but the tail was wrong. Instead of a fan of eyed feathers, a long, soft brush of silver tail feathers balanced the sleek bird.

"Hi again." It wasn't the first time Bain had seen the beautiful creature. Back at Black Rain, he admired the bird that sat in the same cage in the corner of Xavene's open room. But he wasn't allowed to mention the silver aura. Magic wasn't real, and auras were a product of an illness. That was the lie they worked so hard to teach him.

"Why are they keeping you up here?" He couldn't help but notice how diminished its aura was. Maybe the bird had weakened enough to lose favor with Xavene. Bain reached for the door of the metal cage. In Black Rain he would sit by the bird and admire its beauty. When Carbonell and Xavene were out, he would spend hours telling the bird about Erin, reminiscing about their childhood and the strange adventure of becoming elves—all of which would have gotten him in serious trouble if he had been caught.

But the bird couldn't talk to tell his secrets.

Why hadn't he ever tried to free it? "You're not going to bite me, are you?" Bain could have sworn the bird shook its head from side to side. With the wand in hand, he directed the cage door open and cast a touch ward just to be safe.

The bird jumped onto the open door and stretched its wings.

"I'd open the window, but there isn't one." Somehow the bird managed to end up in the only room without sunlight shining through. "If you want, you can come with me. I can get you outside. There are lots of trees. Tons of other birds. Just watch out for the snakes." Bain held his arm out.

It took the invitation and lighted on his forearm. Its grip was firm, but not strong enough to break his skin.

"We only have one more room to check." He cast an invisibility ward over the both of them and stepped into the hall.

The last room revealed a cot. His heart pounded at the prison-like room. No one was there, but it was clearly intended to hold someone captive. There was a bathroom on one end, offering the only comfort. It didn't have granite walls, but the cot was exactly the same as the one he slept on in the black castle. Maybe it *was* the same one.

He wanted to blast the entire room into dust and leave nothing there for Xavene to use. No one should have to endure the nightmare he lived through, the nightmare Carbonell had brought him into. Blood pounded through him, and he could feel it course through his veins.

Erin hadn't been there in the forest to know whether Carbonell intended to deceive them. Maybe this whole thing was a setup from the very beginning. Carbonell told enough truths to get them into Xavene's lair, and now they would be trapped. He tightened his hand into a fist. Why hadn't Carbonell and Aunt Lyndera warded themselves with invisibility? Had they planned to leave Erin and him all along? The whole trip could have been a well-told lie with enough truths to get Erin to follow them here.

They had to get out. Bain ran to the room where the massive green frog stank it up. There were no auras to greet him. Erin and Joel weren't back yet.

34

A Matter of Prince—
Or Principle

ERIN LET JOEL LEAD HER BY THE HAND AS THEY WALKED. SHE didn't really want to explore the mansion alone. No rooms had proved very promising so far. Last time she had found Ella, but even that room was now empty.

"Do you think they're looking for us? Would Carbonell know we made it?" Erin followed Joel into another empty room.

"I wouldn't expect him to save you, if that's what you mean," Joel said.

"Maybe we'll save him."

Joel gave a low chuckle. "That'll be the day."

"Are you mad at me?" She couldn't help asking. His moods were getting hard to read.

"Should I be?"

Erin breathed in. "I don't think so. Are you mad at Carbonell?"

He took her hand and brought her closer. "I'm not mad at anyone. I just don't want to see you get hurt."

"I know, you're here to keep an eye on me."

"Erin . . ." Joel said, looking down at the bare floor. "I can't." He blew out a breath before meeting her eyes. "There's so much you don't know."

"Then tell me."

Joel shook his head. "You know that Ella is my sister."

Erin nodded.

"Ormond . . . Xavene . . ." Joel paused a moment and studied her face. "He's my brother."

She watched as Joel's eyes burned with intensity. The story connected in her head. Carbonell told her about Ormond. There were three children. Joel and Ella. *But Ormond was a prince.* Heat flushed through her like hot rain. "That means you're—"

"A prince too."

"And your mom—"

"Is the queen," he finished for her.

Her arms chilled with goose bumps. How could she not have known? All this time, she thought she knew him better.

"I probably should have told you."

Her laugh was halfhearted as she shook her head. She had no idea what to say.

"But this way you got to know me for who I really am without overreacting to my title."

"Overreacting?" He was a prince. His mom ruled the whole elf kingdom. "But you said you were an officer when I met you."

"I am. My office is crown prince."

"Why crown prince? Isn't Ella older than you?" "She doesn't want it. Ormond forfeited his inheritance, so that leaves me, the youngest one, next in line."

She wondered how he could say it so casually. Next in line to rule the most powerful kingdom in the world—and she was worried about looking stupid at a ball. Her stomach turned to lead. "Do I still have to go to that winter solstice thing?" If she was there with him and everyone else knew he was the prince, then it would send too strong of a message to the kingdom.

"Would you? I know it would mean a lot to my mom."

"Queen Āldera."

"Yes, Queen Āldera. She adores you, you know."

It was too much. "You can't be serious."

He touched her chin lightly, and she couldn't help looking into his light brown eyes. His smile was soft. "I adore you too."

Her heart beat like it wanted to take flight. Part of her wanted to run away and find some kind of reality that made sense, but the other part wanted to stand here, forever lost in his gaze.

She shook her head. "We, uh, better finish checking the

rooms. I think I'm going to see if Bain is back." She didn't wait for his answer as she dropped his hand, breaking the fusion of spells that allowed her to see him.

She left the room, feeling like someone else. Joel was more than a celebrity or Hollywood star; he was a prince. A *crown* prince. Her brain refused to process it. But the pieces were coming together. His brother had become a monster, and now Joel finally had the chance to confront him. That had to be hard.

She was distantly aware of the doors opening and shutting as Joel directed them. It was the same Joel as before—the same boy who brought her breakfast, found her in the dark halls, and helped her a couple months ago when her brother went missing. The same Joel.

She walked silently down the hall. Crown prince. *How come you never told me?* she asked Pulsar.

It wasn't mine to tell.

But you knew all along, didn't you?

Fireborn, there are limitations to even my power. Their secret is protected. No one can share the information unless the royal family permits it.

You mean, I can't tell Bain?

Only if Joel allows it.

The smell of the sleeping frog imp intensified as she approached the room. She covered her nose as she stepped in the doorway. The green flabby imp appeared to be alone.

"Erin," Bain whispered. He flickered into view.

"Oh!" She had to catch herself and whisper. "You have a bird?"

"I rescued it."

She stared at the blue and silver bird. It was regal, in a way. On the top of its glossy-feathered head was a spray of black feathers mimicking a crown. It looked at her with black eyes but made no obvious movement other than its gaze. "It's beautiful."

Erin's heart hadn't slowed from the heavy weight of Joel's news. She wondered if Joel wanted Bain to know. "Bain, there's something I need to tell you."

"Did you guys find anything? Where's Joel?"

"He'll be here soon. Bain, Joel's a . . ." Tears burned her eyes.

How could she have spent so much time with a prince and not known it? It couldn't be true. Then it hit her. Joel's aura never diminished. She already knew it was true, even before she could question it.

"Joel's a what?" Bain asked.

She took a deep breath. "A prince." It touched her that Joel allowed her to tell Bain. Maybe he really did care about her. No matter what life brought, Bain would always be a part of her.

Little one, Joel has a good heart.

The smell of the giant frog turned her stomach. "I have to get out of here."

Bain took her hand, and they stepped into the hall. "There's Joel," he said.

She couldn't see him, but that didn't mean anything. Bain would know. He let go of her hand and dropped his invisibility ward. "Over here," he said, waving.

She heard the hiss of a dart and then silence as it found its target. Bain crumpled to the ground. She turned to see a leopard-like imp fill the stairwell. The bird took flight and made it out an open window. Automatically, she dropped to her knees and shielded Bain with wards.

"We found them," the leopard said.

More imps must have been waiting in the stairwell.

Erin held Bain close. She could feel Pulsar ward them. A hand touched her back and she gasped.

"It's okay," Joel said.

Relief washed over her. She didn't have to do this alone. "Whispering Winds?" she whispered.

"Do it," Joel said.

She closed her eyes and something hard slapped her head and back. They were captured in some kind of net. Erin thought of Pulsar, trying hard to transport them to him, but nothing happened.

Pulsar!

No answer. The net—it must have some kind of magic barrier. "It's not working," she said. "I can't get us out."

The leopard dragged them across the floor and down the stairs.

35
Net Gain

İt didn't take long for Erin to know for sure that magic didn't work inside the net. Every step the imp dragged them down banged her arm, leg or back. She held Bain the best she could to keep him from getting too many bruises.

"Brilliant," Joel said behind her. "Ormond must have invented this. Doesn't surprise me."

She didn't answer. No magical wards meant that the imps could hear everything. Every stair left a bruise as the imp pulled them carelessly down the steps. Finally, they came to a halt on the wooden floor.

"Look at what the cat dragged in," a deep voice said.

Erin twisted around to see the face. Xavene stood there, his ugly black aura spilling off his sharp black suit.

"Ormond. Wish I could say it was nice seeing you again," Joel said.

"Ormond is dead. I'm not the weak prince hoping for a crown like you. There's something even better than merely ruling the elves."

"Like kidnapping your sister?" Joel said.

"Ah, but even that small joy was cut short. A mystery I'm sure you would be happy to explain."

Erin held onto Bain's unconscious body, shifting the weight so that she could see Xavene's face better.

"It was nice of you to bring such treasures with you, Joel. You always were looking out for the best interest of others. Imagine the kind of power these two could give me. It does make killing you less difficult. You never did have as much magic as Ella."

Erin found Joel's hand and squeezed it. She wished she could tell him that everything would be okay, that they would make it out alive, and that Xavene was wrong.

"There are things more powerful than magic, Ormond," Joel said.

"Ormond is dead!" Xavene screamed.

"As is our father," Joel said.

Erin was surprised at the calmness in Joel's voice. It almost sounded like surrender or acceptance. She didn't know.

Xavene laughed. "Oh, yes. Our noble father. The king of the land. The world has not missed him that I can see."

"How could you kill him?" Joel asked. "Your own father."

Erin's arms and legs trembled in the cramped net. She could not see Joel behind her, but resolve flowed through his words. He was not afraid.

"You were there to see it. I'm sure you remember how exceptionally easy it was." Xavene had not moved from where his feet were planted on the bare wood floor.

Erin wondered if Xavene was leery of releasing them. Why hadn't he opened the net? As soon as the question crossed her mind, the answer popped into view. Pulsar. Once the net was removed, she was free to call the dragon, and she doubted he would worry too much about barging straight through the wall to get to her. He would already be here if he knew.

"How did you do it? Whatever happened to being forever an imp?" Joel shifted beside her so he could face Xavene better. "Only you would figure out a way to cheat an irrevocable decree."

Erin would have expected bitterness in his voice, but Joel remained resolute, as if it was a casual conversation with his brother. He spoke as though the confining net did not exist. Maybe he meant to keep Xavene talking, stall the inevitable.

"You always did underestimate magic, Joel. There is so much I could teach you. Did you know there is a way to steal it?" Xavene laughed. "It takes a certain level of finesse, but the end result is well worth it."

"Is that why you kidnapped Ella? To steal her magic?" Joel asked.

"It is an embarrassment that you are my brother and yet you're so painfully slow to come to the obvious answers, but I don't need her anymore. I don't need anyone." Xavene pulled a silver sword from his belt. "Your time is running out, as is your world, your ways, and your kingdom—not that you'll be around to see it."

Erin slowly pulled her eternal blade from its sheath. At least it sat on the side opposite to Xavene and his imps. The emerald blade came smoothly out, and she tested it against the rope net. She lifted Bain's arm out of the way as she slowly cut the first piece of net. Her blade sliced through so easily that she had to catch herself from tearing through the entire side.

Joel and Xavene were still talking, but she couldn't focus on the words. It didn't matter what they said, as long as Joel kept Xavene's attention off her. When her left arm fell out of the net, she pushed against the floor and straightened her back. Her eyes squeezed shut, and she buried her face in Bain's long blond hair as if to hide her horror at being caught again by Xavene.

Pulsar! Maybe he could hear her. If the net was broken, then maybe the spell . . .

Fireborn. Her breath caught as his voice resonated in her head. It was so loud, she wondered if anyone else could hear him too. Her thoughts transported instantaneously to the dragon.

Whispering Winds. Try it first.

She thought of Aunt Lyndera and Carbonell.

Save your brother, Pulsar said. There was no question in his command.

He was right. She couldn't argue at all. Bain came first, and Joel too. They would have to work out something later to find Lyndy. She focused on Pulsar waiting in the trees outside. At first, only a breath of air brushed her cheek, but as Pulsar surged his magic into her, she felt a warm gust of air wrap around them.

"What?" Joel said behind her.

They sat atop the golden dragon still confined by a net, but they were free.

"We're getting out of here, now!" she said. *Where?* she asked Pulsar.

All the way to the kingdom.

She didn't want to risk taking the time to strap into the saddle. Any second Xavene would find them. Instead, she took her blade, dug it into the saddle like an anchor, and forced a picture of the palace into her head.

With Pulsar's magic flowing into her, the trip came instantaneously, with wind ripping around them like a storm. And then they were there. The cold winter air greeted them, with the dimly lit sky shadowing the brown lawn and majestic palace. Even in the dead of winter, Ālfheim was a welcome sight.

"Sorry, Pulsar. We need to get off. We're kind of stuck." Erin transported the three of them to the ground, still wrapped in the net. "I feel like fish pulled out of the sea."

"I've got this," Joel said.

She heard him slice through the ropes, and soon his weight was gone behind her. Joel knelt beside her and cleared the net around her and Bain.

"Let's get him inside to Aelflaed. She'll know what to do." Joel scooped up Bain and strode toward the palace doors.

Erin turned and reached up to touch Pulsar's hot scales. "Thanks." But she knew it wasn't over. She'd escaped with Bain and Joel, but Aunt Lyndera remained behind. She shouldn't have tried to talk her aunt into going along.

And then it hit her. They hadnever found their mother. The weight of the failure crashed through her and took her strength as she crumbled to the ground. Another senseless decision, and this time Bain had to pay the price. "I'm so sorry. I didn't know this would happen. I really thought we'd find her. I was so sure." Hadn't her gift told her that her mom was still alive? Was it really true? Maybe Bain was right.

She curled up against Pulsar's foot and let his warm magic fill her. "What was I thinking? Every time I think I'm doing the right thing, I find another disaster." At least she couldn't cry. Instead, numbness enveloped her.

There had to be a way to fix things. She pulled herself up and climbed Pulsar's golden scales. An ugly gash marked where her blade had sunk into the plush leather of the saddle. She ran her hand over the hole, wishing she knew some kind of spell to fix it.

"Where do you think you're going?" Joel asked.

Before she could answer, he leaped up the scales and mounted the saddle behind her.

"I know better than to leave you alone. You were going back, weren't you?"

She knew she couldn't lie to him. "I guess that means you want to come too."

He wrapped his arms around her waist and leaned into her shoulder. "I wouldn't miss it for the world."

"How's Bain?"

"Aelflaed's taking care of him. He'll probably sleep until tomorrow, but other than that, he's fine," he said.

"Are you sure you want to do this? What if we get caught again?" She could feel his face nudging in her hair.

He squeezed her shoulder. "Let's not get caught."

"Good plan," she said.

His arms tightened across her middle as air gusted around them, sending them back to the Amazon.

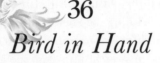

36
Bird in Hand

ERIN LANDED THEM IN THE FOREST NEAR WHERE THE PORTAL from Africa floated between the trees. If Carbonell and Aunt Lyndera made it out, this is where they would come.

"I'm sorry about your dad." Erin let her hands rest on his arms that still wrapped around her middle. Pulsar navigated through the trees as they sat on his back.

"I guess that means we have something in common," Joel said. "Ormond killed your dad before he killed mine."

The thought hit her hard, and she couldn't breathe right. She stared at his tan arms and realized for the first time that Joel had a life without his father too. And even though her dad was something she had only seen in pictures and dreams, she had it so much easier than him. She never knew him well enough to miss him.

"I'm sorry. I shouldn't have said that." Joel's voice was quiet behind her.

"No. I mean, it's not your fault." Her mind raced through images. Her dad unconscious, her mom screaming his name, the burning aircraft diving into the ocean. "How could he have killed my dad before he killed yours? He would have turned into an imp and lost his magic."

"He used my dad's eternal blade. You can't ward against your own blade. There aren't very many who would think to turn an eternal blade on its owner. Guess that makes my brother that much more special."

Erin's head swam, and her throat closed in. She shuddered,

unable to get enough oxygen.

Joel continued. "He was already a mountain lion imp."

"You . . ." she struggled to get the words out. "You saw it happen?"

Joel coughed. A moment passed in silence.

"I came in right after the deed was done. Ormond challenged me to a duel, but he was mocking me. I was so small that I couldn't have won. I watched him jump out the balcony window and run to the forest. I couldn't do anything. My dad was already dead. My mom . . ." His voice cracked. Joel cleared his throat. "My mom didn't know what to do.

"She's kept the kingdom going, but my dad's death has taken its toll. She's been waiting for the chance to pass the crown on. Ella refuses to take it. Absolutely refuses. So it's up to me now."

"But you have lots of time. I mean, she's going to live forever."

"She could, but she wouldn't. Elves can choose to let the magic ebb from them until mortality overtakes them. My mom would do that just to be with my dad again."

Erin rubbed her forehead. "I guess I can see why, but that means you're going to lose your mom too."

"Not anytime soon, but someday."

"That's got to be hard." Erin stared at the foliage around them. Colorful birds darted from the trees. It seemed impossible for so much life to go on around them, oblivious to the winter the other half of the world knew.

"Yes and no. At least I know she'll be with the one she loves. I see the sadness in her eyes, and I want so much to fill that hollow space, but I can't. Only my dad could do that."

Erin didn't know what to say. There was so much more to Joel than she had given him credit for. Maybe she only thought she knew him and maybe that was okay. She squeezed his arm. He found her hand and interlocked his fingers with hers, sending goose bumps up her arm.

She looked out at the forest, where the trees let in shafts of scattered sunlight, giving the world a dark green hue. Some trees had so many vines crawling up the sides that she couldn't even see the bark. The Door of Vines back home seemed exotic, but this place had its own smell and sounds. The animals were mostly familiar to her, and yet seeing the sloth hanging from the tree and watching the bright parrots fill the branches with color was surreal. No wonder her mom had a story from every continent. There was so much in the world to see.

They had to be getting close to the mansion. She knew she had lost track of time, but a mile didn't take very long to cover. A movement caught her attention, and she turned to see a blue and silver bird flapping its wings as it closed the distance between them.

"Look." Erin pointed. "It's the bird from the castle. The one Bain found." It landed on the saddle handles so that it was eye level with her. "You're such a pretty bird." This creature was more than pretty—it was majestic.

The bird held its head high, keeping eye contact, before dropping from the handles and into Erin's lap.

Erin shrieked. Weren't they supposed to be afraid of people? The bird dipped its head and nudged at her arms.

"Uhh . . . " Was she supposed to pet its head?

The bird snuggled against her hand.

"Okay." She sucked in a breath and held it as she reached out to the silky blue feathers. The bird seemed to melt at her touch. As soon as Erin's hand met the bird's head, it relaxed and curled its head around as it fell asleep on her lap.

"Joel, I think the bird is out. What am I supposed to do?"

She could feel him leaning in to get a better look. "Don't let it fall. It would probably get eaten by something if it hit the ground."

She gently stroked the sleeping bird.

"It's pretty, isn't it?" Joel said.

"Yeah." Erin stroked the deep blue feathers. The bird felt warm against her hand, and she didn't want to stop touching the silky feathers. There was something relaxing about the sleeping life on her lap. And the colors—as the light reflected off its body, it shined metallic blue.

The familiar hiss of darts surrounded them. "Joel!" She grabbed his arms to see if he was still conscious. More hisses.

"It's okay. I've got it," Joel said.

"Don't leave me." Erin held to his arms as if to keep him there with her. She didn't want to abandon the bird, but with it taking up her whole lap, she felt trapped. "Pulsar?"

It's about time you let me into the action.

"Right. Just try not to burn the whole forest down."

That's why they call it a rainforest. Now tighten your straps, Fireborn. I'm not going to promise to stay on the ground.

More darts hissed around them. "Joel, strap your legs in. Pulsar's in charge."

37

Getting a Shot at It

ERIN KNEW THAT SHE WAS INVISIBLE, BUT PULSAR WASN'T. HE wanted them to find him. From her perch on his back, she could see glimpses of fur, scales, and skin through the trees as they continued to fire swarms of darts at them. The dragon stayed, too closed in by the trees to spread his wings.

Even with the ward, the darts would fly at her with incredible speed, making her heart race.

"You're going to be fine," Joel said behind her.

She looked down at his fingers laced in hers. "I'm not used to . . ." A dart shot straight at her face, and she closed her eyes. *Ward. Just ward.*

"I've got you," he said.

She could still hear the darts hissing through the trees. Then a familiar sound overpowered the darts. She opened her eyes to see fire blaze from Pulsar's mouth, scorching the trees and blackening the ground.

Silence. Maybe the imps had given up. She searched the trees for any sign of them.

A war cry shattered the silence as the ground around them filled with creatures of every kind—some she had never seen before. There were so many of them.

Erin held onto the bird and focused on her wards as the ground below filled with imps. Growls ripped through the air along with high-pitched screeches and shrieks. The smell assaulted her as the mutated animals closed in around the dragon.

Use your magic and stop some hearts, she said to Pulsar. Maybe everything would be over soon.

The imps carried weapons—metal swords, sabers, and even spiked clubs.

Pulsar blazed another arsenal of fire around him, scattering the imps. Some even fell to the earth, but they moved quickly back in. A black panther with a crossbow collapsed backward but not before releasing an arrow that embedded into a nearby tree. More and more creatures fell, but others were there to take their place. When a tiger imp ran full force with its blade out to the dragon, Erin used her magic to throw the animal into the forest. The effect was satisfying. More imps raced toward Pulsar only to be thrown back by her magic. But there were too many of them. Spears launched from imps farther out but bounced off Pulsar's ward.

"We need to figure out how to get to Xavene." Erin searched the ground, looking for a clearing through the imps. No bare ground was visible.

"I'll be right back." Joel let go of her and was gone before she could protest.

Another flame from Pulsar cleared a path in front of them, and the dragon walked through the blackened forest floor. The roar of the imps grew until it was deafening, sending chills of ice into her veins. She gripped the saddle. Without Joel behind her, she didn't feel as brave. All around were more imps shooting arrows and throwing spears at the dragon. The sight took her confidence. There were so many of them. Could they wear Pulsar down? Maybe there was a limit to how long he could fight this battle.

"Joel!" she called, but it was a worthless attempt over the noise. With his invisibility ward, she would never be able to find him.

Pulsar trudged through a few steps while Erin blasted more imps away with magic. There were so many of them that her efforts seemed futile. Pulsar blocked his thoughts from hers as he slowly gained ground. She felt so alone. The sound of arrows whistling through the trees and the clang of swords bouncing off Pulsar's ward resonated through the forest.

"I'm back," Joel said behind her. "Take this." He handed her a rifle.

She let out a sigh of relief and looked at the weapon. "I don't know how to use this."

"Look. Just fill the barrel with darts and pull the trigger. And don't touch the tips." He sat back and shot into the surrounding army.

It worked. Already a few of the imps had tumbled over, unconscious.

She pulled the rifle up and tried to line the end of the barrel up with an imp that looked like a huge ram. She focused on its chest and pulled the trigger. The dart hissed and shot through the air before imbedding into the brown fur of the charging animal. It tumbled to the earth and rolled, knocking over a spiderlike imp.

She aimed at another and another until her gun was empty and Joel shoved more darts into her barrel. But there were more imps than darts. Pulsar poured fire out in a large circle before spreading his wings. She hadn't even noticed that they were in a clearing wide enough for him to take flight.

Pulsar pumped his wings, leaving the army of imps below. The noise grew dimmer and the sweet air greeted her as they lifted off the ground.

Erin stared at the bright green tops of the trees that filled the land. The sun beat down on them in full force as they climbed higher in the sky.

"It's like leaving the world behind," Joel said.

The roar of imps dissolved with the sound of air rushing at them. "But we still haven't found my aunt. Or Carbonell. Or my mom."

"What do you want to do?"

The green trees covered the land, and only the Amazon River could cut through the world of green below them. "You can't even see Xavene's house from here. It's all trees."

"Good camouflage. He didn't even need to use magic to do that. Smart."

"Do you have any more darts?"

"There's a few here." He stopped. "You've got to be kidding." Joel's voice was flat.

She heard buzzing. Like flies or bees, but deeper. Bigger. Black things lifted from the bright green foliage. Her breath was gone. Airplane-sized wasps and red flying insects no smaller than helicopters lifted out of the trees. The noise. For every mosquito she had ever heard buzzing over her at night, this was all that multiplied by thousands.

"No," she breathed. Hundreds of black mosquitoes filled the air. But they were huge. If the sharp point of their beak ever entered her skin, she was sure she wouldn't live to find out how long it would take for them to drain her life.

The air turned black around them. She couldn't see past the fleet of enormous insects flying straight at them. "Invisible. Pulsar, come on!"

Pulsar warded, but the barrage of flying creatures still came. Long orange legs dangled down from the shiny black and yellow wasps. Red wasps swarmed around them while the mosquitoes filled in every possible gap. They were surrounded.

"Those aren't imps, Erin," Joel said.

She was too terrified to say anything. Their monstrous faces with huge eyes seemed to see the entire world at once. And they were closing in.

"They can smell us and feel our heat," Joel continued. "And there's magic in their sting. Don't get too close."

"What are we going to do?" she asked.

Pulsar answered by diving out of the sky in a free fall to earth. It was a sensation she had almost forgotten. As the cloud of black hovered in the sky above them, she finally understood why Pulsar wanted to practice flying so much. It worked.

They pulled out before reaching the treetops and continued over the forest.

"I can't tell which way's up anymore," Joel said. His grip was iron around her waist.

"It's okay. Just hang on." She craned her neck to see how far away they were from the bugs.

"I'm going to throw up," Joel said.

"Uhm." She didn't have time to come up with a solution before he loosened his grip around her waist. She tried to ignore the gut-wrenching sound, but it was impossible.

The buzzing filled the air, and she saw the red metallic wasps nearly on top of them.

"I just gave us away big time. The smell," Joel said.

The red wasp was nearly on top of them, its mandibles opening and slicing against the other black teeth. She knew the insect wasn't going to sting them—it was going to eat them.

38

One Little Dance

PULSAR FLIPPED OVER IN THE AIR AND STREAMED FIRE AT THE wasp, scorching its wings. Red blurred as the insect spiraled out of the sky. But more crowded in, pointing their spiked stingers at Pulsar's body.

Then the mosquitoes swarmed. Erin froze, paralyzed by fear. She could smell them, a musty horrible smell that was only intensified by the high-pitched buzzing of their wings. She was sure that time stopped. Slowly the wasps' daggerlike stingers shot out like javelins.

"No!" she screamed. Did her voice carry over the invading sound of wings? It couldn't end like this. She didn't want to know if the stinger could penetrate their ward. Joel said they had magic, and magic could kill them all.

White sand on a beach. Clear blue water lapping in crested waves. The vision filled her mind and blotted out the swarm of death around them. The calming sound of the waves crashing against the water.

There might have been a wind, but she didn't notice. The cloud of insects vanished as the landscape transformed. Why did she pick Africa? It didn't matter.

"That was too close," Joel said. "I can't believe you still have the bird."

Erin looked at the blue mound on her lap. She hadn't even realized she was still holding on to it. "It must have been pretty tired to sleep through that." She stared at the silver feathers that crowned its head. "Well, I guess our mission wasn't a complete failure. We managed to save a bird."

Joel patted her back. "And our skin. Sometimes you can't have it all."

Erin flipped the compact mirror closed and changed it back into a watch. She checked the time as she fastened the clasp on her wrist. Why hadn't she thought of making her changing brooch into a flashlight when she was looking for Pulsar? A smile nearly broke through as she realized how obvious it must have been to Joel that she was such an inexperienced älva.

She smoothed the pearl-colored comforter and let her hands rest on the soft mattress. At least Bain's room had comfortable chairs.

"How long are you going to sleep?" she asked.

Bain snored in return.

"Yeah, that's what I thought." She looked at the dark window framed in ivory curtains. Pitch black at only four in the afternoon. Iceland in the winter—it was a wonder everyone didn't hibernate through the cold dark months.

She reached out and took his hand. Aelflaed had assured her that Bain wasn't in any pain. "I brought you a visitor." She glanced at the bright blue bird nestled in his bed. "You two will get along just fine. You've always had a way with animals."

Bain snorted in his sleep, and she looked to see if he was awake. No such luck.

Erin pulled the watch off her arm and transformed it into an iPod. It was going to be a long day. It already had been. As soon as they got back to the palace, Joel went to talk to the queen. His mom. It was going to be so hard to get used to the thought.

He probably wanted to clean up a little too. The Amazon hadn't done him any favors. She took advantage of the hot shower and decent clothes as soon as Joel left her room. She pulled on the sleeve of her sweater. It might have been December, but it didn't feel like Christmas could be coming anytime soon. Time and seasons had lost their meaning lately.

She laid her head on the bed. Maybe it was better that Bain slept. At least he couldn't remind her that she had been wrong about everything. The disappointment left heavy lead in her chest.

A soft knock sounded at the open door. "Can I come in?"

"Joel, hi." She waved him in and pulled a chair close. "Have a seat."

"It's probably going to take until tomorrow to wear off, you know," Joel said, looking at Bain.

"Yeah." She wasn't sure what else to say.

"I see your bird's still asleep."

Erin nodded. She watched Joel take her hand and closed her eyes as the familiar warmth surged through her. It felt so much like magic that she wondered if that's what it was.

"You hungry?" he asked.

She opened her eyes and looked at Joel. "Not really." Her stomach growled, and she looked down at it, smiling. "Traitor."

He stood, still holding her hand. "Come with me." He gently tugged on her hand. "I know just the place."

She looked at Bain, still sound asleep. Joel was right. Her brother wasn't going to wake up anytime soon.

"Okay," she said. She followed him through the long hallways and several staircases. "I can't believe I live in a palace." The tall ceiling shone with light from cascading chandeliers. Even in the halls, exotic flowers grew in pots stationed evenly, as if standing guard. It had only been a few months since her first visit here. Although it made sense that the royal family should live here, she still couldn't understand why Bain and her were given a room in the palace.

Joel squeezed her hand.

"Why *do* I live in a palace? I mean, there's a whole kingdom of houses." She looked up hoping to catch his gaze, but he kept his eyes straight ahead. They walked in silence, and she counted the doors they passed.

It wasn't until the sixth door that Joel's voice broke the pause.

"It was the queen's decision. It has to do with her gifts." He didn't offer more.

Erin didn't want the momentum lost. "What do you mean? What kind of gifts?"

Joel stopped and pulled her hand to his lips, his breath skimming over her skin. "Erin Fireborn."

When he didn't say any more, she stepped closer to him. Her hand was still captured in his. "You can't tell me, can you?"

He reached for her other hand and held them both. A sigh fell from his lips, and he shook his head. "I can tell you, I just don't know if you're ready to hear."

"I'm here, aren't I? If I wanted to leave, I could. A small wish is all it takes, and I'm gone." She gripped his hands a little tighter. "How bad could it be?"

He lowered his hands and held her fingers. In one graceful movement, he wrapped her arms so that they were in perfect ballroom form. He hummed a melody and slowly walked through dance steps.

His body was close to hers, and the smell of his shirt made her want to rest her head on his chest. "You are so strange, you know."

He spun slowly around, keeping his hand on the small of her back while holding her right arm at the perfect angle. "We need better music."

She smiled and rested her head just below his shoulder. "And I need better dancing skills."

"You're doing fine."

The sound of music was faint at first but grew into a harmonized melody. She knew the singing and looked up for the fairies. Wings of every color fluttered above, filling the hallway with a symphony of älvor voices. Joel arched her into a spin before pulling her close again.

As they circled to the music, Erin stopped trying to remember how to dance and just let Joel lead her down the hall to the impromptu music. His arm felt strong behind her back, and it seemed he could make her dance with magic. The music grew faint as they traced down the hall. The fairies departed, leaving Joel and her alone.

When he dropped his hands, she realized how light she felt, as if everything in the world would be right. "Are you going to tell me?"

He took her hand and twirled her out. "Let's talk over some food, shall we?"

She hadn't noticed the doorway leading to a small restaurant. The succulent smell of cooking drifted to her, and she let him lead her to a table. Inside, it may as well have been summer. It looked the same as it had in August. Plants graced the corners, and vines grew up the columns.

She smiled as a glass of water and lemon appeared before her.

"I think you'll like the food here," Joel said.

A plate of salad greens and grilled fish appeared on the table.

She picked up her fork. "Thanks. It's perfect." She waited for him to take a few bites before she spoke. "I really do want to know about your mother."

He let his fork rest in his hand as he looked at her. "She can see things. Know things. Not all the time, but sometimes she sees the future."

She speared a forkful of salad. "Did she see Bain and me coming?" The tart, savory dressing lasted a moment in her mouth as she waited for his answer. "Is that really why we're here?" Ever since the cottage last summer, she wondered why all of this had happened to them. The gifts of speed and strength, heightened senses, the ability to use magic, and finally immortality—it was more than she could have dreamed or deserved.

"Yes, she saw you. She didn't see everything, but enough to know."

"Know what?"

He poked his fork into a piece of fish. "That you belonged in our world."

"There's more." It wasn't a question. There was something he was trying not to say. She reached across the table and rested her hand on his. "What else did she see?"

"She didn't know about Bain. He surprised all of us, but then, having him as your twin explains a lot."

She kept her hand on his and waited.

"You're part of the future of Ãlfheim—the world even. You and Bain will make all the difference." He smiled and chuckled softly. "That's all you're getting out of me right now." He picked up his glass of water and gulped as if to finalize the conversation.

She sighed and picked up her glass of water. "How many times do you think the queen will put up with me failing?" He had been there to see it. She hadn't found find her mom or prove Carbonell's innocence. And worse, she left her only blood relative with the enemy.

Failure is in the eyes of the beholder. Pulsar's voice sounded in her head.

She hadn't even thought about his presence in her head. *I just don't know what to do.*

"Pulsar's right, you know," Joel said.

Her eyes shot up at Joel. "You can hear him too?"

He looked down. "Only when he wants me to."

She shook her head. "How am I supposed to explain this to Bain? I owe him better than this."

Neither Pulsar nor Joel answered. Maybe things really were as bad as she thought.

39
Silver Aura

Bᴀɪɴ ᴏᴘᴇɴᴇᴅ ʜɪѕ ᴇʏᴇѕ ᴛᴏ ꜰɪɴᴅ ᴀ ᴄʀᴇᴀᴍ ᴄᴇɪʟɪɴɢ ᴀʙᴏᴠᴇ ʜɪᴍ barely lit by the late morning sun. The last thing he remembered was waving at Joel in the hallway of the mansion. Even with his eyes closed, he knew he couldn't be anywhere near the Amazon River. Here the air gave hints of sea and ice.

A fluffy pillow was tucked behind his head, and someone had pulled an ivory comforter up to his chest. What day was it? He checked his watch only to remember that it didn't show the date. Somewhere in Africa he'd lost track. He settled his hands behind his head. Nope. He still didn't care what day it was. What difference could it make?

He was back in the palace. That meant that Erin had to be here too. He glanced over at the two chairs that rested right next to his bed. Erin *and* Joel. At some point he would have to track them down. As his eyes wandered across the room, he caught a glimpse of silver and blue. He sat up, his heart racing as he recognized the shape. Hidden in the folds of the comforter, the blue bird from Black Rain slept. Its silver aura barely glowed around it. If it weren't for the shaded light, he might not have even been able to see the aura at all.

"How did *you* get here?" he asked.

The slight rise and fall of its body as it breathed was the only indication that the bird still lived. And the aura. Even if it only barely held onto its magic, it still had some. He thought of the pegasi in the Door of Vines. Their aura had been such a brilliant white that he felt it a shame that everyone couldn't see them the same way he could.

He slipped out of bed and buckled the sheath that held his wand and sword around his waist. It didn't escape his notice that he somehow now wore a clean pair of jeans and a white oversized shirt. At least he had been completely unconscious when they changed his clothes. Even though it was too late to feel embarrassed, he tried to shake the images of Aelflaed from his thoughts. She had long blonde hair and a face so exquisite that he felt awkward in her presence. Not to mention young. He had no idea how old she was.

"We're going for a walk." He scooped up the sleeping bird. Maybe the fairies would know what to do. Aelflaed seemed to be the resident expert on healing and maybe even magical creatures, but chances were, if he went to her, she might send him back to bed.

He stepped silently into the hall, and his socks slipped a little on the smooth marble floor. Maybe he would skate to the älvor. There were several rooms where the fairies graced the trees in the palace, but none were the same as the colony back home. What he would give to be in the Living Garden right now. Adarae and all the others, popping water, the food, their singing—he missed it all.

Things weren't the same here.

The temptation was too great. At least Agnar had given him a shortcut. It wasn't as good as Erin's instant transportation, but it did make getting to Pennsylvania a lot faster. Maybe it was even the right thing to do. He thought about going back to his room to get his boots but changed his mind. That's what touch wards were for. No one would even notice him missing. He could be there and back before anyone realized he was gone.

His feelings for the well hadn't changed much since the last time he plunged into utter darkness. As his stomach climbed into his throat, he held the bird carefully in one hand and gripped the edge of the bucket with the other. Not soon enough, the ride ended, and he ran through the halls of the underground labyrinth.

He loved this place. Even as he passed numerous hallways, he remembered each room. The Steel Door room definitely made the list as his favorite. The Door of Vines didn't really seem like a room in the cabin anymore since the forest directly connected to Älfheim.

He climbed the steps and lifted the trapdoor to the kitchen. Every time he saw this place, he thought of Erin. Drinking soda at the table, visiting with Ella—there were so many good times. And tough ones too. Even as he turned the handle to the front door, he could picture Erin challenging him to choose between her and immortality. If there were ever a moment that had torn his heart in two, it had been then. Erin thought he was a fool for wanting to go through with it and become an elf. At the time, he couldn't see a single downside.

As an älv he could live forever, use magic, run faster than animals could fly, and hear and smell and see things that never could have been possible as a human. What was there not to like?

He looked down at the sleeping bird in his arms. Maybe death had its place in life too. He doubted he would ever really get to see much of his friends from school again. They would get married and have families while he would stay looking like a teenager. For a second, a glimpse of the future flashed through his mind. They would get old and someday be gone. How would it feel to walk the earth while so many people he knew came and went?

The älvor would know.

He opened the door and had to push against the deep snow that drifted against the cabin. He reached for his wand and put a touch ward around them. At least he could keep his feet dry while protecting the bird from the freezing air.

The familiar gate opened against the snow, and he let himself into the garden. Compared with the blinding sunlight reflecting off the white snow, the Living Garden's vibrant colors rebelled against the winter. Even before he could push the gate closed, butterfly wings flashed though the air and several voices greeted him at once.

He smiled at the familiar scent of fruit trees. "I need to talk to Adarae," he said to the nearest fairy. The popping water fountain sprayed next to the flower cups. His favorite had always been the deep orange colored one. It tasted something like orange and strawberries mixed. Tart, yet just the right balance of sweet.

He didn't wait for an invitation before setting the bird carefully onto the soft grass. The feathers gleamed in the sunlight that filtered through the canopy of trees. He stroked its blue feathers and waited.

"Bain, you have come to visit yet again!" Adarae's voice rang like tiny bells.

He hadn't realized how much he had missed her. She landed on the grass next to the bird. Adarae's wings matched the bird's feathers in every way. How had he not realized it sooner? The black patterns that swirled in Adarae's brilliant blue wings made her look like the same brush had painted the two flying beings.

"I thought maybe you could help. When I was in Egypt with Xavene, I saw this bird all the time." He touched the silver feathers on its head and looked at Adarae. "It used to have a better aura, but its light is almost gone now. Like it's dying or something."

Adarae touched the bird with her small hand. "She feels familiar to me."

Bain waited, not sure how to respond.

"I know her." Adarae laid her head against the bird as if listening for a heartbeat. "I know her spirit." The älvor suddenly took flight and hovered just in front of Bain. "Are you certain this creature is a bird?"

He shook his head slightly. "Uh, what else would it be? It can't be an imp. Aren't there magical birds? There are mermaids, after all." Even as he said it, heat flashed through his cheeks. Kelura. Maybe it was worth being an elf if he could swim in the water for hours with her.

Adarae flitted around as if she were pacing in the air. "Did you take it to Aelflaed?"

"I sort of came straight here."

The blue-winged fairy landed once again next to the bird and rested both her hands on the shiny feathers. "Her life is slipping away. It might already be too late to save her." She put her ear once again to its side. "I can almost hear her speak to me, but she is weak. Her thoughts float like wisps of smoke through the air."

Bain watched in silence as Adarae closed her eyes and rested her head on the blue feathers. The älvor began to sing, quietly at first, but slowly and determined. Her tune picked up its tempo and other voices joined in. He looked up to see hundreds of colorful wings fill the air; their voices floating down on him like a shower of heaven. He felt hot tears prick his eyes, but he couldn't understand why. The music was sad, yet hopeful. He didn't know what any of the words meant, but he doubted it mattered.

He didn't have to give as much magic as he did with Pulsar. A little might make the difference between life and death for the bird. He couldn't sit by and watch the bird die. His hand reached out and touched the feathers. It might have been his imagination that the silver aura seemed to shine a little more. More magic. He'd done it before.

40
A Little More Magic

ERIN DIDN'T LET GO OF JOEL'S HAND AS THEY WALKED DOWN THE hall. Pulsar hadn't interrupted their conversation for such a long time that she had to check if he was still within range. He had finished his hunt and was seriously contemplating a late nap.

Since Bain would probably sleep until tomorrow, there was no point in waiting in his room. Joel guided her around the palace, silently keeping her company. The incongruence of plants living as much indoors as out made the palace fascinating. Its bright light and living vegetation made it a stark contrast to the outdoors, where darkness ruled this time of year.

Footsteps echoed in the empty hall, and Erin couldn't help but turn to see who it was.

"Joel, Erin Fireborn, Queen Āldera wishes to speak to you," the älv said.

She didn't recognize the älv who addressed them. "She wants to see me?" It wasn't so unusual that the queen would request her son's audience, but Erin wasn't too excited about facing the queen after her last failed quest.

"This way, please." The älv led them up the stairs and to a room with several sofas circled about. Vines of flowers and leaves grew up the walls and filled the room with its floral perfume. The queen sat on a sofa, her back straight and hands folded in her lap.

Joel led Erin to a seat and then sat next to her.

Erin slowly sucked in a breath of air and tried to appear calm.

At least he decided to sit next to her instead of abandoning her to sit on the other side of the room. He reached over and took her hand. She knew her cheeks flushed red with heat, but it was a price she was willing to pay.

Queen Āldera smiled slightly before her serious demeanor returned. "The älvor have brought troubling news."

Erin waited, wondering where this conversation would lead.

The queen's eyes rested on Erin. "Your brother is with Adarae's colony. It appears he has taken extreme measures to revive a bird you brought back from South America."

"Bain's awake?" She couldn't process the queen's statement. "Is Adarae *here?*"

"He left Ālfheim and went to the Living Garden to seek Adarae's help."

"What kind of extreme measures?" Joel asked.

"He transferred his magic to the bird," the queen said.

Joel muttered something under his breath.

"Is he okay?" Erin asked.

"That's why I called you here. I think it would be best for you to go get him. Travel by the Whispering Winds. Once he's here, we can better assess the damage."

Damage? Erin's heart raced.

"Time is essential. You must go to him," the queen said.

"What about Pulsar?" she asked. She kept promising to never leave without him, but lately she had been breaking her promises to the dragon a lot.

"That is for you to choose." The queen stood and crossed the room to the door, making the conversation final.

Joel squeezed her hand. "I'm coming with you."

Pulsar? she called in her mind, but he was still sleeping. Oh well, he wouldn't fit in the Living Garden anyway. She held Joel's hand in both of hers and thought of Adarae's home. The familiar whip of air caught them, and they transported from the upholstered chair to a garden of grass and trees.

Erin looked around, trying to orient herself with the new surroundings. It had been so long since she had visited this place. She spotted her brother on the grass next to the fountain. "I swear, Bain. I can't leave you alone for a second."

He smiled weakly and covered his face with his hands. "Why did you come?"

"It is good to see you again," a musical voice said.

Erin looked up to see the deep blue fairy she knew so well. "Adarae, is he okay?"

"Take him home—back to the kingdom. And bring her." Adarae lifted into the air and fluttered to where the blue bird watched them from across the garden.

"Okay. Joel, do you think you can get the bird?"

Joel stood and held out his arm. The blue feathers sparkled in the sunlight as the bird stretched out her wings and flew to his arm.

"Why didn't I think of that?" Erin took Bain's hand. "Joel, hold my other hand."

She closed her eyes and thought of the palace. The room with the sofas. A flash of blue interrupted her thoughts. The sofas. Blue wings patterned with black swirls charged through her mind. *The queen's sitting room*. But Adarae's face burned in her mind, making it impossible to focus.

Adarae waited quietly on the edge of the fountain.

Erin reached out toward Adarae. "I think you're supposed to come too. Would you?"

Adarae nodded and lighted on her hand.

Erin carefully lowered her hand to Bain's. She took a deep breath. "The queen's sitting room." She spoke out loud, hoping that it would help her concentrate. No more colors flashed through her mind, and the wind blew around them. She held Bain's hand tightly, hoping that the fairy wouldn't fly off in the breeze.

It was strange to have the grass be replaced by thick carpet. As if by invitation, the bird took flight and landed on the back of the sofa.

"Should we send him to the dungeon?" Joel asked.

Erin turned to look at him. "What?"

Joel laughed and knelt down. "He promised never to give his magic away again. He didn't keep his word, you know."

"You guys have a dungeon?" Bain asked.

"If you don't stop doing this, you're not going to live long enough to find out."

"What do we do?" Erin asked.

"We hope that Bain grows a sense of responsibility," an accented voice spoke behind them.

Erin turned to see Aelflaed. Her pale blue gown matched her eyes, and Erin wondered how her blonde curls could be so long and perfect. But her appearance wasn't the most impressive part of the tall älva. If there lived a soul who could heal someone, it was her.

"Until then, he's going to need to regain his strength," Aelflaed continued.

"Maybe he could touch Pulsar," Erin said. It always worked for her. Every time she touched his golden scales, magic would rush into her.

"It wouldn't do anything for him. A dragon only shares magic with one," Aelflaed answered.

"But he'll be okay, won't he?" she asked.

Aelflaed touched Bain's face. Her expression was thoughtful. "Yes. He'll come through. Do you want me to take him to his room?"

"No!" Bain said. "I'm fine, guys. Really."

"I'll be back to check on him," Aelflaed said.

Erin watched her leave the room. That was it? For some reason she expected Aelflaed to come up with some kind of magic spell that would fix things. "I guess that means we need to get you back to your room."

"Nah. Just throw him in the dungeon." Joel laughed when Bain's eyes grew wide.

41

Pizza, to Go

ERIN STARED AT THE MONITOR. MOST OF THE DIGITAL SCREENS stationed in the enormous computer lab were blank. It seemed like forever since the last time she sat in this room. Only a couple months ago the walls were filled with displays of data from airport seating lists, intercepted cell phone activity, and surveillance camera feeds. Now, silence filled the room.

She clicked the send button on her computer and waited. The long overdue email to her grandpa made her feel a little better even if it didn't tell the whole truth. Her time in Ireland, Africa, and Brazil hadn't exactly been for educational purposes, but exposure to those lands had allowed her to see more of the world. Even Iceland taught her something with its short daylight hours.

Her shoulder muscles tightened, and she massaged the knots of stress. It would probably take Grandpa a while to think to check his email. He didn't use the computer that much. Bain set him up with an email account before they left. She couldn't believe it had been almost a month since then.

It was December 20, the night before winter solstice. Joel had been the one to remind her about the queen's invitation to the ball. That's why she decided to come to the computer lab; it was easier than worrying about what she would have to wear or how stupid she would look dancing in a room filled with elegant elves.

She looked at the screens and considered looking up information about winter solstice celebrations. Her life was so ironic. The most advanced technology in the world was there at her fingertips. Anything she wanted to search for could blink onto the screen. They could track via satellite, listen into cell phone conversations, find nearly any private information, and yet none of it had helped her find Bain. And now none of it would help her find her mom.

She leaned back in her chair. It had been a crazy day. Bain went to bed under Aelflaed's orders. Joel was off doing something—she didn't know for sure what. She thought she would enjoy an evening with the computers, only now that she was alone, she realized she wasn't happy. She found it impossible not to recap all her recent failures. Maybe she should give up and move back home with Grandpa. It didn't seem like she had a real purpose here.

She shook her head. She was probably just tired. Tucking the chair back, she headed out of the room, and for old time's sake, she cast an invisibility ward. The last time she left the computer room alone, Carbonell kidnapped her. A shudder raced through her. The halls were dimly lit and empty.

She pulled her changing brooch out and turned it into an iPod. The music helped her feel a little less creeped out. For every step she took, her mind relived the day when invisible hands captured her and rendered her powerless. She had no magic and no dragon, just her and the invisible hands. Her heart raced.

The thoughts were driving her crazy. Erin took off into a full sprint and made it to her room in less than a minute. As she closed the door behind her, she released the invisibility ward. Her hands trembled as she fumbled for the light switch.

Light flooded the room, and there by the balcony stood Carbonell. A scream pierced the silence before Erin could stop herself.

"Shh!" Carbonell had his finger to his lips. He opened the curtain of the balcony to reveal Pisces and Lyndera.

Erin wasn't sure if she ran or transported over to her aunt. "You're here!"

Lyndera opened her arms and took Erin in with a hug. "Yes, child. It turns out Carbonell has a few tricks up his sleeve." She reached up and patted Pisces. "Go on. Find some grass."

Erin backed up as the horse unfurled his wings and lifted from the balcony.

"I'm starving," Carbonell said. "You think you could find us some food?"

Erin pulled out her iPod and changed it into a watch. "It's kind of late."

"I was hoping you could use your little trick. Pop in, get some food, and come back. I'm in the mood for pizza. Pepperoni, olives, sausage, and mushrooms. Thick crust. Don't even bother with the low carb option." He pulled out a wallet and handed her some bills. "You know that little pizza joint back in your hometown? It should still be open."

"You want me to go to America for pizza?"

He stuffed the cash into her hand. "And breadsticks with sauce. I would give anything, anything to have that right now."

Erin looked at her aunt. "Uhm, do you want anything?" She couldn't believe she was really going to go get a pizza from another country.

"I'll eat whatever he's having," Lyndera answered.

They were serious. Her aunt's hair was pretty frazzled, and both were filthy. "I'll be right back." She couldn't help smiling. Maybe there should be practical advantages to having wings of light. Wind blew softly around her before her bedroom was replaced with the entrance to the restaurant.

"Carbonell, you owe me," she said as she stepped into the delicious pizza aroma.

When she returned to her room, Carbonell and Aunt Lyndy were sitting at the small table, talking. "Dinner anyone?" Erin set the food out for them, and Carbonell took a quarter of the pizza from the box.

"Oh, I could hug you," he said.

"Uh, that's okay," she said. "So, what did I miss?"

Aunt Lyndera opened her purse and pulled out a recliner. "Have a seat," she said, patting the chair. "We both want to apologize for dragging you to Xavene." Aunt Lyndera eyed Carbonell.

"It was my choice," Erin said.

Lyndera patted her arm. "I know, dear, but you wouldn't have come if Carbonell hadn't put you up to it. Xavene's powers are beyond anything I could have imagined. Did you know he could steal magic?"

"Yeah, he told us. That's why he kidnapped Ella—to steal her magic."

Lyndera pulled the breadstick apart. "Ah, but he's figured out that he doesn't need elves anymore."

"I don't get it," Erin said. "What else is there?"

"Really big bugs," Carbonell answered before nearly emptying a liter of root beer. "After you rescued Ella, he discovered that any form of magic would do. Have you seen the kinds of things that fly around his place?"

Erin nodded. She doubted she would ever forget.

"There are more magical insects in the Amazon than anywhere else in the world. And they're huge. All he needs is a helicopter and his magic-sucking nets, and presto, he's got a month's worth of magic." He reached for another piece of pizza. "I had no idea how much Xavene had figured out. The imps are talking about him turning all of them back into elves. Do you realize what that means?"

Erin pulled a breadstick out of the bag. "That they won't stink so bad?"

Aunt Lyndy smiled.

Carbonell shot her a stern glare. "If he turned the imps into elves, what's going to stop him from taking over the kingdom? Technically, he is the rightful heir." He picked up another piece of pizza. "But even that won't be enough for him. If Xavene has his way, he'll have his hands in the human world too.

"Imps everywhere will seek him out. Xavene won't need to search for an army anymore because they'll come crawling to him from every corner of the earth." Carbonell stuffed half the piece of pizza in his mouth.

"How do we stop him?" Erin asked. The haze of light around Carbonell had improved so much that she wondered why she'd ever doubted him. Everything he said had to be true. "You should tell Queen Āldera."

"Can't, love. She'd have me arrested. We never found your mom, remember?" He wiped his mouth with a napkin.

"Then I'll tell her. I can even take her to him," Erin said.

"You can't go back there, Erin." Aunt Lyndera stood and wrapped her arms around her. "I think I'm going to stay here for a while and keep an eye on things."

Erin's heart sunk. The feeling of being babysat made her want to disappear. She smiled at the thought. Invisibility was an option.

"Thanks for the pizza." Carbonell stood and wiped his hands on his jeans. "Lyndy, do you mind if I take Pisces?"

"Where are you going to go?" Erin asked.

"I don't know yet. I'll think of something." He stood there for a moment, looking at them. "I'll see you soon, I promise."

Erin watched him jump over the edge of the balcony to the lawn at least one story below. Being an elf definitely had its advantages. "Do you want to take the bed? I can sleep on the floor."

"Don't be silly." Lyndera pulled her leather bag from the chair. "I brought my own bed."

42
No Pressure

ERIN WALKED DOWN THE HALL, HER HAND IN JOEL'S. FOR ONCE, she was glad that he was a morning person. Aunt Lyndera had no problem with her going for a walk with the prince. If anything, she seemed pleased.

"Last night," Erin started. She had to tell Joel, but she couldn't help feeling worried about how he would take the news.

Joel looked at her but said nothing as he waited. She explained everything, talking a little too fast. "He said that Xavene is the rightful heir, Joel. How can that be true? He's not a real älv anymore."

He stared straight ahead as they walked.

"What is it?" she asked. Joel's muscles tightened, and he clenched his jaw. A heavy feeling settled in her stomach as the silence drew on.

"Carbonell is right. Ormond is the rightful heir."

"I don't understand."

Joel didn't answer as he led her into his favorite room. The last time he brought her here, he called it the thinking room. Colorful fish swam in the crystal water that pooled under the cascading waterfall. He sat down and took her hand in both of his.

She listened to the waterfall, glad there wasn't complete silence. The sound was comforting.

"There is one law that could make a difference," Joel said. His voice was low, and if Erin didn't have superior hearing, she doubted she would have caught his words.

"What law?"

Joel smiled, but it didn't hide the seriousness in his eyes. "There is more to taking the throne than being the oldest son or next in the blood line." He dropped his eyes and stared into the pool. "The law requires marriage. Ormond isn't married. None of us are."

Realization hit her, and she gasped. "He wanted to marry my mom. She would have been queen."

Joel nodded.

"But he could still force his way in and become king anyway, couldn't he?"

"Erin Fireborn Farraday." Joel's voice cracked slightly as he said her name. He took a deep breath. "This . . ." He shook his head. "This is the hardest thing I've ever had to do."

Erin watched him. The intensity in his face was fierce. "What is it?"

"My mom's vision about you—the part I didn't tell you."

Erin's heart raced. "What did she see?" Her voice came out as a whisper, but she knew he heard her.

His eyes were fixed on hers. "She saw you as queen. You were my bride."

She knew he was waiting to see how she would react, but she couldn't move. She could hardly breathe.

He continued. "If I married first, I would become the rightful heir. The fact that Ormond and Ella are still single leaves it open for any one of us. Ormond will convince everyone that he is innocent, and since he looks like an älv, most everyone will believe him. The way it stands now, the first to be married is the next in line for the throne."

"What about Ella?" Erin's whole body quivered, and her breath came out halted. "Couldn't she just get married and become queen?"

"She is not in love with anyone, and even if she were, she does not want the throne. The position isn't taken lightly. It is a lifelong service, one that requires complete devotion."

"You do realize that I'm only sixteen, don't you? I can't exactly get married and become a queen either." Her head spun as she tried to find a solution. She had only known Joel for a few months.

"I know." A smile appeared suddenly, and he laughed.

"What could possibly be funny?"

"I really thought you would run screaming when I told you. Or disappear to the Bermudas." He chuckled softly before returning to his sober mood. "I want you to think about things. We'll wait and see what Ormond does. We don't have to do anything right away, but if it comes down to him or me taking the throne, you will be the one that determines the fate of our kingdom."

"No pressure," she said.

He smiled again. "No pressure."

Erin sat in front of the tall mirror, watching her aunt. Earlier, two gowns had been delivered to her room. She looked down at her lap, where deep purple satin gathered in layers as it fanned out against the floor.

"You have nothing to be nervous about, Erin." Aunt Lyndera pinned a curl into place. She held another bobby pin in her teeth as she arranged Erin's hair.

Erin attempted a smile but couldn't make it convincing. Even with the distraction of the ball, she couldn't help but dwell on what Joel had said. Just when she thought she would take some online classes and try to salvage what should have been her high school years, she faced saving a kingdom by marrying an älv she had only known for a few months.

"Joel is such a good dancer, he'll pull you through. And look at you, child. You're absolutely gorgeous." Lyndera arranged the golden circlet among the red curls. "I wish I could have been there the day you crossed the bridge." She pinned another curl and let a few curls fall around Erin's face and down her neck.

"Thanks, Aunt Lyndy." All of the annoyance she had felt about having her aunt stay with her melted away. She was grateful to have her aunt there to send her off to her first dance. Her mom would have wanted it like this.

"I should have paid better attention all these years. I should have been there for you and Bain. The more I think about it, the less I know what I was thinking," Lyndera said.

"It's okay. Really. Grandpa Jessie has always taken really good care of us. We've been fine."

Aunt Lyndy shook her head slowly. "Still." She turned and grabbed her leather purse off the bed. "I have something for you." She handed Erin a small white box. "Your mother gave it to me."

Erin opened the box. "It's beautiful." On a chain of diamonds rested a purple butterfly.

"Let me help you with that." Aunt Lyndy fastened the necklace. The butterfly rested at the hollow of Erin's throat. "It's perfect."

Erin stood and hugged her. The sensation of her aunt's arms wrapped around her filled her with comfort. Maybe she really could make it through the evening.

"We can't stand around like a couple of old ladies." Lyndy stood back and looked at her. "You really are perfect, Erin."

"I promise I'm not."

Aunt Lyndy kissed her cheek. "I'm going to get changed." She picked up her cream-colored gown and headed to the bathroom.

Pulsar, what am I going to do? At least she always had him to talk to. It took a while for her emotions to slow down long enough to let him into her mind, but when she finally showed it all to him, he didn't seem surprised. Maybe dragons saw the world a lot differently than people.

You will go dance at the ball, eat desserts, and try to find someone for your brother to dance with.

At least you haven't lost your focus, Pulsar.

You can only overcome one obstacle at a time, little one. Greet the future as it greets you. You will ruin yourself if you try to solve every problem at once.

Thanks. She knew he was right. He was probably always right. They were just going to have to figure out how to keep Xavene from taking over the kingdom. Maybe it wouldn't come down to her getting married. Joel would think of something.

Aunt Lyndera emerged from the bathroom, her hair miraculously smoothed straight. Erin couldn't believe the transformation. The cream-colored dress draped just right, making her aunt look sophisticated. "You look great. Is there someone you're hoping will sweep you off your feet tonight?"

"You're the guest of honor, love. I'm just along for the ride."

A knock sounded on the door.

"That must be Joel. Do you want me to get it?" Aunt Lyndera asked.

Erin's heart thudded in her chest. She wasn't ready to see him yet. Not after everything they'd talked about.

Pulsar's deep voice sounded in her mind. *Go on, Fireborn. And try not to trip on your dress.*

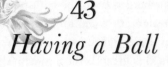

43
Having a Ball

THE BALLROOM SPREAD SO FAR OUT THAT ERIN COULD HARDLY take it all in from the upper level where she stood. Below, swirls of color filled the floor as couples danced to the lively music. Trees sprouted from the ground and bloomed into branches filled with bright green leaves.

The room was dim and thousands of shimmering lights scattered across the ceiling like stars. In the center of the ballroom, a majestic evergreen stood tall, decorated with candles and bows. It was the only indication that Christmas was only four days away. Everything else felt foreign—beautiful and breathtaking, but still foreign.

"Are you ready?" Joel asked.

She shook her head. She doubted she would ever be ready to face a crowd of elves, but now they were even more incredible with their gowns and fancy clothes.

Joel squeezed her hand. "You'll be fine."

The music stopped, and all eyes were on Anjasa. He stood in a jetted out section of the balcony visible to the room below.

Butterflies filled Erin's stomach as she listened. Anjasa announced the queen first, followed by Ella. Applause filled the room. Joel held her hand as he guided her to the edge of the balcony.

"Prince Joel," Anjasa announced, "and the Guest of Honor for this year's Winter Solstice Celebration, Erin Fireborn Farraday."

The sea of faces looked up at them from below as the sound of clapping echoed in the hall. Erin didn't know if she should wave or just stand there, feeling conspicuous, with a smile glued to her face. In a split decision, she waved at the audience with her right hand while her left still firmly clasped Joel's.

Joel nodded at the audience and wrapped Erin's arm in his as he guided her away from the balcony. "That wasn't so bad, was it?" he whispered in her ear.

She shook her head, the smile on her face refusing to budge. The grandeur of the ballroom cast its spell. Music drifted up from the level below, and a current of energy filled the air.

"Come on," Joel said, leading her to the staircase.

The dance floor was alive with beautiful elves dancing. Dresses of every imaginable color swirled around them, and even more variations of suits and tuxedos accompanied the movement. Not all of the men chose black suits. Some of the suits seemed like they were from the eighteenth century. The dresses surpassed age and time, with some of the styles defying anything Erin had seen.

Erin hardly noticed when Joel began dancing with her. Maybe it was the stunning people around her that stole her attention. When she tore her eyes away from the view and looked up at Joel, she was surprised to see him staring back down at her. A smile played on his face.

"You're a natural, you know," he said.

"What are you talking about?" she asked.

He spun her out and wrapped her back in only to slowly turn, her arms tucked in front of her as he held her close. "Dancing. You're doing great."

Shivers ran up her arms. "You had to remind me."

He twirled her and locked his arm behind her back. "It's not every year I get to dance with the Guest of Honor. Last year it was a guy."

She laughed. Her nervousness made everything funnier than it should have been. "Where's Bain?" She hadn't seen him at all since they came. She hoped he wasn't stuck sitting by himself somewhere, waiting for the hours of torment to end.

"I don't know. Do you want me to have someone find him for you?"

Joel's arm felt strong under hers. She didn't know if he wore cologne, but he smelled wonderful. His tall shoulders made her want to rest her head on his chest. How could her heart pound and feel ready to melt at the same time? All she wanted to do was dance with him. Maybe forever.

"Erin?" he asked. "Do you want to go find Bain?"

"That's okay. We'll check on him later." If Joel hadn't spun her out again, she might not have been able to resist the urge to nudge a little closer.

Bain sat at the small table with a cup of punch and a small plate of desserts. He watched Erin blush as Anjasa announced her and caught glimpses of her and Joel dancing through the crowded floor. At least she seemed to be having a good time.

Carbonell surprised him when he sat down at his table, invisible. Bain would know that plum-colored aura anywhere. When Aunt Lyndera joined him at the table, he had a hard time not showing his surprise. He had so many questions.

"Let's go for a walk, shall we? They always decorate the indoor patio for the ball. Do you want to see?" Aunt Lyndera asked.

Bain wished he could see Carbonell's face. The three of them wound through the room until Lyndera led them out to a moonlit garden. The temperature dropped from the crowded dance floor, and smells of flowers and bushes gave the garden a tang of freshness. He would rather spend the whole evening here than in the ballroom.

Aunt Lyndera took Bain's hand, and Carbonell came into view. Bain realized that Carbonell and Lyndera were shielded by a combined invisibility ward. Carbonell dressed up for the occasion with an expensive-looking black suit with no tie hanging on the unbuttoned neck of his white shirt.

"Sound ward too?" Bain asked.

Lyndy pulled him into a hug before letting Bain go, his hand still in hers. "Yes, Bain. So good to see you again. You look great."

"What's going on? How did you get here?" Bain asked. Seeing the two of them was such a relief.

"We didn't get caught," Carbonell answered.

"What about the imp that saw you? Didn't he tell Xavene about you?" Bain asked.

"I still had a few darts. After we put Sledjon to sleep, we had to get rid of him." Carbonell lifted Lyndera's hand, which was still in his. "It was your aunt's idea to take a little trip with the imp."

Lyndera smiled at him, blushing a little. Bain couldn't help noticing how completely different she looked with her polished straight hair draping over her shoulders and an evening gown that contrasted her striking colors. He watched Carbonell, whose eyes were locked on hers.

Bain cleared his throat, interrupting their moment. "Where did you go?"

Carbonell laughed. "With the help of another portal and Pisces, Antarctica. Kind of cruel, I suppose, but we figured it would take him a while to find his way out of there."

"Antarctica? I guess that explains why we never found you. How long have you been back?" Bain asked.

"Last night," Aunt Lyndera answered. "We stopped in and saw your sister."

Bain nodded. "What do we do now?" he asked.

"You need to keep your eyes open, Bain," Carbonell said. "Xavene has power. We found where he's been dumping wasps in the Amazon. He's been stealing their magic. His resources are nearly limitless. If he ever runs out of bugs, he'll move onto the other magical creatures." Carbonell gave him a meaningful look. "Like mermaids, for example."

Bain tried not to show his surprise. He hadn't thought of Kelura for a while.

"My guess is he's going to come here and claim his place as king," Carbonell said.

"You don't think that would really happen, do you? It's too obvious. He's an imp," Bain said.

"You can see that, Erin can even see his black aura, but to everyone else," Carbonell shook his head, "he looks like Ormond."

"What are you going to do about this? You worked with him. You know him better than anyone else. How are you going to stop him?" Bain asked. He was surprised at the anger that rushed through him. The months he spent in Black Rain, being lied to, the horrible headaches—it was Carbonell who carried out Xavene's orders. If there was ever a time for Carbonell to show his true colors, it was now.

"I don't really know what I can do. He's got an army. He can change imps into elves, Bain. Do you realize how dangerous that is? For all we know, there could be members of his forces right here at the ball."

Bain looked out at the trees that lined the walkway. "But I would know. So would Erin."

Carbonell chuckled softly.

Bain shot him a look. He couldn't tell if Carbonell was mocking him.

Carbonell raised his hand to calm Bain. "It's not what you think. Xavene thought you would make a powerful weapon because you can see magic. No one can do that. Even now, I'm sure he wishes you were on his side. But what he missed, what *I* missed, was that you and Erin will be his downfall. You and your sister can spot his army. You'll always know. No matter how well he deceives the rest of the kingdom, you two will know."

"We might be able to see him, but he's still got his traps." Bain looked down at his aunt's hand. She had been quiet for a while, and he wondered what she was thinking.

"Yes," Carbonell answered. "But I still think we can win."

44

Paper Airplane Fit for a King

BAIN SCANNED THE DANCE FLOOR FROM THE BALCONY. HE COULD see so much from this vantage point. The mixed colors of magic and gowns meshed into a kaleidoscope. There were so many black suits below that he wasn't sure he could pick out a black aura. Maybe Xavene knew that. Bain wondered if Xavene would even come.

He leaned his elbows on the balcony as he watched the dancing below. Even from here, the golden glow of his sister's aura was brilliant against the other colors: pure gold, just like her dragon. Bain wondered what Pulsar was up to. He doubted the dragon would want to have anything to do with this kind of occasion.

His thoughts wandered as the swirling colors below moved to the rhythm of the music. Already, he had lost track of Carbonell's aura. There were too many auras crowded together. He doubted his aunt would have much luck finding anything either. It hadn't been a great plan, but it was all they had. Find Xavene. Well, find him if he happened to be here.

Their plan didn't include what they would do if they actually found him. They didn't have cell phones. For all the advanced technology the elves possessed, they didn't use much of it very often. He wondered if immortality made things seem less urgent.

Bain tried to stay focused. If Xavene were here, what would he do? It didn't seem likely that he would go for Erin. Not only was she with Joel, but she had the power to transport. She didn't make a very easy target. Bain's eyes scanned the ballroom. If Xavene wanted to make a statement about his power, this would be the event to attend. The kingdom's whole älvin population was here.

"The queen," Bain said. Why hadn't he thought of it sooner? He searched the flooded room for Queen Āldera's light blue aura. Usually, it was easy to spot. Most auras had a bold color, but the queen's aura defied the vibrant colors.

She wouldn't be alone. Anjasa and others were sure to be at her side. Bain found the throne at the head of the room empty. Maybe she was dancing. A foreboding settled in his chest. *Find Erin.* It's all he could think. *Find Erin.* The thought reverberated in his head.

Erin's gold glow shined bright on the dance floor. He could take the stairs and risk getting lost in the crowd. No. He needed her now. Bain pulled the sword pin from his jacket and stared at it. In truth, he'd only tried to use his changing brooch a couple of times. His mind stormed through the possibilities. If she only had a cell phone.

He smiled as he remembered Carbonell's trick.

> *I need to see you. Come up here and bring this note—I don't want to lose my changing brooch. I'm waiting where you waved to the audience.*
> *Bain*

Bain shot the paper airplane into the air and directed its flight with his wand. Material manipulations. Master Ulric would have been proud. The note floated down over the heads of hundreds of elves. Hopefully no one would look up to see it. When it bounced off Erin's shoulder, Bain's heart skipped a beat. Erin didn't even turn to see what hit her. He flew the airplane a little higher and aimed it at her cheek. Just before it crashed into her face, Joel caught it.

Bain dropped his wand and watched Joel open the note. Joel's eyes lifted to where Bain stood invisible.

"Wait!" Bain said. But it was too late. Joel hadn't seen him. Bain broke the invisibility ward and watched his sister.

She took the note from Joel and after a second, glanced up at the balcony.

Bain waved at her.

A half second later, Erin and Joel stood beside him.

"What's going on?" Erin asked, handing Bain the note. "Are you just bored? You really should ask someone to dance. You don't have to sit around alone all night."

Bain pretended not to hear her. "Joel, do you know where the queen is?"

Joel turned and scanned the ballroom floor. "She's usually . . ." He leaned over the railing, studying the room below. "I don't see her."

"Do you think Xavene would come here?" Bain asked. The sinking feeling had only increased.

Joel turned to face him. "We need to find her." He headed to the door.

"Wait!" Erin called. "Where do you think she is?"

Joel stopped at the door and turned around. "I don't know. Maybe Ella's with her." He shook his head. "We could really use Ella's help right now."

"You could use my help too." Erin grabbed Bain's hand and pulled him toward Joel. "Just tell me where you want to look and we'll get there a lot faster together."

If it weren't for Pulsar's navigational help, Erin doubted she would have been able to transport them successfully to each place Joel requested. The search had already covered most of the rooms Erin was familiar with, and in a breathtaking stop, she even got to see the queen's personal chambers. No hotel could ever impress her again.

With each room, the sense of urgency increased. Joel didn't say much. Bain said nothing. Most of their communication involved shaking and nodding their heads.

"No," Joel said. His face grew pale. They had been all over the palace already.

Erin was sure Joel was going to throw up. "What is it?"

Joel grabbed her hand and barely managed to grasp Bain's arm. "The throne room."

"I don't know which one it is," Erin said. The look on Joel's face scared her.

"The bridge. The room you crossed the bridge in to become immortal. The river." Joel's intensity increased. "The throne room."

Pulsar projected the map in Erin's mind. The only time she had been there was when Bain and she crossed over the bridge and stepped forever into immortality. The image of the room spread in her mind as Pulsar helped her concentrate. She barely noticed the light wind that whipped around them as they transported.

The first sensation to hit her was the sound of rushing water. Memories poured into her mind: the polished wooden bridge, the queen at her throne, all the masters presenting them with their gifts, and most of all, the rush of magic that poured through her as her own golden circlet was placed on her head by the queen

"No!" Joel screamed.

Erin spun around, jolted from her reverie. There, by the queen's throne stood Xavene, his ugly black aura polluting the air around him. His arms were wrapped around the queen, and he held Queen Āldera's own eternal blade to her throat—the queen unable to ward against her own sword.

Erin's heart pounded in her chest. Xavene was going to kill her. Right there, in front of them. Erin's mind raced, trying to find a way to stop the inevitable.

Pulsar! she screamed in her head.

"Here we are again, just like old times," Xavene said, twisting the blade in front of the queen. "At least this time you're big enough for a proper duel, eh, little brother? I wouldn't want to deny you that opportunity again."

"No one's going to believe you're innocent," Joel said evenly.

Xavene laughed. "I have everything worked out. You don't need to worry your little head about it. You're not going to be around to watch, anyway."

The glass window. I'm coming in. Ward yourself, Fireborn.

Erin's eyes shifted to the enormous glass windows that rose like walls of a cathedral. *He'll still kill her. You might be able to save us, but what about the queen?*

"Let's trade then," Joel said. "You can have the throne. You don't need to kill her to become king. You're already the firstborn. I think the people will give their support more readily if suspicion of murder doesn't cloud their view. We can coronate you tomorrow."

Xavene lowered the blade a few inches, and the queen took a visible breath.

"I'll even leave the kingdom if you want. Give you some space," Joel continued.

Erin's breathing constricted. Joel said he would abdicate the throne. He couldn't.

"And what about you, Mother?" Xavene said in a condescending tone. "Are you willing to step down and let me rule as I see fit?"

The queen stood tall, her expression determined. "I would love to see our family find peace."

Xavene lowered the sword and smiled. "You're right. This is even better than I planned. If the people see that I have the queen's blessing, they will welcome me with open arms."

Wait for it, Fireborn, Pulsar boomed in Erin's head. *He can't be touching her or you'll transport him too.*

"The only downside to this, really, and don't take it wrong," Xavene said, lifting the blade into the air, "but it can be terribly irritating to have another person in line for the throne. I'm sure you'll understand."

Erin's gaze did not lift from the queen. She heard Joel draw his sword. Xavene let go of the queen and advanced toward Joel.

Now! Pulsar said.

Whispering Winds transported Erin across the room to the queen. She wrapped her arm around Queen Āldera and together they vanished from the throne room. The sound of rushing water was replaced with music as they landed on the balcony of the ballroom.

"Your majesty." Erin let go of the queen and wrapped her arms around her middle. Her satin gown was cold from the wind. "It was all I could think of."

The music bounced cheerfully throughout the hall, mingled with the sounds of conversations from below. No one seemed to notice their sudden appearance.

Queen Āldera looked at her, and Erin couldn't decide what emotion hid behind her composed expression.

45

The Smell of Victory Stinks

BAIN WATCHED XAVENE ADVANCE, HIS BLACK MAGIC AURA SPILL-
ing around him. Joel drew his sword. Xavene kept coming, so
Bain pulled his blade too.

"There's nothing you can do, Ormond," Joel said. "You can
fight me, but you'll never win."

Joel blinked invisible, but Bain could still see his orange aura.
Bain followed his lead and warded with invisibility too. "Now
what?" Bain said to himself. No one would hear him with his
sound ward in place.

"Coward," Xavene said. "You shouldn't waste your time. I will
find you, whether it be today or at night while you sleep. I'll find
you."

Bain heard a sound over the rush of the water. He turned
to see imps lining up in front of the river, shoulder to shoulder. Hundreds of them. Where did they all come from? As they
formed a tight line, they marched forward. Realization hit him
like a lead ball. A net strung between the imps and filled the
floor behind them as they surged forward. They were going to
find them.

Bain froze as he watched them lay the trap. If Joel and he
jumped over the line of imps, they would be caught in the magic-
draining net. Joel's orange aura moved along the wall toward the
corner, and Bain followed him. The net was large enough to spread
the entire distance of the massive floor.

"We could really use Erin about now," Bain said, not daring

to drop his sound ward. He made it to Joel's aura and reached his hand out toward the orange glow. He couldn't get through. Joel must have a touch ward too.

The army of imps quickly closed the distance. Xavene walked in front of the line as they carpeted the floor with their net.

Bain looked up, hoping to find something that could offer hope. No trees grew in this room. There was nothing but a tall glass wall to meet the ceiling. "Oh!" Bain almost laughed. Tiny pinpoints of light filtered in against the distance. At first he only saw a few, but then more and more trickled in until there were too many to count. Even with their invisibility wards, the älvor could not hide from Bain.

A bright silver aura accompanied them, but the bird was not invisible. The blue bird flew with the älvor as though it were one of them.

The line of imps had almost reached them; the net spread over the whole floor from the river to them. Bain covered his nose. One of these days he'd have to learn a scent ward. The smell emanating from the wall of imps was unbearable. Bain could hardly breathe.

He held his eternal blade in front of him as he waited for the imps to collide with him. The colors of light that floated toward them began to rain down on the imps. Flashes of electricity blazed from the älvor as they attacked the imps. Many of the imps fell back onto the net, but each recovered and moved forward. Even with the fairies helping, they were hopelessly outnumbered.

The imps swatted at the invisible fairies like flies. Bain tried to decide if it would be worth it to cut down a few imps with his sword. As he watched chaos erupt from the line, he wondered if it would be necessary.

The room shuddered as glass erupted from the wall above him. Bain looked up to see shards of glass raining down and Pulsar's bright gold aura flying through. "It's about time," Bain said.

The ceiling was tall, but it was cramped space for a flying dragon. Bain watched the dragon's aura circle around. Already, the imps had broken formation and fled over the net as the fairies sent electric volts at them.

In a steady stream, Pulsar sent a blaze of fire at the imps. The smell of burning fur and flesh instantly attacked Bain's nose. The odor sickened him. Another flood of fire met more imps. Bain tried to decide if he should cross the net. Nothing that touched it had an aura. He wondered if it would drain his magic and transfer it to Xavene.

Pulsar couldn't stay in one place very long as he flew, and even though his arsenal of fire was impressive, the dragon couldn't get to every one of the imps. Bain watched Xavene's black aura. Even Xavene hadn't dared to breach the net. Imps scattered through the room, most seeking an exit.

Bain couldn't resist the idea that came to mind, shaking his head as he considered the risks. He inched closer to Joel's aura and dropped his invisibility and sound wards. "Come on." Bain reached his hand out to Joel, hoping he would understand.

For a second, Joel flickered into view. A grin grew on his face. "Okay, what have you got?" he asked, grabbing Bain's forearm.

The brief moment that it took for them to communicate was all Xavene needed to discover their location.

"He's coming. I guess there goes our element of surprise." Bain looked at the net lying on the floor next to his feet. "I wanted to sneak up on him and push him onto his own net. I figured we'd have a better shot at it if it was two against one."

Another round of fire spewed past them.

"Maybe we still can," Joel said.

Bain studied the sliver of space between the wall and the net. "I don't know. There's not much room."

"You can see him, can't you?" Joel asked.

"Yeah."

"I can't, so I'm not going to be much help. It's up to you. Think of Xavene as a really big basketball."

Bain slid his blade into his sheath and pulled out his silver wand. He had to focus to summon a decent amount of magic. He wanted this to work the first time. "We should get a little closer."

Walking toward the foul black aura made Bain's stomach turn. He raised his wand and pointed it at the dark cloud. Bain took a deep breath and surged his magic through the wand as he pushed Xavene's form onto the net. It was easier than he expected. Maybe they had the element of surprise after all.

Bain watched as the black aura disappeared and a huge mountain lion took its place. The transformed imp stood on its hind legs and roared in fury.

Bain's heart pounded in his ears. The sight of the mountain lion took him all the way back to his runs in the forest near his house. Even before Bain became an elf, the imp sought him out. Xavene could have destroyed him then. Why hadn't he?

As the oversized mountain lion charged at him, the vision flashed through his mind of the last time he saw him in front of the cottage. With the memories flooding through him, he lost track of his magic. Bain barely noticed his wards coming down around him as the lion closed in.

The imp bared its teeth as it sped toward him. Bain couldn't move. Couldn't think. All he could see was the brown fur and dark eyes.

"No!" Joel yelled.

Bain hit the ground as Joel yanked him out of the lion's path. The momentum carried Joel onto the net. Xavene turned on him, swinging its massive paws at Joel. It bared its teeth and let out a terrible roar. Bain grabbed his sword and joined them on the net. Here there would be no magic to save them. It was muscle and claws against blades. The beast was too big for Joel to take alone. He thought of everything Agnar tried to teach him about swords, but fighting a monster was so much different than sparring with an elf.

He narrowly missed a deadly swipe from Xavene's claws. Joel's sword slashed in a blur, and stripes of fresh blood colored the tan fur. Bain faced the mountain lion, his sword flashing. Xavene came down at them with the full weight of his massive body. Bain stabbed his sword into the lion's arm. Joel thrust his sword at Xavene, sinking it into the lion's shoulder.

In a blur of fur, the mountain lion roared and at lightning speed lunged at Joel. Bain didn't hesitate to thrust his sword at the lion's head, but Xavene was too fast. The mountain lion knocked Joel to the ground, and Bain's blade clattered as it hit the floor.

"It's over," Xavene growled through his beast form.

Bain looked for his blade. If he could get to his sword, maybe there was still a chance.

"Did you really think you could win?" Xavene asked Joel.

Bain could hardly see Joel underneath the lion's body. As soon as Bain's feet left the net, he could feel a ward surround him. He reached down and picked up his silver blade. Was his aim good enough? Bain could feel the magic surge from the sword. It would be a just cause killing Xavene. The imp didn't deserve to live.

Bain lifted his arm, ready to throw his sword through the lion's side. It would be the first time Bain killed. Maybe. He didn't know if anyone had died at Black Rain when Erin helped him escape in Egypt.

The hilt of the sword nearly left his hand when Pulsar suddenly shot a fiery stream at Xavene. Orange flames scorched his fur, and the smell of burning flesh filled the air. Xavene leaped up and bolted for the door. Pulsar followed, sending a trail of fire across the already smoking room. Other imps rushed after him, pouring out of the room as fast as they could run.

Bain crossed the net and helped Joel up. He looked out at the smoldering expanse of net. Some of the imps escaped, but Pulsar had taken many of their lives with fire. Their motionless bodies smoked as the remains of fur burned.

Bain coughed at the putrid smell, gagging. "We've got to get out of here."

They both studied the carnage that ran the entire length of the floor.

"Right," Joel said.

The sound of voices echoed across the racing river. At first, Bain thought he only imagined them, but more voices and the sound of feet joined in. On the opposite side of the river, elves lined up, still in their fancy ball gowns and suits.

A mahogany bridge appeared over the river.

A breeze whipped through Bain's hair, and Erin materialized beside him. She wrapped her arms around him in a hug. "You're okay!" She let go of Bain and pulled Joel into a hug next. "I was so worried about you two. You ready to get out of here?"

Bain nodded and grabbed Erin's free hand. "I'm thinking Hawaii sounds nice."

"Very funny," Erin said.

Another gust of wind wrapped around them, and they were gone.

46
A Bird from a Thousand Dreams

Erin sat at the table across from Bain. Joel was next to her, with Aunt Lyndy sitting across from him. The ballroom was hollow without the swirling dresses, music, and subdued voices filling it. The party was over.

Erin leaned her elbows on the table. In spite of the many disasters, the whole night could have been so much worse. Pulsar had blocked her out of his mind as he fought the imps, a fight that could have cost her brother's life . . . and Joel's. Her heart sickened at the thought.

And maybe it was her fault. Her emotions had been wrapped up in the moment. The problem was, neither Pulsar or Erin knew for sure why they didn't seek each other out. There were definite limitations to their relationship even if it seemed fail-proof.

Erin looked around the table. None of them were talking but seemed lost in thought, just like her. She noticed Bain glance up and followed his stare to see butterfly wings float into the ballroom. After all they had done to fight off the imps, Erin couldn't believe she had forgotten about the fairies.

Another pair of wings caught her attention. "Look." The metallic blue bird flapped its wings amid the fairies. "It's so beautiful."

Bain gave Erin a quick glance.

"No," Aunt Lyndera whispered. "It's not possible." She clapped her hands over her mouth. "I . . . It's . . . " Her words came out in quick bursts.

"What is it?" Erin asked. She'd never seen her aunt react like this. Erin met Bain's questioning look, and she shrugged. Maybe their aunt knew some of the älvor.

The blue bird landed on the white linen tablecloth. Its long plume of silver feathers fanned out like a peacock tail.

Aunt Lyndera stood and reached for the bird's face. "It's you." Tears flowed down her aunt's cheek, and Erin was pretty sure Lyndera was going to climb up on the table. Erin was wrong. Her aunt didn't climb onto the table but pulled Erin into a hug. Then did the same to Bain.

"What am I missing?" Erin asked, Lyndy's arm tight around her still.

"Bless my stars, you two." Lyndera dropped her arms and grasped both of their hands. "It's your mum."

"What?" Bain asked.

Aunt Lyndera squeezed Erin's hand. Erin stared at the bird and wondered if her aunt had lost her mind.

"Julia—your mother. She's here!" Lyndera let go of their hands and reached out to the bird. "But why can't you change? What happened to you?"

Erin watched. "What do you mean, *change*?"

Aunt Lyndera turned to face the twins. "Your mother had a most unusual gift. We all have gifts. Your gift is to see truth. Bain's gift is to see magic. Your mother's gift was a secret. She could transform into a bird. No one knew but me."

"We found this bird at Xavene's mansion. It was in Egypt and then again down at his place by the Amazon River. How could . . . ?" Bain broke his words off.

"She was with Xavene." Lyndera said.

"Her magic," Bain said. "When I first saw the bird a couple months ago, she had a little bit of magic. But this last time her light was nearly gone. Do you think . . . ?"

"Xavene was stealing her magic," Erin finished. "He must have used nearly all of it. That's why he kidnapped Ella."

"But then he figured out that he didn't need elves anymore to steal magic," Carbonell finished.

Joel scooted back his chair as Carbonell suddenly flickered

into view. Carbonell was sitting right next to Joel. Bain didn't show any surprise, and Erin guessed he had known Carbonell was there all along.

"You!" Joel shouted. "You're not allowed here."

"Hush," Aunt Lyndera said.

Erin looked at her aunt in shock.

"Julia is here. The agreement was that Carbonell wasn't allowed back unless he brought their mother with him." Lyndera's voice was firm.

Lyndera turned and pulled Erin and Bain from the table. "Listen. That's your mum over there. Ormond did something to her, but it's her. I don't know what the two of you are capable of, but you have to try something." She shook her head.

"Bain, with your wand." Lyndera slid the wand out of his belt and handed it to him. She took Erin's hand and rested it on top of Bain's. "And Erin, with your dragon, surely the two of you can do miracles. For land's sake, it's your own mother!"

Lyndera turned and left the two of them standing there, their hands still touching.

Bain winked at her. "What's the worst thing that could happen?"

Pulsar, are you in on this?

I'll make sure you don't hurt yourself, Fireborn.

"Okay. Let's see what we can do." Erin turned and faced the table. The bird watched them carefully. Its eyes were so intelligent that Erin wondered if it understood everything they said. She looked around at the faces at the table. "We've never had to do this in front of an audience before." Erin laughed nervously.

No one smiled.

"Give me your hand," Bain said.

Erin was relieved to have Bain take over. He held her fingers in his and reached out to the blue feathers that felt like warm satin. Erin's heart sped up as she thought about transferring magic. How much magic would be enough? How much was too much?

"We need Pulsar," Erin blurted.

"Very well," Joel said. He stood and reached his hands

upward. The ceiling that looked like a star-filled sky opened up. As the sides of the windowpanes parted, a chill of air seeped into the room. The real night sky looked so much like the ceiling that it was hard to tell where the glass ended and the sky began.

Pulsar's golden scales cast prisms of light as it reflected the starlight. He tucked his wings in as he cut through the opening of the roof. Pulsar's talons grabbed one of the trees as he slowed his dive into the ballroom. The dragon's claws slid on the marble floor as he landed.

Erin couldn't help but smile. Maybe it was when Pulsar looked clumsy that she loved him the most. It made her feel a little better about her own lack of gracefulness. Of course, Pulsar was almost never clumsy.

It was the floor, little one, Pulsar said to her.

I know. Thanks for coming. She waited as Pulsar walked to their table. When he was close enough for her to rest her hand on his cheek and still touch her mom, she nodded. "Okay, I'm ready."

Bain put his hand over hers and pointed his wand at the bird. "I just want to tell you," he said to the bird, "if we mess this up, I'm really sorry." He looked at Erin. "Okay. Let's do it."

Hot magic poured through her body as Pulsar's energy surged through her. She wished she could see the magic like Bain could. The table began to shake, and the others stood and backed away.

Erin focused on the bird, and the feathers seemed to melt under her hand. The bird trembled, and Erin worried that they were hurting it. A loud clap sounded. It felt like lightning had struck the table. White light blinded Erin, and she was sure her hands were no longer touching the bird. Heat blasted in front of her. She warded with Bain in her protective cover.

"That was it," Erin said. Either they had succeeded or they had blown up the bird. The blinding light refused to dim.

It is enough, Fireborn. Look.

Erin couldn't see anything but white light. She closed her eyes and let her mind reach into Pulsar's vision. The table was gone. In its place stood a tall älva with red hair and a shimmering blue dress the same color as the bird's feathers.

"Mom?" Erin opened her eyes, and the light had subsided enough to see an outline.

The älva wrapped her arms around Erin and Bain. The touch of her skin, the warmth that radiated from her, Erin knew. Even if she had dreamed about her mom a thousand times, no dream had ever come close to showing her who her mom really was.

Julia looked at the twins. Her smile showed perfect happiness. Erin couldn't help notice the curly waves of red hair that contrasted her mom's porcelain skin. All her life, Erin had wished for silky blonde hair and a tan. Looking at the striking lady before her, everything changed. If she could look like her mother, she couldn't ask for more.

"I have waited so long," Julia began. "You two have grown up." A few tears escaped and ran off her cheeks, and she turned to Erin. "Erin, I don't know how I survived for sixteen years without you." She turned to face Bain. "Bain, I fear that every girl within a hundred miles is in danger of a broken heart. Look at you. Both of you." She pulled them into another hug.

Erin reached her arms up and returned the embrace only to feel Bain's arm wrap around her too.

"I missed you too, Mom," Erin said. The missing piece finally found its place.

When Julia finally let go of them, Lyndera was there. The two sisters held each other close.

Erin stepped back, noticing Carbonell; his smile was warm but thoughtful. Erin walked over and stood between Joel and Carbonell. "I guess that means you're off the hook," she said to Carbonell.

"Off one hook and caught on another," Carbonell answered. "I don't know how to tell you this, but," a broad smile crept on his face, "I think I'm in love with your . . . aunt."

Erin laughed softly. "If it's any consolation, I think you'd make a pretty good uncle."

Joel reached over and took Erin's hand. She pulled his hand into both of hers and noticed Bain standing next to Carbonell. In a strange way, everyone there felt like a part of her. The only one missing from the reunion was Grandpa Jessie.

47
No More Secrets

ERIN STOOD IN FRONT OF THEIR HOUSE IN PENNSYLVANIA. SNOW covered the ground and trees, making her neighborhood look like something out of a winter catalogue. She glanced over at Bain. He had a knit cap pulled over his ears and a black scarf around his neck. At least he looked the part.

The whole thing reminded her so much of coming home for Thanksgiving. They wanted to surprise Grandpa then, but this time the surprise was on a completely different level. Erin eyed her mom, who stood even taller than Bain. Her ivory trench coat set off her red hair and her long, shiny black boots only added to her sleek line.

"Are you ready?" Julia asked.

Erin didn't know if she'd ever be ready. How was Grandpa Jessie going to take this? Their mom was returning after sixteen years of absence. Not to mention that they were supposed to be in school in Iceland. How did finding their mom work into any of this? Erin's stomach twisted. This was going to be a disaster.

Julia took Erin's hand with her gloved hand. "Okay, darlings. Let's get this over with."

"Amen," Bain said.

Erin looked over at him as he looped his arm through hers. Between her mom and her brother, Erin guessed they would drag her into the house if necessary.

Go on, little one. I'll be here if you need an escape. Pulsar waited in the field across from their house. At least in the middle of winter they didn't have to worry about him crushing the crops.

I can get away anytime I want, Erin countered. But she didn't want to. Stuck in between her mom and her brother wasn't such a bad place to be.

"Are you sure Grandpa Jessie won't have a heart attack?" Erin asked. They were almost to the door.

"There's only one way to know," Bain answered. He let go of Erin and ran to push the doorbell.

"You're so cruel," Erin said.

Bain smiled back, his arms folded in front of his chest. The door opened, and Grandpa Jessie looked out at them.

"You made it!" Grandpa Jessie said. "Come in. It's freezing outside."

Erin glanced up at her mom, wondering if she had gone invisible. That would explain why grandpa didn't seem to notice their guest. Sure enough, where her mom should have been there was nothing.

"That's cheating, you know," Erin whispered to her.

"It's okay," Julia said. "I've got a plan. Go on in, and I'll meet up with you later."

"It's still cheating," Erin said, trying to keep her face serious. She shook her head and walked into the warm house. Even though Erin loved the kingdom, stepping into her own house made her feel different. Better. She hadn't realized that she missed this place. Garland swags with bright red bows hung from the banister. It was the same as when she left, but seeing it again made her smile.

Erin peeled her coat off while Bain took their luggage upstairs.

"The ham is in the oven. It should be done here in a couple hours," Grandpa Jessie said.

"Mmm, smells good," Erin answered. She thought about the rolls she usually made and doubted there would be enough time to make them before dinner. It was already Christmas Eve. They always celebrated with a nice dinner. Erin wondered if maybe there was bread in the freezer she could pull out. It wouldn't be the same.

"How's school treating you?" Grandpa Jessie asked.

Erin was glad that Grandpa didn't have her ability to see whether people were telling the truth. "It's good." She followed him down the hall, and Bain caught up to them. Erin shot him a glance. He must have moved at superhuman speed to already be back. Grandpa Jessie didn't seem to notice.

"What about you, Bain? Are you keeping your grades up?" Grandpa Jessie asked.

"Uh, sure," Bain answered.

Erin watched as his aura dimmed. Hers must have done the same thing.

Grandpa Jessie smiled. "It's good to see you kids. I still can't believe I let you go clear across the world for school."

"It's not that far," Bain said. "Iceland is just across the ocean."

"It's far enough," Grandpa Jessie said.

They walked down the hall, past the living room, and made their way to the kitchen. Maybe it was habit. They usually pulled something out of the fridge and snacked while they talked, especially if they had been gone for a while. Grandpa Jessie would suspect something if Bain *didn't* want to eat the moment he walked in the door.

Erin stopped in the doorway and stared. She almost screamed but swallowed the reaction. Grandpa Jessie and Bain filed into the dining room and stopped too. No one said a word.

There, in the kitchen, Julia flipped over a big glob of dough. Her coat hung on the coat rack by the back door, and she was wearing an old apron. Julia pretended not to notice them as she set the dough in the bowl and held her hands over it. Instantly, the dough began to rise, too fast for her not to be using magic. Soon the dough spilled over the edges of the bowl, and she punched it down again.

Erin watched as the dough quickly rose again and her mom took pieces of it and created perfectly shaped rolls. It was all Erin could do to keep her jaw from falling open.

"Merry Christmas, Jessie," Julia said as she patted another roll onto the pan.

Erin could have died. Not only was her mom suddenly in their kitchen after sixteen years, but she had just performed magic in front of Grandpa Jessie like it was commonplace.

"Julia?" Grandpa Jessie said. He didn't move but watched her from where he stood.

Julia smiled and untied her apron. "I thought it would be nice to spend a Christmas together. It's been a long time." She looked around the kitchen and then at Bain and Erin. "Too long." Julia turned and picked up a tray of mugs. "Why don't we go in the other room and catch up."

Grandpa Jessie took the tray away from her and set it on the table. When he turned back around, he opened his arms and took her into a strong hug. "Oh, sweetie. I've missed you." He sniffed, still holding her close. "I always wondered. Always."

When he let go of her, she had tears in her eyes too. "Robert's gone," she said. "I couldn't save him. There was nothing I could do. He died before the plane even hit the water. I'm so sorry."

"But you're back," Grandpa Jessie said.

Julia picked up the tray of steaming mugs. "It's a long story."

"Let me help you," Erin said. She took the tray from her mom and tried to keep her own tears from sliding down her cheeks.

Bain smiled and directed one of the mugs into the air and over to his hand.

Erin stared at him, wondering if he'd lost his mind. Bain shrugged and sipped at the drink.

Erin turned to her grandpa. "You knew." It wasn't a question. "All this time, you knew, didn't you?"

"Let's go have a seat," Grandpa said. "I think we have a lot to talk about."

Erin followed them into the living room, still carrying the tray. Everyone found a place to sit, and Erin warmed her hands on her mug. She had a feeling that things would be different after today.

"How do I start?" Julia said. "I don't know how much you two know, I don't even know how much Jessie knows, but let me try to explain. If you get lost, let me know." She interlocked her fingers and rested her elbows on her knees. "Ormond wanted to marry me, but I didn't want him. I ran away, all the way to Pennsylvania.

That's when I met your dad." She glanced at Grandpa Jessie.

"It's pretty simple. We dated, fell in love, and were married. I felt so safe here. With Ormond gone, I thought I would go on living life as though it didn't matter that I was . . . different. But I wanted honesty too. Robert knew that I could do magic, and so did your grandpa. I told them about the kingdom and the elves. I figured everyone would be better off if they learned it from me.

"The only way they could really trust me is if they knew the truth." She looked at Erin. "I guess that's where you get your need for truth."

Erin could only look back at her. There were no words.

"Then you two were born," Julia said. "Nothing better has ever happened to me. You were both perfect. I guess I should have known you would be human, but I wasn't sure how it would work. It didn't matter. The ones that made my life exquisite were all mortal. I never would have guessed that you two would change."

"But, Grandpa, how long have you had us pegged?" Bain asked.

Erin shook her head. Her brother had a point. All this time she thought she had been the one living a lie.

"When you said Iceland, I had to wonder," Grandpa Jessie said. "But the real clincher for me was when you came home last month looking just like your mom. Same eyes. Shot up about six inches, I'm guessing."

Bain's smile was broad and Erin couldn't help laughing softly.

"I'm fine with it all," Grandpa Jessie said. "Except I still haven't heard where you've been the last sixteen years." His eyes were on Julia. "Wouldn't mind hearing that story."

Julia nodded. "After the accident, I tried to make it back." She bit her lip and shook her head. "Ormond found me. He trapped me at his place and used me to siphon off magic. I was stuck. There was no way out, and no way to change." She gave Bain and Erin a meaningful look.

Erin realized her mom meant she couldn't transform back into an elf. Maybe Julia still had secrets she kept from Grandpa Jessie.

"It turns out," Julia continued, "that Erin and Bain found me. They rescued me. They might have had a little help along the way, but that's the short version of the story."

"Is that how you studied Ireland, Africa, and the Amazon jungle?" Grandpa Jessie asked Erin.

Erin's cheeks flushed red, and she nodded. She had kept Grandpa Jessie in the loop more than she realized.

"Oh, but she didn't tell you who her study partner was," Bain said.

Erin shot him a hard stare, hoping he could read her thoughts. *You wouldn't.*

He always does, Pulsar answered in her mind.

"It wasn't you?" Grandpa Jessie asked Bain.

"I think our little Erin has her sights set on someone with a little more status. Someone with potential." Bain winked at Erin.

Erin couldn't glare back at him. Everyone was looking at her.

"Who?" Grandpa Jessie asked.

"Only Ormond's little brother, the crown prince Joel." Bain smiled back at Erin, victory written all over his face.

"No," Grandpa Jessie said. "That can't be true."

Erin's cheeks burned hot. What could she say? She pulled her watch off and held it in her hand. A moment later she handed the changing brooch to Grandpa Jessie.

"Oh." Grandpa Jessie watched the tiny screen intently.

"I want to see," Bain said.

"Me too," Julia scooted closer.

"Here, I've got an idea." Erin took the changing brooch back and faced the empty wall.

Images from the projector came to life on the wall. She showed her and Pulsar flying over the ocean, Aunt Lyndera's house, sitting on the beach roasting marshmallows, and Joel dancing in the hall with her.

Silence filled the room. Erin knew she couldn't stop there.

The screen blinked a picture of Joel and Bain standing in the scorched room, their blades in hand, the queen announcing Xavene's return to the ballroom of elves, and finally, Erin skipped to the picture she saw through Pulsar's eyes, her beautiful mother walking through a brilliant explosion of light.

The lens blinked off, and Erin turned the projector back into a watch.

"Thank you," Grandpa Jessie said after a long pause of silence. "Thanks for bringing me there with you."

Erin glanced up at him. "Thanks for not freaking out about us being elves."

"Or not going to school," Bain added. "You did figure that part out too, right?"

Grandpa Jessie smiled. "It seems I'm not your legal guardian anymore. You two have your mom now. It's up to her what you do."

"Well, if I'm in charge," Julia spoke up, "I say we eat. I'm starving."

"Me too," Bain agreed.

"Some things haven't changed at all," Grandpa Jessie said as they headed into the kitchen.

The rolls had somehow been magically baked during their conversation, a trick that Erin intended to learn from her mom.

Grandpa Jessie sat in his chair and smiled as the dishes floated from the kitchen to the table. "Just like old times," he said.

Erin watched, leaning on the kitchen counter. Maybe she would have to sneak out later and visit Joel in the kingdom. There had to be certain advantages to being the only other person besides the princess with wings of light. She smiled at the thought. She could never be trapped. Finally, she could have both worlds.

About the Author

NEARLY A NATIVE OF IDAHO, LAURA BINGHAM WAS BORN IN IOWA and moved to Idaho at age four. She graduated from Ricks College with an associate's degree, and from Boise State University with a bachelor's degree in biology, as well as a certification to teach all science subjects in secondary education in the state of Idaho. In her backyard stands a dance studio, where she teaches youth of all ages clogging and Irish step dance.

Her grandparents and other relatives live in the beautiful Pennsylvania hills where she adores visiting and eating home-grown blueberries. She lives in Boise with her husband and five young children, including her own set of boy-girl twins. Visit her at www.laurabingham.com.